Duty to Investigate

J.W. Stone

WARRIORS PUBLISHING GROUP
NORTH HILLS, CALIFORNIA

DUTY TO INVESTIGATE

A Warriors Publishing Group book/published by arrangement with the author

PRINTING HISTORY
Warriors Publishing Group edition/July 2013

Cover photo: Marines during their deployment with Regimental Combat Team 1. U.S. Marine Corps photo by Sgt. Nathaniel C. LeBlanc.

ISBN 978-0-9853388-7-9

PRINTED IN THE UNITED STATES OF AMERICA

10 9 8 7 6 5 4 3 2 1

PROLOGUE

On the second day of the Second Battle of Fallujah, Captain Chris Douglas, the Executive Officer of Kilo Company, rode in the passenger seat of the up-armored Humvee as he monitored the radio net, writing in his notebook and relaying orders to the platoon commanders. A news reporter occupied the rear passenger seat, and the first sergeant sat to the rear of the driver. The Humvee drove close behind the Marines of Kilo Company, who, in turn, followed behind the Army armored battalion.

The overcast sky drizzled rain, turning the powdery Iraqi dust into a slippery slime that coated the streets and increased the difficulty of moving through the bombed-out houses. From time to time, the Humvee passed uncollected Iraqi bodies stacked at the side of the road while Navy corpsmen loaded the wounded into ambulances. The deafening noise of artillery, tank guns, and smaller ordnance thundered from all parts of the city.

Captain Douglas concentrated on the accomplishment of the Company's mission. He cared about nothing as much as his Marines and told himself that if he did his job perfectly, he could save lives. He cursed his luck and the fact that he had to babysit some Chicago newspaper reporter in the middle of the largest battle fought by the Marine Corps in 40 years. As a professional, he never complained about an order, but in his mind the idea of an embedded reporter appeared more brainless than issuing the malfunctioning Johnson Automatic Rifle to Marines on Guadalcanal. Civilians had no place in combat, and consequently, it didn't matter if the reporter, Anne Merrill, seemed intelligent and brave, wanting to report the accomplishments of his Company. But he wanted her to stay out of his way.

On the day of the battle, he asked the reporter not to get out of the Humvee. She didn't argue, but every time he got out, she nevertheless got out too and started taking photographs. When he yelled at her, she returned to the Humvee, but at the next stop, she jumped out again, moving with the grunts and snapping photographs.

Next, he ordered her to stay within 20 feet of the Humvee, but that didn't work either. If he left the area of the Humvee, she followed.

He then ordered the first sergeant to make certain she did not exit the Humvee. At the time, he thought if the first sergeant could control all of the young men and women in the Company, then he should be able to manage a civilian reporter.

Douglas cursed out loud when he saw Anne Merrill just smile at the first sergeant and proceed to go anywhere she wanted. He chewed out the first sergeant three times before conceding defeat.

"I give up, First Sergeant. If something happens to her, it will be on the back of the assholes that sent her out here. Just let her take care of herself."

After that, Douglas let Anne Merrill go everywhere that he went, and that included every part of the battlefield.

Kilo Company turned south on Nazal Street, and the lead elements reported being in sight of Al Hareery School. Douglas passed this information to the Battalion Intelligence Officer, who quickly replied that he had analyzed the situation reports and warned that insurgents occupied most of the mosques and schools in Fallujah as strongholds. The Intelligence Officer recommended that Douglas designate the Al Hareery School as a Company objective and that the Battalion Operations Officer prepare a coordinated attack on the school. Douglas concurred and ordered Kilo Company to pause two blocks from the Al Hareery School in order to plan the attack.

He watched as the reporter stepped out of the Humvee and bolted towards the school.

જીજ્

1400, 9 November 2004
Al Hareery School
Fallujah, Iraq

Anne Merrill worked her way to Kilo Company and fell in with the lead platoon. She stood behind a block fence next to a foul-smelling pile of garbage and snapped photographs of the school using one hand to shield the lens from the increasing rain that soaked through her jeans in an irritating pattern that looked like she had peed in her pants. The school complex seemed like a small prison, with three flat-roofed stucco buildings surrounded by another fence—a large classroom building with windows and two doors, a small two-story building, and a shed in the back. The two-story building appeared extensively damaged with one wall completely missing.

The turret-mounted .50 caliber machine guns on the Humvees blasting away at the buildings made Anne's camera shake, and the rounds sent dust and plaster everywhere. Bursts of return fire poured out of the school windows, and Anne heard the zip and pop of the insurgents' bullets flying over her head.

She stopped taking pictures, crouched low behind the wall, and put her hands over her ears. A squad of Marines hustled past and formed a stack line along the wall next to the front gate. She took a deep breath, leaped to her feet, and raced toward the squad. As she approached the line, she fell, crashed into the back of a corporal, and lay in the mud, sprawled on her back. Another Marine came from the rear, grabbed Anne by the shirt collar, and deposited her next to the wall. The troops forming the stack ignored her.

Climbing back on her feet, Anne heard a sergeant yell something and saw the stack surge through the gate. Without thinking, she ran as fast as she could and followed the grunts to the side of the school near the front door. Her knees trembled violently, and she pressed her body firmly against the brown stucco wall. She clenched her camera and tried to concentrate on getting a great photograph. Before she could aim the camera, the squad rushed inside the school with their rifles at their shoulders, pointing them from side to side.

Anne pressed on, but inside the school realized the squad had turned right while she had turned left. Cautiously, she made her way back toward the right and entered a schoolroom. She paused and raised her camera. A Marine across the room, holding his pistol with both hands, pointed the weapon at the opposite wall. Anne instinctively pointed the camera toward him and hit the shutter button.

The Marine spun toward her, pointing the pistol at her head. Anne screamed, dropped the camera, and threw up her hands.

"Don't shoot!" she cried.

The Marine raised the pistol toward the ceiling, said nothing, and turned back toward the opposite wall. Anne realized that she was standing in a pool of blood, and her eyes followed it to its source: the bodies of Iraqi women, children, and an old man. They were on the floor and facing the opposite wall, the backs of their heads blown open. Anne looked back at the Marine, who moved from one dead Iraqi to another while still holding his pistol with two hands. Two Marines rushed into the classroom from an adjoining room. They were followed by four other Marines from Kilo Company. Anne heard one gasp. "My God!" he exclaimed. "What the hell happened in here?"

Anne saw that in addition to the Iraqi bodies by the wall, there were several dead Iraqis in the middle of the room. The Marines gawked at the carnarge.

A second later, the platoon commander charged in, glanced at the bodies, and shouted an order to a sergeant. "Secure this area. We have to keep moving."

The platoon members rushed to collect weapons and check bodies. Anne started snapping photographs, including close-ups of the head wounds and victims' faces. No one tried to stop her. Anne rushed over to the platoon commander. "Aren't you going to conduct an investigation?" she asked.

The platoon commander looked annoyed. "It's probably a tribal dispute. It happens all the time here. My orders are to do whatever it takes to keep up with the armored battalion, and there's no time for an investigation."

The Executive Officer, Captain Douglas, arrived moments later and immediately stared at Anne when he walked into the school. He turned with a disgusted look and addressed the platoon commander. "What the hell is *she* doing here?"

The platoon commander shrugged his shoulders.

"Where is the STA team leader?" Douglas demanded.

A Marine ran over to Douglas. "Sir, Corporal Nelson is the STA team leader."

"What happened here, Corporal?"

"Sir, I don't know. I wasn't here."

"What do you mean, 'you weren't here'?" Douglas shot back. "Your team was here, but you weren't? What kind of bullshit is *that*, Corporal?"

The Corporal stood in silence, a painful look on his face.

"Who else is on the STA team?" Douglas asked angrily.

"Sir, the other members are Lance Corporal Case, PFC Goldman, and PFC Hale."

"Get them over here."

The three Marines ran over to Douglas and shouted simultaneously, "Reporting as ordered, sir."

"What happened here?" Douglas asked.

A massive explosion shook the school. The concussion knocked Douglas sideways and flattened a Marine standing in the doorway. Anne staggered to a wall and sat dazed and confused. She couldn't hear and felt something flowing from her right ear. Marines took cover next to the walls.

A second mortar round came quickly, followed by a third. Anne saw a Marine next to the north window go down. A corpsman ran over and started tending to his wounds. The next mortar round hit a Humvee parked outside, scattering it over the schoolyard and causing secondary explosions.

Douglas shouted at the platoon commander. "I better call this in to Battalion. We'll have to come back for the Iraqi bodies."

Part 1

Chapter 1

0456, 07 November 2003
Beck Residence
Chicago, Illinois

Mike Beck glanced across the bed, saw the blond hair of a beautiful young woman, struggled to remember how she'd gotten there, and slowly recalled that they met on the plane from Boston the night before. She rolled over and stretched, as trusting and content as one of Mike's ex-wife's cats, causing the sheet to slide below her breasts. Mike hurried to her side of the bed.

"Sorry; I have to catch a plane," he said. "Why don't you sleep in and make yourself at home? There's coffee and eggs in the kitchen and you can just lock the door on your way out. I'll call you when I get back in town next week."

She smiled again and rolled back to the middle of the bed. Within ten minutes Mike shaved, showered, and dressed. He walked to the kitchen and pushed the start button on the coffee pot. He then opened the briefcase that had been left near the door of his home office by his assistant, Brenda Higgins, and took out the folder titled USMC PENSACOLA. The folder was bound in the same manner as a deposition transcript and included several tabs: orders, a packing list, itinerary, rental car numbers, frequent flyer numbers, phone numbers, lodging reservations, and restaurant lists. This was the first time Mike had seen this folder, but he'd seen hundreds of similar folders prepared by Brenda. In fact, she prepared a new one for every trip.

A second folder inside Mike's briefcase was titled ARAMEX v AGCO and held Mike's personal laptop. During the trip to Pensacola, Mike planned to read both the folder and everything on the laptop. Never having done any previous work on the case, he expected to appear in court to try the case on the following Tuesday.

Mike opened the folder to the PACKING LIST section and returned to the bedroom. He quickly went down the list, putting everything into the suitcase: the Marine Corps dress summer uniform, black shoes, cover, ribbons, belt, socks, white T-shirts, and a selection of civilian clothes.

When Mike returned to the kitchen, he peered out the window and observed the front gate open. He knew Brenda had gotten up at 3:30 a.m. to take him to the airport, which seemed utterly ridiculous since he could easily have driven his car and left it at the airport parking lot. Mike knew better than to negotiate the issue with Brenda and just took it for granted that anytime he left town, she would show up at his door an hour and a half before flight time. Indeed, Brenda insisted on dropping off and picking up Mike from the airport on every occasion, business or personal, and many unknowing secretaries, paralegals, and associates incurred Brenda's extreme displeasure for offering rides to Mike.

At age 38, Brenda exuded a powerful sexuality, with raven black hair, dark eyes, and a stunningly beautiful face. If critically examined, Brenda might be considered a little overweight, but few men saw her that way. Instead, most were infatuated with her beautiful eyes, perfect skin, and ravishing breasts. This morning, Brenda pulled her vehicle to the side of Mike's house, parked, and entered through the back door.

As Mike walked into the entryway, Brenda, with a smile on her face, asked, "Did you decide to buy yourself a used Honda Civic?"

Mike ignored the question.

"Let me guess," Brenda said. "Is she a court reporter, a cocktail waitress, or just a horny housewife?"

Mike continued to ignore Brenda as she faked a disgusted look.

"Are you ready to go?" she asked.

"I think I have everything."

Mike and Brenda spent the trip to the airport reviewing the work he'd left for her at the office.

Brenda pulled over to the curb at O'Hare International's Terminal Four and got out to help Mike unload and to say goodbye. When Brenda leaned down to pick up Mike's briefcase, he couldn't help but notice her substantial cleavage and that she wore a lacy black bra. He also noticed that she wore a new and very attractive outfit. Mike looked Brenda in the eyes.

"That's a nice outfit. Is it new?"

Brenda blushed. "Yeah. I picked it up on sale. I'm getting so fat that I can't fit into my old stuff anymore."

As Brenda pulled away from the curb, a surge of emotion overwhelmed her. She took a deep breath and tried to concentrate on the traffic. Even the smallest compliment from Mike had that effect on her. She knew he had an eye for the ladies, but she sometimes wished he had more of an eye for her.

CRBD

1500, 07 November 2003
Naval Reserve Center
NAS Pensacola, FL

Lieutenant Colonel Mike Beck, U.S. Marine Corps Reserve, was drunk when he walked off American Flight 333 from Chicago to Pensacola, stepped to the side, and dialed his civilian law partner, Sidney Johnson, using his cell phone.

"Did we get a verdict in the Boston case?" Mike asked.

"Mike! We got a verdict all right. Hell, we kicked their asses! No, we murdered the sons of bitches. Sixty-five million in compensatory damages and one hundred million in punitive damages."

"Sid, you did a great job working this one up for trial. The motion to exclude their expert witness was a work of genius."

"Listen, Mike, your cross-examination won this case. This one's going to send shockwaves up the insurance boys' asses, and by the time you get back from temporary duty, we'll have settlement offers on half our big cases."

"I hope you're right, Sid."

"Oh, I'm right. Have a good time in Pensacola and try and stay out of trouble. I'll see you on Tuesday."

Mike continued walking from the gate to the cocktail lounge. Its small size made it easy to spot his friend, Steve Way, sitting at the bar, talking to a salesman in a wrinkled suit. Steve would talk to anyone, especially after a couple of beers. His ability to communicate with people made him a great trial lawyer, but it also made him a pain in the ass as a friend.

This red-haired farm boy from southern Indiana, six feet tall and 180 pounds, believed above all else in The American Way of Life. He always seemed in a good mood and could make people feel better about the world and themselves. Mike sat on the vacant stool next to his friend.

"Hey, Wrong Way. You ready to get into some trouble?"

With a warm smile, Steve gave out a yell. "Mike! Damn, you're looking good, old buddy."

Turning toward the bartender at the end of the bar, Steve yelled over the crowd, "A beer for my compadre and two more over here."

The bartender walked away from a small crowd waiting to order and brought three beers. Seeing the bartender's reaction and looking at Steve, Mike knew he'd already consumed a lot of beer.

"When does the Colonel get in?" Mike asked.

Wrong Way slurred his reply. "He's already here. He checked in at the Bachelor Officers' Quarters a couple hours ago."

Mike decided to drink one beer, dump the salesman, and get to the Bachelor Officers Quarters' at the Pensacola Naval Air Station as soon as possible.

CB&O

1850, 07 November 2003
Naval Reserve Center
NAS Pensacola, FL

Lieutenant Colonel Beck and Major Way hustled into the conference room and found seats among the other instructors on the Trial Advocacy Team. Many had been on the team for years, and Beck considered them his closest friends. They'd flown in from New York, Boston, Philadelphia, St. Louis, and Los Angeles. The Team included 20 of the leading trial lawyers in the United States who were drawn from the Air Force, Army, Navy, and Marine Corps Reserves.

At exactly 1900, the officer in charge of the Trial Advocacy Team, Colonel Max Dickenson, USMC, marched into the conference room. The training officer shouted, "Attention on deck!" All instructors stood at attention, a common military courtesy, but one that was rarely practiced in the legal community. However, it seemed a natural reaction with regards to Col. Dickenson.

"It's great to see all of you again," Dickenson said. "The training officer is passing out this year's course schedules and tentative assignments. I'm sure you all brought your calendars, and I would like you to check for conflicts this evening and resolve any issues with the training officer before we leave on Sunday. He is also giving you the case file for next year, which we will review tomorrow. Dinner this evening will be at Maxi's at 2100."

♋♌

0450, 08 November 2003
Naval Training Center
NAS Pensacola, FL

Mike Beck and Steve Way stayed in downtown Pensacola, drinking until past 0200, but Mike still got up at five in the morning for a six-mile run. He had a pot of coffee brewing and sat in front of the television, watching the news and lacing his running shoes when someone knocked on the BOQ door. Mike opened the door and was surprised to see Col. Dickenson standing in the corridor.

"Good morning, Mike. You have the coffee on yet?"

"Yes, sir. Should be ready in a second."

"I figured you would be going for a run and wondered if you would mind if I tagged along."

Mike could smell the ocean breeze when the two walked out of the BOQ room and down the three flights of stairs towards Gate Two. The sun was barely visible to the east, and sea birds were starting to squawk. The civilian gate sentry gave a quick look at their military identification cards and did his best to give Col. Dickenson a proper salute. The two proceeded out the gate and started running south on Pensacola Drive. Both were long-distance runners and in great shape. Mike held back to let Dickenson set the pace. After a couple of miles, Dickenson started talking.

"Mike, we need to discuss your Marine Corps career."

A loud laugh burst from Mike's gut. "Sir, I don't have a career. Everyone knows that. I've been passed over for promotion three times."

"I thought you would say that, but I have a plan, and I'm hoping to convince you to go along with it. First, Mike, I have rated you above everyone else on the trial advocacy team for the past three years, and I meant every word in your fitness reports. You set the kind of example that the course needs to motivate the students to be the best trial lawyers, and I intend to do everything in my power to see that you stay on the team."

The colonel stopped talking to catch his breath, keeping up the pace while ascending the overpass. Beck took the opportunity to interrupt.

"Sir, because of my failure to get promoted I have a mandatory retirement date in less than a year. I've enjoyed the program and would like to stay on as an instructor, but it just isn't possible."

"Well, Mike, will you hear me out? It doesn't take a rocket scientist to figure out why you've been passed over. You have the best fitness reports I've ever seen, every award imaginable, and a first-class physical fitness score. The problem is that the only reserve billet you've had is as a member of the trial advocacy team, and you haven't even signed up for a command and staff course. But I have a way to fix both problems."

Without slowing down, Colonel Dickenson turned his head and proudly smirked. "There is a billet opening for Staff Judge Advocate at the Fourth Division. The reason the billet has never been filled is that the general already has a full-time civilian attorney with the Office of General Counsel, someone who does everything for him and who hasn't seen the need for a reservist. But the OGC lawyer happens to be an old friend of mine, understands the need to get you promoted, and is willing to play ball with us."

The faster he talked, the faster Dickenson ran, and Beck worked hard to keep up.

"The best part is the drill site—New Orleans. All you have to do is enroll in the Command and Staff course and study one weekend a month in New Orleans. The next time you come up before the promotion board, you'll have a non-trial advocacy billet, a fitness report from a two-star general, and the Command and Staff course. I think the the promotion board would react favorably to someone sticking it out and doing all that without a guaranteed promotion. All right, now you can talk, and I'm going to shut up."

Beck slowed to turn at the halfway point and then started to answer. "Sir, while on active duty I was a prosecutor and a defense counsel. I've never done anything as a reservist except teach trial advocacy, and I've forgotten anything I learned at the Basic School about being a Marine. In short, I don't know jack shit about operational law or being a staff judge advocate. What if I got mobilized?"

This made Dickenson cackle. "Mike, if things get bad enough for the Fourth Division to be mobilized, I'm taking my family to Canada."

They both burst out laughing, and Dickenson continued. "Besides, you aren't really going to be a staff judge advocate.

Leave that to the OGC attorney. You just worry about finishing the Command and Staff course."

"Can I think this thing through and make sure I can do it?"

Dickenson had a curious look on his face. "There's a kicker. There is also a Deputy Staff Judge Advocate billet open at Fourth Division. I have it reserved for Major Way. Think about how lonely you must be in your big ten-million-dollar mansion in Chicago and think about what in the world you intend to do with all your money. I'm betting that one weekend a month with your buddy in New Orleans is about the most fun you can expect in life. But think about it and give me an answer on Sunday."

After that, Colonel Dickenson stopped talking and picked up the pace. He made one last comment to Beck as they split up back at the BOQ. "Mike, let's keep this secret among us girls. Don't even tell Wrong Way. I really don't want a dozen instructors coming to me asking why they can't have the billet. Check?"

"Check, sir. I won't say anything to anybody."

Chapter 2

When Anne Merrill walked into Joe O'Daniel's office at 7:00 a.m., he said nothing—just picked up the phone. "Frank, can you come down here?"

He tossed Anne some handwritten notes and went back to reading the article on his desk.

Anne already knew a lot about Frank Tobolski. He had worked as a reporter at the Dearborn News Service for 28 years. At 56, he stood five-feet-three inches tall and had a beer-belly, 20 extra pounds, and a balding hairline. He usually wore a clip-on tie and a brown polyester sports coat, the sleeves of which strained against his thick arms. He cut his hair in a flattop and possessed a square jaw and a protruding brow. You didn't have to be from Chicago to instantly know he was Polish.

"Frank, I want you and Anne to get on this story," O'Daniel said. "There's an old lady sitting on her porch who says she will not allow herself to be evicted. The story should make a good lead for tomorrow's edition. You can let Anne write the story before deadline."

For the first time, Anne saw Joe look nervous. He obviously expected an argument from Frank Tobolski. Frank said nothing for a long time and then read the handwritten notes.

"OK, Joe. It doesn't look that interesting to me, but if you want to pay me for wasting my time, that's up to you. We should be back before noon."

Frank turned to Anne. "Get your camera, and I'll get us a van. Meet me in the parking lot in five minutes."

Anne stood in the parking lot for three minutes before Frank walked out of the building.

"Anne, you drive," Frank commanded in an impatient voice. "I've done a hundred of these stories, and it's kind of hard to feel sorry for some moron who doesn't have enough sense to pay their property taxes."

As the DNS van pulled up to the Oliver home, Anne noticed two Chicago Police cars, a half-dozen neighbors in the yard, and several reporters. Anne got out of the van. Frank walked over, grinned, and whispered in her ear. "Don't screw this up, sweetheart. It's your big chance to impress the boss."

Anne pushed her way through the neighbors and started snapping photographs. Mrs. Oliver sat in a folding lawn chair on the small front porch. She wasn't crying, but an intense look of pain painted her face. A German shepherd lay next to her chair with a scared look on its face. Anytime someone got within 30 feet of the porch, the dog stood, snarled, and charged, barking and growling. Three police officers stood off to the side; two discussed their options, and the other looked bored. A fourth officer sat in the car, talking on the radio.

Anne Merrill instinctively disregarded Frank's instructions, took a deep breath, and walked past Mrs. Oliver to the bored-looking police officer. As Anne approached him, the bored look on his face vanished.

"Officer, I'm with DNS," Anne announced. "Can you tell me what's going on?"

The officer pointed to a man carrying a clipboard. "He's trying to evict the old lady, but he can't get past the dog. He called in for help, but it's a civil matter. Law enforcement can't do anything without a court order, and then that's the sheriff's jurisdiction."

When Anne looked over, Frank was already talking to the man with the clipboard. She also saw that the officer on the radio had gotten out of the car and was headed toward them.

"The sergeant says to tell him he will have to get a court order," the officer said. "Let's hit the road."

When the police and process server left, Anne walked over to Mrs. Oliver. This time the dog didn't growl, but wagged his tail instead.

"Hello, Mrs. Oliver. My name is Anne Merrill, and I'm with *Chicago News*. Maybe I can help you. I'm sure the Cook County Treasurer doesn't want any bad press. Can you talk to me?"

At that point Frank came over and, in a voice loud enough for both Anne and Mrs. Oliver to hear, explained. "Not a tax sale. The process server said the house was sold at a trustee's sale three weeks ago because Mrs. Oliver stopped making her mortgage payments. He was just here to take possession on behalf of the new owner."

Oliver was silently staring into space, tears running down her face.

Frank looked at Mrs. Oliver and Anne. "Better call Joe and tell him this is a bust. Come on. Let's get back to the office."

Anne placed one of her business cards on the arm of the chair. "Look, when you feel better, call me at this number," Anne said. "I promise I'll do what I can to help you."

Anne and Frank piled back into the van and headed back to the DNS office as fast as possible. Frank went straight to Joe O'Daniel's office and reported.

"Not her fault, Joe. It was just a wild goose chase. No interview. No story. Nothing."

Joe looked at Anne.

"Joe, I agree it's not the story you envisioned," Anne stated, "but I'm not so sure that there isn't a story here. My story concept is a series on how elderly people are losing their homes."

Joe looked bored with Anne's response and looked at Frank. "You can follow up on elderly people losing their homes. You know—does the government have statistics, foreclosure records, and know that people are moving into care facilities because mortgage companies and banks are putting the bite on 'em. Just don't let it interfere with your other assignments."

Anne smiled, but Frank rolled his eyes as they walked out of Joe's office.

⊂ॐ∾

1130, 11 March 2004
DNS Office
Chicago, Illinois

Anne returned to her office and checked her voicemail. Mrs. Oliver had already left a message, and Anne immediately returned the call.

"Mrs. Oliver, this is Anne Merrill at DNS. Can you tell me more about your problem?"

Mrs. Oliver seemed confused, but after a moment she started talking. "Honey, I'm scared. I always pay my mortgage. This is just a mess. I don't have any place to go." Mrs. Oliver started bawling in the phone.

"Who has your mortgage document, Mrs. Oliver?"

"Well, honey, I just don't know. I've never seen it. I guess my husband had it, but he never showed it to me. It might be in the safe deposit box at the bank."

Anne asked Mrs. Oliver questions for 30 minutes, but the old woman clearly didn't have much of a grasp of business or record-keeping.

"Mrs. Oliver, would it be possible for you to come down to my office and bring all of your records?"

"Well, that is awful sweet of you, but I don't have the money for a cab right now. Maybe I can come see you when I get my check on the first of the month."

"No, we can't wait. Would it be all right if I came back to your house tomorrow morning to talk about this?"

"Yes, dear, you come back anytime you want." Her voice was kind but sad.

"Great. We'll be back tomorrow. Bye now."

⊂ॐ∾

1115, 12 March 2004
Oliver Residence
Cicero, Illinois

Mrs. Oliver beamed from ear to ear when she opened the front door and the Shepherd dog wagged his tail. "Please come in. This is my dog, Handy."

Anne knelt down to pet Handy, and Frank waited on the porch, sighing.

"Please come in," Mrs. Oliver said.

The reporters entered the home.

The immaculately clean house had not been remodeled in 50 years, and the living room was an homage to fake wood paneling and shag carpet. The room was a shrine to her deceased husband and included a wooden box with an American flag, another box with ribbons and medals, and dozens of photographs on the walls. On the opposite wall was an assortment of other items that had the Marine Corps emblem printed on them. Frank Tobolski carefully examined the medals and turned back to Mrs. Oliver.

"It looks like your husband was a Marine," he said

"Yes. Gerald was a Marine. He served in Vietnam."

Anne asked every possible question and learned that Mrs. Oliver lived off her deceased husband's military retirement and Social Security. On the first day of each month she called a cab, rode to People's National Bank, cashed the check, and obtained cashier checks to pay her mortgage and utilities. She asked for the balance in cash and picked up her groceries on the way home. This was the only time she left the house. When she returned home, Mrs. Oliver mailed the mortgage payment to Newport Financial. She had no payment coupons and no proof of any kind that she had actually made the payments, but she insisted that she'd sent $185 every month.

"Mrs. Oliver, do you have family or friends to help you?" Anne inquired.

At that, Mrs. Oliver started crying. "My family is all gone, and Gerald and I never had children. I don't want to go anywhere. You probably know that none of the apartments will take pets. I just can't lose Handy. He's all I have left."

She lowered her head and continued sobbing.

☙❧

0930, 13 March 2004
Forrester & Seubert Law Office
Chicago, Illinois

John Forrester read the weekly billing report as the firm's most junior associate sat down and tried to adjust the broken conference room chair. He sat the billing report down and looked at his partner, Bob Seubert.

"How are we progressing this month on the Newport foreclosures?" Forrester asked.

"We completed six, but one went sideways. For some reason, our process server called for police assistance, and several news reporters showed up. The debtor is an old lady in Cicero and won't leave the premises."

"Did the TV station cover the story?"

"Not yet."

"Look, Bob, you know we can't have any publicity on these Newport cases. Do whatever it takes to get her out—and do it fast."

Chapter 3

0440, 16 March 2004
DNS Office
Downtown Chicago, Illinois

Anne Merrill saw less than ten vehicles on the road when she turned off the I-290 onto LaSalle. She thought of how she had ended up working for Joe O'Daniel.

Dr. Nichols could never say no to his only daughter Anne, and, as expected, she made straight As in college, obtaining a Bachelor of Arts degree in photography from the University of Illinois. She dated a good-looking pre-med student from a wealthy family. They graduated in May and had a June wedding. Dr. Nichols expected that Anne would live the life of a wealthy housewife and start having babies. It didn't turn out that way.

Anne remembered her husband Brian's admission to medical school and how she looked for a job as a photographer. She got lots of interviews, but the prospective employers always took one look at her and insisted on referring her to a modeling agency. When she became bored with modeling, she went back to school for a masters in photojournalism at the University of Missouri while her husband completed his internship at Barnes's Hospital in St. Louis.

Between the demands on Anne's study time and the lengthy hours her husband spent at the hospital, the two lacked time to develop a close relationship. When they left St. Louis for Chicago, Anne knew that their marriage had already turned cold. It lasted another two years, when Brian fell in love with a nurse and decided to divorce Anne. Anne felt relieved to be out of the marriage. She'd merely been going through the motions. She was someone who pushed to get things done, and a stagnant marriage had not been what she'd signed on for.

A year after the divorce, Anne applied for a position with the Dearborn News Service, a company that owned both the *Chicago News* and a local television station. Anne was aware that the *Chicago News* was notorious for its support of local Democrats, and at the time Anne went to work she knew that the newspaper depended on its core anti-Bush readers for its circulation numbers and profits. Every edition contained some article bad-mouthing the Republican Party.

Joe O'Daniel, the Vice-President of Operations at DNS, ran both the newspaper and television. He offered Anne a job as a television reporter. At first she turned down the offer, but Joe persisted and offered a deal. Anne could pursue her photojournalism career as long as she also worked for the television station. It was double duty, but Anne figured that at least she would stay busy—and it would be easy. She was ambitious, and now that she was divorced, she would enjoy channeling her professional energies into her job.

ᗠᗡ

0500, 16 March 2004
DNS Office
Chicago, Illinois

When she arrived at the office, Anne began researching everything she could find on Newport Financial. A dozen companies with similar names existed, but none of their customer representatives Anne spoke to would admit having any record of Mrs. Oliver's loan. Finally, Anne asked Frank to interview the process server.

Four blocks from the old Cook County Courthouse, the process server occupied a rundown office in a 12-story building that now housed fringe government agencies without budgets to make lease improvements. No name appeared on the door, just a piece of cardboard stuck inside one window that listed basic information: Michael H. Berne,

Registered Process Server, 222 N. 44th Street, Chicago Illinois, 60602.

"Get ready, Anne. When he opens the door, you snap his photograph."

Frank pounded on the door and then stepped back. When the process server opened the door, Anne flashed a picture. The process server stood well over six feet and weighed over 250 pounds. He looked like the quintessential bully.

"Hi. Michael. Frank Tobolski from DNS. I'm sure you were expecting us sooner or later."

Berne crossed his arms defensively and responded. "Now why would I be expecting *you*?"

"Because of Mrs. Oliver. We were there the day you called the police."

Berne paused, suspicious of his visitors. "If I talk to you, are you going to take my name out of the story?"

Frank looked Berne in the eye. "I want to do a story on the people that hired you. I promise that no one will know the source of any information you provide. Your clients will never know where I got their names."

The process server thought a while and smiled the same smile a wolf shows a cornered lamb.

"I have been working for one of those law firms uptown," Berne said. "The name is Forrester & Seubert on La Salle. I work for Mr. Seubert's assistant, Brian Townsend. They send me a couple of files every week and pay me a flat fee of a thousand dollars for my services. My job is to get the owners to move out and sign a release. I'm authorized to pay them ten thousand dollars in cash. Until Mrs. Oliver, every case has been the same. The people claim they made their mortgage payments and don't know anything about a foreclosure. However, they all fold their tents when I make it clear that I'll give them the ten grand just to avoid any trouble."

Without thinking, Anne interrupted. "Did you offer Mrs. Oliver the money?"

"I offered Mrs. Oliver the standard ten thousand. She wouldn't consider it. I should have sent the file back to Forrester & Seubert, but that damned dog went crazy on me. He attacked me right there on the porch. I screwed up and called the police. I thought they would explain that her house had already been sold, but the cops couldn't get close to the dog or the old lady. Brian came over the next day to tell me I was fired."

Anne decided to let Frank ask the questions and kept quiet.

"You say that homeowners claim they make their mortgage payments?" Frank asked.

"Sure, but not only on the Forrester & Seubert cases. I serve a lot of eviction notices, and believe me—everyone says that they paid."

"Did you ever wonder why Forrester & Seubert was paying you a grand to give away ten thousand dollars?"

"Of course, but ask yourself why a downtown firm is doing foreclosures? I figure they must have some high-powered client who doesn't want to take a chance that his name is going to be connected to kicking people out of their homes. Maybe a movie star or politician."

"So you really think this is on the up-and-up." Frank pressed the issue.

The process server nodded his head. "Are you going to tell me that Mrs. Oliver couldn't be a little confused about when or where she sent her payments? When I asked her where she was sending the money, she gave me the address of her insurance company."

Frank nodded his head. "I guess we'll find out when we trace her checks."

০৪৪৩

When they returned to the DNS office, Anne's telephone messages included one from Mrs. Oliver. Anne returned the call and discovered that Mrs. Oliver had been served with an eviction summons. The plaintiff's attorney was Robert

Seubert of Forrester & Seubert, 120 N. La Salle Street, Chicago, Illinois. Anne rushed down to Frank Tobolski's office with the news.

"Well, this story will probably go nowhere, but at least no one at DNS will be complaining about it," Frank said. "Forrester & Seubert are big-time Republicans. I think John Forrester has been chairman of the Republican Fund Raising Committee since you were in high school. O'Daniel is going to love this, and we'll both get a raise if we can nail a Republican law firm. Mr. Oliver was a Marine. I think I know someone who can help."

Frank clasped his hands and smiled smugly. A reporter scored points where he could.

CB80

1200, 17 March 2004
Johnson and Beck's Office
Chicago, Illinois

When Mike Beck returned to the office from the morning motion calendar, the receptionist informed him that Mr. Johnson needed to see him. Mike went straight to Sidney's office.

"Hey, Sid. What's up? You need to see me?"

"Yes. I'm trying to prevent a widow from being thrown out of her house by some mortgage company. Her husband served with me in Vietnam, so I thought I'd give it a shot. Got a heads-up from some guy named Tobolski at DNS. I had Karen Schuman do the research. She says there isn't a damn thing we can do after they have completed the trustee's sale and recorded the deed. But I have to do something. Hell, I'll buy the house back if I have to. I already deposited eight grand in our trust account in order to help her. I think the eviction hearing is on Friday."

After listening to the rest of the facts, Beck concluded that even with the $8,000, the only thing to buy time was to file bankruptcy. He remembered Sharon Steinberg, a bankruptcy lawyer in Calumet Park. He telephoned her from Sidney's office.

"Sharon, I'm doing a pro bono for a widow with an eviction hearing on Friday. I think with some time I can reach a settlement. Any chance you could file a bankruptcy for her while we figure this out?"

Steinberg sounded excited to help. "Sure, but if the hearing is on Friday, she better get in to see me today. She'll need the filing fee and a list of her creditors."

Beck took a quick look at his calendar. "No problem. I'll bring a check for the filing fee and will have her over at noon, if that's convenient."

"That will work perfectly, Mike. See you then."

ೞ෨

At noon, Beck met Tobolski and Mrs. Oliver at the bankruptcy lawyer's office located in a strip mall off Interstate 57 and Burr Oak Avenue. Tobolski walked up and shook Beck's hand.

"I've heard of you, Mr. Beck. Thanks for helping us out."

"My pleasure, Frank. I'm sure that between the press and the law, something can be done for Mrs. Oliver. The military service angle won't hurt either."

Steinberg shook her head and moaned when Tobolski explained that Mrs. Oliver had no checking account, paid her bills with cashier's checks, had no proof of making her mortgage payments, and didn't keep financial records of any kind.

"Well, Mike, I can't promise anything," Steinberg said. "I don't think there's anything that can be done once the foreclosure sale is completed. Without any records, the bankruptcy judge may allow the eviction to go forward. If you can't come up with anything fast, the bankruptcy court will probably allow the state court to proceed."

Mrs. Oliver didn't seem to have a clue what any of Steinberg's talk meant, but Beck convinced her that she wasn't going to be thrown in the street. Frank made it clear that she

should call the minute she heard anything from Sharon
Steinberg.

ഓൽ

1830, 19 March 2004
Forrester & Seubert Law Office
Chicago, Illinois

After work on Friday, Bob Seubert and John Forrester walked
to a bar four blocks from the office. The place looked crowd-
ed, but they grabbed a corner booth. Bob Seubert explained
what had happened in the Oliver case. John Forrester
appeared nervous. "Where is this thing headed?" he asked.

"I've done the research. The deed was recorded and
there is no way that the bankruptcy court or any other court
can set aside the foreclosure. Since the foreclosure is complete, it cannot be restructured in the bankruptcy, and the
bankruptcy judge will have to allow the eviction to proceed.
That old bitch will either have to settle with us or get her fat
ass out by the end of next week." He paused. "Don't worry so
much, John. I have this under control."

Chapter 4

Colonel Dickenson's plan worked perfectly. His OCG attorney friend, Dave Darwin, had no trouble convincing the commanding general at 4th Division to appoint LtCol. Beck as Staff Judge Advocate, and Maj. Way as Deputy Staff Judge Advocate.

The 4th Marine Division Headquarters, nothing more than a warehouse built by the Navy during World War II, faced the Mississippi River, with its back against a rundown section of New Orleans. The Bachelor Officers' Quarters also faced the river, but from the other side at Naval Base New Orleans, an old and almost abandoned naval port. Beck discovered that staying in the BOQ required taking a motor launch across the Mississippi River each day.

After checking into the BOQ, Mike and Steve headed to Bourbon Street for barbequed shrimp and a night of drinking. At Murphy's Tavern, a coed wearing a Baylor University T-shirt that stopped about four inches above her hip-hugging blue jeans asked Mike to dance. Steve danced with her girlfriend. At midnight, the four started hitting the bars up and down Bourbon Street until Beck's date told her girlfriend to stay at the House of Blues until she returned.

She took Beck to her room at the Marriott and, without saying a word, quickly took off her clothes and lay on her back, smiling drunkenly at Beck. He stared at her completely tanned, small, round breasts with deep rose-red nipples. Even drunk, she was incredibly beautiful. After sex, she immediately passed out, and Beck strolled back to the House of Blues to retrieve Way.

Beck didn't want to risk being late the next morning and woke Maj. Way at 0530 to drive to the parking lot next to the boat launch. The cold air rolling off the river felt more like San Francisco than New Orleans. At 0630 the gate to the dock opened, and Beck walked down to the water for a quick ride across the Mississippi River.

As the boat left the dock, he noticed heavy fog farther out on the river. He also realized that he had no concept of the width of the Mississippi River at New Orleans. As the boat entered the fog, Beck could not see more than 50 feet, but he could hear the sound of foghorns from other vessels on the river. He braced for a long, cold journey across the river.

After a successful crossing, Beck and Way had no trouble finding the location of the law center at 4th Division Head-quarters. A gunnery sergeant met Beck and Way and showed them the vacant space that served as the Staff Judge Advo-cate's office on drill weekends. The gunny also handed Beck a folder left by the OGC attorney containing a draft opera-tions order for an upcoming exercise and a Post-it-note: "Lieutenant Colonel Beck, please prepare the operational law annex to the operations order."

Beck handed the folder to Way.

"I never had to do one of these things."

As a consequence, Beck worked feverishly to complete the assignment, but wasted most of the day reading the operational law books in the law center. The operations order described a fictitious international crisis requiring U.S. military intervention. Generally, Beck figured out that the operational law annex had to address the legal issues in-volved in the operation, but realized it would take days to identify and research the issues.

In desperation, at around 1900 the two men dug into the file cabinets in the law center in hopes of finding an opera-tional law annex from some previous operation. At midnight they hit pay dirt and found an extensive file on the same operation for the previous year.

"I wonder why the bastard didn't think to give us this with the operations order!"

Using the previous year's file, Beck knew what to do. He concluded that the entire annex needed editing and furiously started a total rewrite. At 1645, he placed the final draft on the OGC attorney's desk. Beck and Way headed back across the river to the BOQ with just enough time to shower, pack, and taxi to the airport for the trip home.

Chapter 5

C lifford Jones stared at a map in the front seat of a black Chevrolet Suburban headed north on the Baghdad-to-Ramadi Expressway and looked at the approaching cloverleaf intersection. He yelled at the driver, "Get off here!"

The driver reacted to Clifford's instructions, and the Suburban, followed by three Mercedes trucks and another black Suburban, headed west on Highway 10 towards the center of Fallujah, Iraq.

The trucks hauled restaurant equipment from Taji, Iraq to Camp Ridgeway, and since trucks got hijacked every day in Iraq regardless of whether they were transporting goods for Americans or Iraqis, the trucks needed escort by armed security contractors. Unfortunately, the four American security contractors in this convoy had arrived in Iraq only days earlier, did not know about a safer route to Camp Ridgeway, and did not appreciate the that chances of getting three loaded trucks through Fallujah without being robbed were slim to none.

Since the map did not depict the Fallujah streets, Clifford set it aside and picked up his 9mm semi-automatic AR-15 rifle. As the group proceeded, he and the driver did their best to stay on Highway 10 but veered right instead of left at Andalusa Avenue and headed past the Government Center and toward the old railroad bridge. After three blocks, a traffic jam stopped the convoy.

Clifford slid his seat back to cover the rear and immediately heard the automatic weapons firing. Soon, he saw the

Jordanian drivers jump out of their trucks and run. He yelled again at the driver. "Take us back! The rear guard may be in trouble!"

Somehow, the driver pulled a U-turn and headed back down Andalusa Avenue while Clifford shouldered his AR-15 and pointed it out the passenger window. In seconds, Clifford saw the other two contractors lying dead in the street, bloodstains on their backs.

As Clifford and his driver headed east, a crowd soon forced them to stop. The Iraqis swarmed over the trucks and the Suburban, looking for something to steal. Clifford yelled at the driver to keep going and to run over the Iraqis. Within minutes, Iraqis shot both Clifford and the driver.

More and more Iraqis poured into the street and pulled the bodies of the Americans from the vehicles. The Fallujahans beat the bodies with shoes, sticks, and metal pipes. Someone brought out a five-gallon can of gasoline and poured it on the bodies and the Suburbans. Huge clouds of black smoke billowed into the air, bringing more Iraqis to the scene. As the flames died down, Fallujahans with shovels assaulted the bodies, chopping off heads, legs, and arms. The crowd dragged what was left of the bodies to the old railroad bridge and strung the dismembered body parts up with ropes. The Fallujahans smiled, cheered, and danced with joy.

Chapter 6

On Monday morning, Beck jumped out of bed, showered, and headed to the office to finish preparation for the trial starting Tuesday. At his office, Beck made a pot of coffee and turned on DNS at 4:30 a.m. and listened to the lead story of the shooting of the American security contractors in Fallujah. A call came in on his private line, and since only a few persons knew the number, at this time of day it usually meant a call from one of his Marine Corps buddies. He recognized Steve Way's voice.

"Lieutenant Colonel Beck, have you considered that I can write you up for abuse of subordinates. It's a serious offense for a commanding officer to force a reservist to work thirty-six straight hours on a drill weekend. This weekend was about as much fun as studying for a law school exam."

Beck laughed before responding. "First of all, I don't remember you studying for law school exams, and second, has anyone explained to you that Marine officers do not whine? You can't expect to screw off your entire twenty-five years of service."

"Mike, you know me! I have to have at least two nights a week of drinking and partying just to function. If I can't count on my drill weekends to get drunk, I'm going to end up hung over in trial during the week."

"OK, Deputy. As your superior, I promise you time for at least one beer and a bowl of gumbo next drill weekend. Hell, if you stop whining, I'll even buy."

"Man, you're getting easy in your old age!"

Way hung up, and Beck went back to preparing for the trial when Sidney Johnson walked in.

"Mike, have you seen the news this morning?"

"I sure have."

"I feel sorry for those bastards. They were over there trying to help, and no one deserves to die like that."

Sid stared blankly at Mike. "I tell you what's worse. I just heard that the President is ordering the Marines into Fallujah. I think the American people are about to feed the Marines one more shit sandwich."

"Let's hope you're wrong, Sid."

CRBO

0700, 5 April 2004
Stateline Trucking
Joliet, Illinois

Jeremy Case felt exhausted by his new life, working at Stateline Trucking and partying with his friends. It seemed they did something different every day. On top of endless hunting and fishing trips, they shot pool, played card games, and attended every sporting event known to western civilization.

Every payday, Jeremy managed to hand his mother $400, and for the first time in her life, Francis Case did not live from paycheck to paycheck. She had a little extra money in the house, and Jeremy saw signs of a new prosperity, such as utility bills paid on time and food in the house at the end of the month.

The new life ended after four months. Jeremy received a note to report to the loading supervisor who, in turn, told him to report to the manager at the end of his shift. The manager handed Jeremy a check and a letter of recommendation.

"Jeremy, I'm sorry about this. You're a good employee. The problem is that I have to let three people go, and you've been here the shortest period of time. I have explained that in the letter of recommendation. You turned out to be one hell of a forklift operator, and I wish you the best."

Jeremy understood his firing, but the thought of telling his mother that he had lost his job caused him great despair.

Each day, Jeremy got up, had dinner with his parents, and pretended to go to work at Stateline while in reality staying out late every night.

ೞೱ

The tree stand proved perfectly located. At about an hour after daylight, Jeremy Case held the rifle to his shoulder for five minutes and saw no sign of a deer. He cursed his luck and concluded that the only deer in the woods had probably been taken by another hunter and that he'd missed his opportunity. Slowly, he calmed down and began enjoying the woods once more. Although he could barely move with the weight and bulk of his hunting jacket, Jeremy started to get warm. Then he heard a second round of shots from nearby hunters: BLAM, BLAM. His heart started pounding.

He watched and waited. This time, for some reason, Jeremy sensed the deer had headed his way. The bright and cold weather meant that, when shooting from a tree stand, there was a danger of shooting high. He would be careful to take that into account.

The small whitetail buck shot into the cornfield, running at an angle. Jeremy realized that he could never hit it on the run, and he quickly lost sight when the buck ran into brush on the edge of the field. Soon the buck came out and headed through the hardwood timber. Jeremy only glimpsed his target as the buck moved in and out of the trees. Finally, at about 150 yards, he saw the buck run into a brushy opening in the woods. The buck never came out of the brush.

Jeremy scanned the area through the Redfield scope, and in a short time could see the buck's white belly. His head was behind a large tree, and the rest of his body was blocked by small brush. The buck was frozen.

As he stared through the scope, Jeremy could see the buck's front leg and chest area. He took a deep breath, steadied the Weatherby, and slowly squeezed the trigger. BAM! Without hearing protection, the roar of the Weatherby was deafening. The buck shot forward, running faster than before. At 50 yards, the buck went down.

Jeremy felt a thrill travel along his spine. Maybe he was a natural. And maybe—just maybe—it proved that he could do other things with his life. In fact, he'd been watching more and more television, and he thought of a rather large organization that might be willing to give him a job.

Chapter 7

Brenda Higgins buzzed Mike Beck on the intercom. "I know you're getting ready for the R & T trial, but I thought you would want to talk to Mr. Darvin from the Marines in New Orleans. Knowing that you spent the weekend there with Wrong Way, I expect he wants to talk to you about some criminal charges involving underage girls."

"All I have to say is that she looked twenty-one and swore she was nineteen." Brenda laughed and put Dave Darvin through.

"Hello, Lieutenant Colonel Beck. This is Dave Darvin. How did you and your Deputy enjoy New Orleans this weekend?"

Mike was not sure he trusted Darvin. "Oh, it's a great city with some great historical attractions."

"Well, you know you made one hell of a first impression on General Scott. He said that your annex to the operations order was the best he has ever seen. In fact, I consider that a hell of a complement since I wrote the last annex."

"I'm glad the general found the annex user-friendly," Beck said. "Did I get all the legal points correct?"

"I did a chop on it and changed a couple of things, but I agree with the general. It's one hell of a good job. Mike, you know that no good deed goes unpunished in the Marine Corps, so the bad news is that General Scott wants to know if you can work your schedule to drill next weekend and brief him at ten-thirty on Sunday."

Dave Darvin paused for Beck's answer.

"I have a commitment I can't get out of next Sunday," Beck said, "but I could come down Friday night and drill one day on Saturday, if that works?"

"That'll be fine. If you have a military résumé, I wouldn't be bashful about handing a copy to the general. And make sure you have some sort of mobilization plan worked up."

Mike Beck decided that it was time to swallow his pride. "Dave, I can go to New Orleans this weekend, but preparing that kind of brief is impossible in so short a time. If the Fourth Division did get mobilized, Scott's in a world of shit if he has to rely on me and Major Way."

Dave Darwin laughed. "Here's what we'll do. Forget the résumé. Just gloss over your background. After reading your annex, the general is already convinced you're the best staff judge advocate in the history of the Marine Corps. Just show up here at seven-thirty Saturday morning and I'll have everything put together for you. I can get a copy of the plan First Division's using right now and tweak it a little."

Beck was still a little in shock at even the possibility that a real Marine Corps general would be looking to him for advice. "All right, Dave. I just don't want anyone thinking that I'm up to speed at this time."

"Don't worry. We'll get you there."

Beck's case settled on Thursday morning, and he called Colonel Ray Moore at NAS Pensacola. "Sir, I was just assigned as Staff Judge Advocate at Fourth Division and need some help. I'm supposed to put together a mobilization plan, but don't have a clue where to start."

Colonel Moore explained to Beck what Marine Corps judge advocates were doing in Iraq. He talked about his job there as the Staff Judge Advocate the previous year, convinced Beck was worried for nothing.

"I'm happy to do anything I can to help, Mike, but you're getting geared up for nothing. There is a zero chance of the Fourth Division going to Iraq. It's never going to happen."

છ૪ૐ

1000, 5 April 2004
DNS Office
Chicago, Illinois

Joe O'Daniel welcomed the possibility of discrediting the chairman of the Republican Fund Raising Committee, John Forrester, but he didn't have the patience for an investigation. Whenever Anne tried to talk to him about it, he would respond that it seemed a waste of time. "If it's worth publishing or if you nail Forrester, I might throw you a few bucks for the story, but I'm not promising anything."

Joe assigned her more and more television stories. One was the killing of the Americans in Fallujah. The photographs made Anne sick to her stomach, and she couldn't comprehend why the people of Fallujah hated Americans so much.

DNS had a list of retired military officers willing to give interviews, and Anne would cover the national story, followed by a sound byte from a local expert. She spent two weeks covering the Fallujah story, always critical of the administration.

Three weeks later, Anne was assigned the story of a Marine staff sergeant killed in Fallujah. His family lived in Park Ridge and agreed to a press conference. By the time Anne arrived at the house, the camera crews were set up, and in a short time the door opened and the family came out.

Anne intended to take photographs and ask questions, but the spectacle of the news reporters immediately repulsed her. She detested the attitude of the reporters and the kinds of questions they asked. Anne refused to take any photographs and returned to tell Joe O'Daniel that she wasn't covering the story.

By now, Joe knew better than to argue with Anne Merrill.

Chapter 8

By 0830, Beck had prepared for his briefing with the general, and Darwin suggested that he use some time to pay a courtesy call on the 4th Division Chief of Staff just to let him know that he was aboard.

Beck thought Lieutenant Colonel Vic Carter looked about the same age as himself. Beck estimated him at six feet tall and 240 pounds, with a muscular build and the huge arms of a serious bodybuilder. He wore his graying hair in a grotesquely short Marine-style haircut. He knew the nuts and bolts of how a Marine Corps division operated and had the capability to perform any billet, from corporal to commanding general. His gruff personality and constant use of profanity suited an officer who had served in the infantry his entire career. Vic Carter was a little volatile as a lieutenant colonel, and he was the only officer in the Division who had been passed over for promotion as many times as Beck.

Carter jumped up, swaggered around his desk, and shook Beck's hand. "You sure answered the mail on the annex. It's the first fucking thing I've read by a lawyer that made any sense. You must have been a grunt before law school."

Beck grinned at the compliment. "No. I went straight from the Basic School to Naval Justice School."

Carter continued in his loud voice. "Well, I'm pleased as shit to have you on board. Most SJAs just sit around with their thumbs up their asses and try to rain on my fucking parade."

"I will damn sure try not to do that," Beck answered, continuing to smile.

"I appreciate your volunteering to be Fourth Division's Staff Judge Advocate. That took some guts. I'm sure you knew that Fourth Division is headed to Iraq. We'll need lawyers to sit on the floor and drink tea with those assholes. Try and teach them democracy."

Beck struggled to conceal his surprise at the comment about going to Iraq.

"Mike, it's going to be a tough job for reservists in Iraq, but we are the Marine Corps, and we will improvise, overcome, and adapt. Right, Mike?"

Beck nodded his head. "No shit, Vic—you're sure we're going to be mobilized? My lawyer sources say it's not going to happen."

"Oh, it's going to happen, Mike. Maybe you didn't mean to volunteer for a combat assignment, but you best get your seabag packed because you're fucking going—and soon."

ଓଙ୍କ

At 1020, Mike Beck walked down the hallway to General Scott's office. The door to Scott's office remained closed, but Beck could hear voices inside. He didn't want to interrupt Gen. Scott, but wasn't sure if the general might be waiting for him and consider him late for the meeting. Finally, at 1045 Beck put Darwin's laptop under his arm, knocked on the door, and heard someone yell, "Come in."

"General, I'm Lieutenant Colonel Beck, the new Staff Judge Advocate. I'm here for the ten-thirty brief."

General Scott walked around the desk and extended his hand. "Welcome aboard. This is the Assistant Division Commander, Colonel Hall. By the way, good job on the operations order annex."

In his 24 years of active and reserve duty in the Marine Corps, Beck had never been inside a general's office—hadn't even been introduced to a general—and he did not know what to expect. He guessed Gen. Scott to be only a few years older than himself. He was of medium height, weight, and build. It immediately struck Beck that MajGen. Scott looked more like the chief executive of a large corporation than what he had pictured as a stereotypical Marine Corps general. He also looked like someone you would meet playing golf at one of Chicago's exclusive country clubs.

Scott motioned Beck toward a small round table with four chairs at the other end of the office. Col. Hall took the opportunity to leave, claiming that he needed to talk to the Personnel Officer.

Beck sat down, handed Gen. Scott a paper copy of his PowerPoint slides, put the laptop in front of the general, and started his presentation. During the briefing, Scott interrupted Beck frequently, asking insightful questions and commenting on the proposed judge advocate lay-down.

"Mike, I'm sure that the mission in Iraq won't be completed for years, but I think we'll be going sooner than later. My concern is that by the time we go, there won't be any lawyers left to take with us. I want you to drill down into this and lobby all your lawyer contacts to perfect our plans for deployment."

CRTBO

1656, 11 April 2004
Louis Armstrong Airport
New Orleans, LA

Beck checked his bags and walked up to the Red Carpet Club, hit the buzzer, and asked the bar attendant for a Jack Daniels on the rocks. While waiting for the flight back to Chicago, he started having second thoughts about the assignment of Way as his Deputy.

Mike and Steve went all the way back to the class of 1977 at the University of Chicago Law School. He never understood how the hell Steve got admitted to law school in the first place. Steve seemed totally out of place with the faculty and other students and landed on academic probation after the first semester and stayed there until he graduated four years later.

After graduation, Mike took the bar exam in Illinois, passed on the first attempt, and reported for active duty as a lawyer in the Marine Corps. With Steve's horrible academic performance, it took him an extra semester to get his law degree, and he failed the Indiana bar exam three times. He received no interviews and no job offers. Two years after Mike Beck received his commission as an officer in the Judge Advocate Division, Way applied to the Marine Corps. Luckily for Way, the Marine Corps recruiters demonstrated no interest in his class standing or academic acumen, and so both men ended up as lawyers in the Marine Corps.

Beck divorced his first wife, but Way, with two kids, remained married to Wendy. Beck preferred being left alone, but Steve and Wendy felt it their Christian duty to make sure Beck got at least one home-cooked meal a week, so when he wasn't drinking and whoring around Washington, D.C., Beck would be at Way's rented apartment in Quantico, eating Wendy's cooking and getting drunk with Steve.

Sitting in the airport, Beck realized that Way was his best friend, but wondered if Wrong Way could do the job if they went to Iraq. He wasn't sure.

ಅನಿ

0430, 12 April 2004
Johnson & Beck Law Offices
Chicago, Illinois

Mike Beck sat in his office, drinking coffee and waiting for Sidney Johnson to show up. Yesterday, he doubted whether Steve was up for the task. Today, he doubted his own readiness. At that moment, Beck heard Sidney Johnson walking down the hall.

"Hey, Sid. You got a minute?"

"Sure, Mike. How was New Orleans?"

"That's what I want to talk about. The Chief of Staff tells me that the Fourth Division is being mobilized and sent to Iraq."

Sid stroked his bald head the way he always did when he was thinking, and then shook his head. "I don't remember the Marine Corps activating the Fourth Division during Vietnam. But if it does happen, don't worry. You'll do fine. Besides, I can hold the fort down until you get back."

Beck hoped he was right.

Chapter 9

A week after his firing, Jeremy drew down his checking account to $500 and knew he had to do something. Since he wasn't working, he had time to think about the killing of the Americans in Fallujah. One morning, he drove to the Armed Forces Recruiting Station on Michigan Avenue. By chance, he found a parking space next to the Marine Corps Recruiting Office and remembered the old veteran at the American Legion asking him if he was a Marine. He walked inside.

The recruiting office had a waiting area and four glass offices in the rear, and Jeremy could see a tough-looking sergeant talking to a young man at his desk. Another Marine sat in the adjoining office. Jeremy walked over, knocked on the side of the door, and said, "Sir, can I talk to you?"

Master Gunnery Sergeant Lopez stood up. He looked old and wore green trousers and a khaki shirt with rows and rows of ribbons. He had a way of standing ramrod straight, feet set slightly apart, as if daring someone to challenge his authority. He extended his hand. "Master Gunnery Sergeant Lopez. Can I help you?"

"Yes, sir. My name is Jeremy Case, and I wanted to find out about getting a job in the Marine Corps."

Lopez did not hesitate for a second. "Son, we don't offer jobs here. If you are looking for a job, you need to walk on down to the Air Force Recruiter."

At first, Jeremy thought the old Marine was just preparing for his sales pitch but soon realized he was dead serious and expected Jeremy to leave. When Jeremy walked out of the recruiting office, he didn't go to the Air Force office, but went to a bar instead.

The next day Jeremy drove back, walked inside the Marine Corps Recruiting Office, and saw that the old Marine was busy talking to someone in his office. Jeremy waited in the reception area for Master Gunnery Sergeant Lopez to finish his conversation.

"What can I do for you today, Case?" asked Lopez after several minutes.

"I want to enlist in the United States Marine Corps," Jeremy answered, looking the old Marine in the eye.

"Come into my office."

When they went inside, Lopez closed the door. "I have just one question for you, Case. Why?"

Jeremy had to think about it. "I want to serve my country, and I want my mother to be proud of me."

Lopez reached in his bottom drawer, pulled out some paperwork, and asked Jeremy for his driver's license. After taking down Jeremy's personal information, Lopez stopped. "Look, Case, if you've smoked grass within fourteen days, it's going to show up on your piss test. Do you want to continue or come back next week to finish the paperwork?"

Jeremy tried to think when the last time he'd lit his pipe. After mentally counting the days, Jeremy replied, "We can finish the paperwork today, sir."

"That's good, Case. I can already tell that you're going to make a good Marine."

Chapter 10

0900, 12 April 2004
DNS Offices
Chicago, Illinois

Everyone but Anne gave up on the Oliver investigation, and Frank said that some of Mrs. Oliver's Marine friends were already looking for another house. Anne, however, just kept plugging away. In the second week of April, she received a call from Mrs. Oliver's bankruptcy lawyer, Sharon Steinberg.

"Anne, we have the discovery from Newport Financial," Steinberg informed her. "Here's what happened. Newport Financial purchased the note and mortgage from People's Mortgage Company and wrote to Mrs. Oliver requesting proof of insurance. They had a right to do that under the loan documents. Mrs. Oliver never responded, and so Newport purchased a policy of insurance and wrote to Mrs. Oliver informing her that her monthly payments had increased to cover the cost of the insurance.

"Mrs. Oliver kept sending the old amount. Those payments weren't accepted, but instead placed in a suspense account. Newport Financial wrote to Mrs. Oliver three times, telling her that her payments were short and would not be accepted. Again, Mrs. Oliver ignored those letters and that is why her house went into foreclosure."

The bankruptcy attorney paused, and Anne asked the obvious question. "Can they do that?"

"In fact, they had a right to do everything they did. I also looked at the foreclosure file. Not surprisingly, Forrester & Seubert did everything right, and I don't see any way to set aside the sale, so if they want to play hardball, even with the money in Johnson & Beck's trust account, Mrs. Oliver is in the street."

"So there's nothing we can do for Mrs. Oliver?" Anne pleaded.

"Here's the good news. Robert Seubert says his client is willing to give Mrs. Oliver a chance to refinance her home. In turn, we dismiss the bankruptcy and deliver Newport Financial a release of all claims, and they will convey the house back to her if she pays all amounts due under the mortgage, including foreclosure costs and attorney fees, within sixty days. They also want an assurance from us that there will be no adverse news coverage. We can use the money in Johnson & Beck's trust account as the down payment and should have no trouble refinancing. I'm going to talk to Mike Beck and meet with Mrs. Oliver tomorrow at eight o'clock. You're welcome to attend, if you like."

"Sure," said Anne. "Sounds good."

❧

Frank Tobolski volunteered to pick up Mrs. Oliver the next day. Anne met them at Sharon Steinberg's office. Mike Beck could not make the meeting and had not yet heard about the settlement offer.

Steinberg explained the legal presumption that if notice is sent by first-class mail, it's presumed to have been received by the addressee. Sharon Steinberg strongly recommended that Mrs. Oliver accept Robert Seubert's settlement offer.

❧

1800, 15 April 2004
Case Residence
Downers Grove, Illinois

Jeremy Case drove home, turned on the television, and tried to think of what he would tell his parents. His mother walked in the back door at 6:00 p.m. and yelled for her son to carry the groceries in from the car. After the groceries were put away, Jeremy asked his mother to come into the living room and clicked off the television.

"Mom, will you sit down? I have to tell you something."

Francis Case sat down, looked Jeremy in the eyes, and expected to hear something bad.

"Oh, God, Jeremy. What in the world has happened?"

"Mom, I enlisted in the Marine Corps."

Jeremy waited for a reaction from Francis Case.

"I don't understand," his mother said. "You have the job at Stateline, and you are doing so well."

Jeremy knew he couldn't lie anymore.

"I got laid off at Stateline four weeks ago. They said they liked my work and gave me a letter of recommendation, but that's not why I joined the Marine Corps."

Jeremy hesitated and then continued. "Most of the guys at Stateline are veterans. They did their duty for their country. I just can't stay in Chicago all my life and look back when I'm sixty and think that I never did my part."

Francis Case had tears in her eyes. She started to sob and forcefully hugged Jeremy for a long time. "You are the sweetest young man in the world. I don't understand this, but I know it means a lot to you. I love you no matter what you have to do."

"What do you think Dad is going to say?"

Francis Case thought for a moment before answering. "Well, it's a shock, but I know when he has a chance to think, he's going to be proud of you, just like me. How long before you have to leave?"

"The recruiter said they're probably going to send me out right away."

At that moment, Ian Case walked in the front door. He could see that something important was happening. "What's going on?"

Francis Case answered. "Jeremy has enlisted in the military. In the Marine Corps."

Ian Case looked bewildered. He stared at Francis Case, then at Jeremy and back at his wife. "Are you OK with that?"

Francis Case stood up and walked to her husband. "Yes—I think it's wonderful that Jeremy has the courage to stand up for what he believes in. I'm so proud of him."

Ian Case was confused but was not going to question his wife. "Well, Jeremy, if it's all right with your mother, it's all right with me. Congratulations, son."

Chapter 11

Anne Merrill spent hours studying the documents received from Sharon Steinberg. She conducted an extensive investigation into the employee who signed the mailing certificates for Newport Financial, Charlene Lawson. According to the computer reports, Charlene Lawson owned nothing in her name. However, the credit report showed a different story. She had loans for a 2002 Pacemaker doublewide mobile home, a 2003 Ford Expedition, a 2004 Ford F-150, a 21-foot Pro-Bass boat, three ATVs, a 2003 Harley Davidson motorcycle, a swimming pool, a hot tub, and numerous appliances. Lawson's monthly payments exceeded $12,000 a month. The co-borrower on the loans was Bruce S. Garrett, and a computer asset search under his name listed him as the owner of the mobile home, vehicles, and other assets. He also owned a vacation home on Lake Michigan.

The next day Anne Merrill waited outside Frank Tobolski's office.

"Frank, look at this credit report I have on the Newport employee who signed the mailing certificate. Where is she getting all this extra cash?"

Frank carefully examined the credit report and the mailing certificates. For the first time since she had known Frank Tobolski, he appeared excited. "This is it Anne! Those bastards are paying her under the table to shit-can the notices. No wonder Mrs. Oliver didn't respond. You ready to pay Lawson a visit? Let's see if she leaves the office for lunch."

"Frank, how are we going to identify her? I don't have a picture."

"I'll get the photograph from my friends at the Department of Motor Vehicles. Just be ready to leave here at ten-thirty."

At 11:30 a.m., Frank and Anne stood on the street outside the entrance to the Plaza Building. At 12:15 p.m., Charlene Lawson walked out of the building and headed toward the mall. Frank and Anne followed. Charlene walked to the Panda Express, ordered a meal to go, and started to head back outside. That's when Frank went to work.

As Frank approached Charlene, he quickly flipped his wallet open and shut.

"Mrs. Lawson, I'm Frank Tobolski with the Illinois Bureau of Investigation. Will you follow me, please? I need to ask you some questions, and I don't want to go to Newport Financial's office."

Charlene Lawson appeared ready to faint, and her hands shook violently by the time the three sat at one of the tables inside the mall.

"Ms. Lawson, we have a sworn statement from a dozen witnesses, copies of your bank records, and photographs of you throwing unopened mail in the trash. I have enough to convict you right now, but I want Robert Seubert. You're going to answer my questions today. If you do, I could care less about you. If you don't cooperate, you're going to have a long wait at the Cook County Jail."

Lawson stared at the unopened Chinese food. "I'll cooperate. Bruce doesn't know where I get the money. He's innocent."

"Like I said, Ms. Lawson—I want Robert Seubert. I doubt you ever spoke directly to him. Probably only to Brian. Is that right?"

"Yes."

"How did you get paid?

"By Brian. In cash. I meet him at the mall on Fridays at noon. He hands me an envelope with the money and a list of the files that I'm supposed to trash the next week."

"All right. That's all I need. You don't tell anyone about this visit. You keep doing exactly what you've been doing, with no changes."

Lawson fought off the tears. "Yes, sir. I understand."

ᎧᎦ

1500, 18 May 2004
DNS Office
Chicago, IL

Joe O'Daniel seemed beside himself. He promised Anne and Frank a raise and anything they wanted and put every reporter at DNS on the story. A full-scale investigation on every player was ordered, including all partners, associates, and employees of Forrester & Seubert. Joe O'Daniel expected the Oliver story to be front page for months.

The Chicago Police arrested Brian Townsend on Friday, and he promptly spilled his guts. Using Brian's statement, the police arrested Robert Seubert the next day. Newport Financial settled with Mrs. Oliver by conveying her house back free and clear.

Robert Seubert and John Forrester were ordered to pay restitution to all victims, given one-year probations, and were disbarred. Brian Townsend received one year of jail time. Charlene Lawson got probation.

Joe O'Daniel soon forgot about the promises to Anne and Frank. Neither really cared. Frank's stories returned to the front page, and that's all he really wanted. Anne just wanted Mrs. Oliver to get her house back.

However, after the Oliver story ran its course, Anne surprised everyone. She walked into Joe's office and told him she was holding him to the promise that she could have anything she wanted. Anne Merrill wanted to go to Iraq as an embedded reporter with the Marines. O'Daniel knew that not many reporters would be volunteering for such hazardous duty, and he agreed, believing that Anne was making the biggest mistake of her career. Still, it might help DNS expose the folly of the Bush Administration.

Chapter 12

Lieutenant Colonel Carter scheduled a special drill in May to review the 4th Division's mobilization plans. By this time, Beck had convinced himself that Sidney Johnson and Steve Way were right—no way could the 4th Division actually mobilize, and everything suggested another big training exercise.

When Beck and Way arrived at 4th Division Headquarters, Beck picked up his green notebook and headed to the conference room. There were already 20 officers inside. A PowerPoint slide appeared at the far end of the room stating MOBILIZATION BRIEF.

The active duty officers were, at this point in their careers, burnt out on staff meetings. Since they had over 12 hours of work to accomplish each day, the meetings seemed like a waste of time.

All legal issues were considered confidential, and since his private brief to Gen. Scott, Beck had never been asked to brief anything. There were only two occasions when a legal question came up. On one of those occasions he had been well informed and articulate. However, on the second occasion he had been half asleep when he heard the general say, "Mike, am I correct on that?"

Since Beck didn't have a clue what the general had been talking about, he just stood up and replied, "Spot on, sir."

This tactic was obvious and elicited a thundering laugh from the rest of the staff.

Fortunately, the general was not perturbed. "Ah yes; great sucking up."

The general then explained the issue. Beck, uncertain of the answer, ended up saying, "Sir, I will double-check that."

The nametags on the conference table and select gallery chairs suggested another degree of the importance of the present meeting. In fact, the meeting's significance relegated most of the 4th Division Staff to gallery chairs.

In short order, the room filled with generals and admirals. A lieutenant colonel heralded, "Standby," followed with, "Attention on deck."

The commanding general of the 4th Division, Major General Scott, entered the room, followed by the commanding general of the 1st Marine Expeditionary Force from Camp Pendleton, California: Lieutenant General Bailey.

"At ease, ladies and gentlemen. Please take your seats."

Beck had a good angle on LtGen. Bailey. He had never seen a three-star general, but Bailey made a good first impression. Looking at Bailey, Beck considered the myth that warriors have a singular look, which persisted because it was advantageous in maintaining uniforms, personal grooming, and physical fitness. The Marines on the recruiting posters were right out of Gentlemen's Quarterly: tall, athletic, good looking, healthy, and strong. Of course, Beck knew that none of the great Marines looked anything like poster Marines. Instead, the great ones came in all shapes and sizes. Their strengths were not external but below the surface.

It soon became apparent that a wave-top PowerPoint slide show was not going to work with LtGen. Bailey. He had his own agenda, and started around the table with incisive questions for each staff member. An extensive amount of time was spent with intelligence and operations. The discussion moved from general concepts to specific details. He seemed to be interested in everything. All aspects of the mobilization operation were covered in detail. The brief lasted two hours.

At the conclusion of the brief, Bailey told everyone to put down their pens because he wanted to say a few things. "Ladies and gentlemen, thank you for a professional brief. I am honored to be here. It is obvious to me that a great deal of work has gone into your mobilization plan, and I intend to approve it today."

Bailey paused, and it was obvious that even the general was hesitating about what he had to say next. "I came here today because I consider this an historical event, and I wanted to inform you of the decision in person. We're here because of what happened on September 11th. Some extremists decided that America had to be punished. They attacked our homeland and killed our mothers, wives, and children. The Fourth Division has not been mobilized since the Korean War. But ladies and gentlemen, the Marine Corps needs the Fourth Division again. The President is ordering a full mobilization."

There was dead silence in the room.

"You will deploy to Iraq in thirty days." Again, dead silence. "Good luck and God bless."

At that, Bailey stood up and the aide barked, "Attention on deck." All stood at attention as he walked out, followed by MajGen. Scott.

The Chief of Staff stood grinning. "Ladies and gentlemen, we have our orders. Let's get to work."

Chapter 13

0600, 21 May 2004
Edson Range
Camp Pendleton, CA

Private Case, along with 200 other recruits, placed himself in the sitting position at the 200-yard line of Edison Rifle Range on a beautiful southern California morning at Camp Pendleton. His movements were practiced and precise. Everything that morning felt fantastic. The weather seemed perfect, with a slight ocean breeze. His M16A2 rifle was perfectly clean, lubricated, and adjusted. Even his fresh digital camouflage uniform felt good against his skin.

This day, however, felt different from all the rest. In fact, it proved different from any other day in Jeremy Case's life. He had never before been able to focus on anything the way he concentrated this morning. Private Case became a different person at the rifle range.

Each day he improved. He no longer had to think about how to sit, kneel, stand, or lay down. Each position felt perfectly natural, as if there could be no other way to do these things. He had mastered it all. His left hand formed a perfect V under the forearm, the rifle butt fit firmly in the pocket of his shoulder, his right hand held the pistol grip in so that the trigger pull was precisely the same each time, his elbow was in exactly the right position, his cheek was welded to the stock, and his breathing was controlled. Most importantly, he was completely relaxed.

Case waited for the range officer to finish his announcement. "All ready on the right. All ready on the left. Shooters, when your targets appear, you may commence firing."

He sat looking down the barrel. It was not necessary to force the rifle on target. Instead, Private Case simply moved his right leg, leaned a little forward, twisted his butt slightly, or made a slight body adjustment.

He checked the sight picture. He could feel himself breathing. With both earplugs and hearing protectors on, the world was perfectly silent. He tried to feel the wind, but it was so light that he couldn't. Instead, the only thing he felt was the concussion from the rifles of other Marines.

He started to squeeze the trigger. Time slowed. His mind analyzed a dozen things before the rifle discharged. He exhaled and stopped breathing. He still felt no wind, the sight picture was perfect, and the sight was dead-center of target. When the rifle discharged, the target instantly went down.

When the target came up, there was a four-inch white circular marker stuck in the bullet hole. The round had hit dead-center. Case took one deep breath and started the process over again. It was another bull's-eye. And another. And another.

The firing continued at the 200-yard line for the sitting, kneeling, and standing positions. By the time he moved to the 300-yard line, Private Case knew that he had enough points to score expert. At the 300-yard line, Private Case was not surprised that he shot a perfect score in the sitting position. He had done that several times in the last week, but what surprised him was when he also shot perfectly in the standing position. That had never happened.

The final series was the prone position at the 500-yard line. This was Private Case's best position, even better than the sitting position. Indeed, shooting at the 500-yard line had become a daily mystical experience for Case. The target itself was just a blur, and Case recalled that it was nothing like shooting the .270 Weatherby with the Redfield Nine power scope. Still, almost every time he squeezed the trigger, a white marker would appear. Today was no exception, and Case racked up another perfect score at the 500-yard line. It might be a range record, or even a Marine Corps record.

He would be promoted to private first class and honored at the graduation parade.

Part II

Chapter 14

The temperature had reached over 115 degrees Fahrenheit when Beck and Way stepped out of the transient tent and attempted to get their bearings to find the chow hall. They had spent a day, night, and another day on a chartered Boeing 737 traveling from California to Kuwait. The trip required the plane to refuel three times, and the men had cobwebs in their brains. They had not had a drink of alcohol in two days, the longest period of time for both of them in over 30 years.

Camp Victory felt like a space station on the desert planet Arrakis from the novel *Dune*, a depressing environment of tents, port-a-johns, and diesel generators. Beck's uniform lay hot against his skin. The desert wind burned his nostrils, and within minutes his clean boots and uniform were covered in fine white dust.

The Marines now called the chow hall a D-FAC, short for dining facility, and at Camp Victory the D-FAC occupied a gymnasium-sized mobile home built and operated by Brown & Root, one of the American companies providing support services to the military.

After breakfast, he and Way returned to the transient tent as the rest of the Marines started crawling out of their racks.

Beck knew that, as a time-honored tradition, Marine Corps officers traveled with the troops, sharing the same hardships. This motivated the enlisted Marines, but it wasted valuable working time of the senior staff. Mike Beck had attempted not to waste an hour of available work time in his 25 years of being a trial lawyer, and he planned on working every minute on the trip to Camp Baharia. Accordingly, he packed an excessive supply of reading materials: Operational Law Handbook, Law of War Documentary Supplement, Field Manual 27-10 on the Law of Land Warfare, Rules of Engagement Handbook for Judge Advocates, MAGTF Handbook, and the Joint Staff Officer's Guide.

Beck appeared to be the only Marine in the tent not wearing a set of headphones. Because he didn't want to stand out, he pulled out his MP-3, put on his Bose headphones, and continued to study Field Manual 27-10.

രദ

1300, 7 June 2004
Transit Billeting
Camp Victory, Kuwait

Lance Corporal Case and the rest of the Surveillance and Target Acquisition Team—Corporal Nelson, Private First Class Goldman, and Private First Class Hale—sat in the front row of the tent in Camp Victory, attentively listening to Captain Pascal, the Battalion Staff Judge Advocate, lecture on the rules of engagement.

Case had arrived at Camp Victory with 3re Battalion, 4th Marines the day after Beck. Case had been in the Marine Corps for four months and had already received six lectures on the rules of engagement: at Boot Camp, at the School of Infantry, as part of his check-in at 3rd Battalion, on his assignment to the Surveillance and Target Acquisition Platoon, as part of the pre-deployment package at Camp Pendleton, and at a short brief given by the Army staff on arrival at Camp Victory.

Nevertheless, the commanding officer of 3rd Battalion was a hard charger and didn't plan to let his Marines sit around Camp Victory on their backsides. On the first day, the unit's flight got cancelled, and he ordered a training plan to be hastily put together to use the down time for additional lectures on convoy operations, internal security, patrol procedures, Iraqi road systems, basic Arabic, and handling prisoners.

Captain Pascal considered himself lucky. He brought four thumb drives and six CDs for every PowerPoint lecture given by any Marine Corps judge advocate in the last five years. Capt. Pascal could sleep while the other officers worked on their lecture slides.

On the first day, Pascal lectured on detainee processing, how to complete detention forms, and the proper methods to transport prisoners. To his surprise, Pascal ran out of new subjects, and on the sixth day went back to the rules of engagement, even though he knew the subject had been repeatedly covered.

Pascal started the lecture he had given many times. "Positive identification is required prior to engagement. PID is a reasonable certainty that the object of attack is a legitimate military target. This means you must comply with the Law of Armed Conflict concerning discrimination of targets. PID is a determination based on reasonable military judgment."

He moved on. "Proportional force. Force employed must be proportional. You may use necessary force, including deadly force, to protect yourself, unit, or coalition forces."

The Geneva Conventions were also reviewed. "Do not engage anyone who has surrendered or cannot fight due to sickness or wounds."

Up to this point, the Marines had difficulty concentrating because most of them had memorized the basic concepts. At the conclusion of the lecture, new ROE cards were handed out to the Marines. These cards added the special rules to the standard ROE that were to be followed.

⁂

1500, 8 June 2004
Headquarters, MNC-I
Camp Victory, Iraq

Anne Merrill had a direct flight from Chicago to Kuwait, changed planes, and landed in Baghdad in less than 24 hours.

A public affairs officer, an Army major, met Anne Merrill and ten other reporters at Baghdad International Airport, with the responsibility for finding quarters for the reporters and getting them to the joint briefing the next day. She had spent the last four weeks planning, coordinating, and executing the reception of embedded reporters for the upcoming operation in Fallujah. Anne and the other reporters rode an armored bus with blast-proof windows—the Rhino Bus— from the airport to the former palace grounds of Saddam Hussein, now called Camp Victory. The camp had been built around a large man-made lake, with balconies and wonderful views that replicated the palaces of European royalty. On the inside of the palace, designs included 50-foot ceilings, marble floors, magnificent stairways, large paintings, chandeliers, and gold-plated fixtures.

One of the palaces now served as the dining facility, administration offices, and activity center for the Joint Billeting Center, which also had a number of mobile trailers parked around it. Anne was assigned a room in one of the trailers next to the water.

The next day, Anne and the other reporters attended a briefing at the palace occupied by the Multi-National Corps Iraq, or MNC-I Headquarters. The public affairs officer spent an hour using a PowerPoint explaining the embedded reporter rules and the agreement Anne would have to sign. The officer also explained Anne's options of staying at Camp Victory, moving to Camp Fallujah, or being assigned to a combat unit. Without hesitation, Anne requested to be assigned to a Marine Corps combat unit.

Chapter 15

Haitham Rasheed rubbed his eyes, slowly rolled over on his sleeping mat, and hit his back on a beat-up AK-47 rifle. Haitham and all of the men in the Rasheed family kept next to their sleeping mats what the interim Iraqi Government allowed Iraqis for protection: a rifle with a 20-round magazine. If the Americans found anything more, one could end up in prison.

Haitham carefully descended the unfinished concrete stairs, exited through the side door to the outside sink, filled it with fresh water in preparation for the washing ritual for his morning prayer, and spoke out loud before washing, saying, "In the Name of Allah." He then returned to his sleeping room, positioned himself, and completed his morning prayer.

The house belonged to Haitham's uncle, Ghazi Rasheed. Uncle Ghazi was a large man for an Iraqi, six feet tall and 250 pounds, and exhibited an air of quiet authority. He had a kindly face, a potbelly, long arms, and huge hands. He always wore a *dishdasha*, or man-dress, and a red checkered *keffiyeh*, or headdress. Uncle Ghazi was a profoundly religious man and was extremely proud of his pilgrimage to Mecca. Every decision in Ghazi Rasheed's life, whether trivial or monumental, was made on the basis of what would please God.

Uncle Ghazi's house sat on the side of a potato field surrounded by date palms, with no roads, electricity, or water. Access to the house came from a dirt path that ran to a canal bank and then two miles south to the village of Saqlawiyah.

The house had been under construction for as long as Haitham could remember. First the kitchen had been built, then the large bedroom, the prayer room, the sitting rooms, and the additional bedrooms. Even as a boy, Haitham worked with his father on the house.

He remembered walking across the field to harness the donkey and the walk down to the canal, listening to the men's conversations while waiting for the brick truck at the highway. When there were enough bricks, water could be carried from the canal, and the mixer, built in England and powered by a one-cylinder Ford engine, could be started. The cement sacks were carried all the way from the plant outside Fallujah. Sand and gravel were occasionally stolen from the side of the highway or railroad track. Haitham and his relatives would mix concrete in the mixer and, day by day, pour the floor. After the floor was laid, the brick walls went up, then dozens of wooden poles were used to support plywood forms to pour an eight-inch concrete roof. Even though the house had no utilities, it looked large and impressive.

After his father died in the war with Iran, Haitham and his mother had moved in permanently. Today, Haitham would not work on Uncle Ghazi's house. Uncle Ghazi had lost his job, there were no government rations, and even the Fallujah cement plant remained closed. Before Haitham reached the bottom of the stairs, his aunt started yelling at him. "Hurry! Your cousin is ready for school. You better not be late again."

CRACO

Haitham stood outside the school. Since there was nothing to do at Uncle Ghazi's house, Haitham decided that he would spend the morning waiting with the group of desperate out-of-work men under the large tree next to the canal across the street from the school. Like Haitham, these men had nothing better to do than sit and wait the four hours before the boys came to school and the girls went home. Today, the group of loafers included a father, an uncle, and two grandfathers. One of the uncles talked about going to Najaf.

"My cousin tells me that the Americans are building schools in Najaf," the uncle said. "They pay anyone whose house was damaged in the fight. If you can lay bricks or even dig a ditch, you should go there. You are sure to find a job."

"That's good if your family is Shiite," the father replied. "But it is a long way, and I don't think anyone in Najaf is going to hire a Sunni from Saqlawiyah."

"No. The people in Najaf are not like that. I have been there, and I know. There are a lot of Sunnis in Najaf, and we are all Iraqis. As long as you can get the work done, no one cares who your family is."

A grandfather joined the debate. "I have traveled to the Ali Shine, and it is an expensive journey. Better not to risk it unless you have arranged a job for when you get there."

This debate went on slowly for most of the morning. When the school bell rang, the group walked across the street to the school. Boys dressed in school uniforms were lined up on the side of the street while a stream of little girls poured out of the gate. Haitham walked his cousin back home, thinking of the talk he had heard during the day. Haitham had made up his mind. He would talk to Uncle Ghazi about his right to a job in the family.

The dinner that evening consisted of canned beef, with tomatoes and potatoes from the garden. Afterward, Uncle Ghazi and Haitham smoked on the roof and talked for hours about what had passed in the last year and what might be the future.

"Americans cannot stay in this country, but we must be wiser than Saddam Hussein and carefully pick when to fight the Americans. The Sunni and the Baath Party will again rule Iraq. This I know for certain. Let the foreigners spill their blood while we make plans for our future."

"I want to work for the family," Haitham said. "I do not want to join the Jihadists."

After much thought, Uncle Ghazi spoke. "Perhaps my brother Khalid in Ramadi can help you. He was very close to your father and will want to take care of you if he can. I will give you enough money to return if things don't work out. Promise me you will think always about what is best for the family."

○8○

1400, 11 June 2004
Doctor Khalid Rasheed's Office
Ar Ramadi, Iraq

The taxi looked worn out, with the padding in the backseat gone, so that Haitham's rear end kept bouncing on the floorboards. The route to Ramadi consisted of freeways with two lanes in each direction, overpasses, and interchanges, but after Saddam Hussein completed the freeways in 1980, the government did nothing to maintain them, so most of the metal signs and guardrails had been stolen and deep pot-holes appeared every few miles. The trip required a series of short races with the taxi driver accelerating to 80 miles an hour and then braking to swerve around a pothole or an abandoned vehicle. The violent maneuvering, heat, and blue exhaust blowing in the windows made Haitham sick to his stomach. Fifteen miles outside Ramadi, the driver started screaming.

"Those fucking pigs! They shouldn't be here now!"

Haitham saw ten cars backed up by the same number of military vehicles traveling at about 25 miles per hour. It seemed crazy, but the taxi driver started passing the cars on the right, one after another, until he was directly behind the last military vehicle, which had a large sign which read: STAY BACK. DO NOT APPROACH OR PASS VEHICLES.

Inside the vehicles, American soldiers pointed their guns to the rear and watched the taxi. The soldiers looked like aliens with their helmets, body armor, and goggles. The taxi driver kept closing in on the left side of the convoy.

"Stay back," Haitham pleaded. "Please. You are going to get us killed."

The driver didn't answer. He just kept yelling out the window. "You are fucking pigs! You are fucking American pigs! You don't own this road. Get out of my way."

Of course, the soldiers could not hear a word the driver said. They just kept staring and occasionally made a motion with their hand waving the taxi back. The convoy never pulled over, but continued at 25 miles per hour all the way to Ramadi, through the city, and toward the town of Hit. Finally, the taxi was able to pull off the freeway and had no trouble finding the hotel, a four-story building located on a busy intersection in downtown Ramadi.

The hotel lobby appeared dark and cold, and no one sat at the front desk. Instead of ringing the bell, Haitham sat down and waited for someone to return. After ten minutes Haitham recognized the person coming down the stairs as his cousin, Ahmed. Ahmed was a slip of a teenager with thick bushy hair and olive skin. As he got closer, Ahmed also recognized Haitham and greeted him with a friendly embrace. "Ahmed, I am here to see Uncle Khalid whenever he has time."

Ahmed replied in a friendly voice, "Sure. I will let him know you are here, Haitham. Follow me and you can wait in his office."

Inside, Uncle Khalid's small office papers were stacked in every available location—on the desk, the chairs, and even the floor. Haitham remembered Uncle Khalid Rasheed as tall and trim, with a fine head of gray hair and a well-trimmed beard. He always wore a western suit and white shirt and had an engineering degree from the University of Baghdad. He never obtained his certificate, preferring instead to operate several businesses before purchasing a hotel on Zuba Street. Uncle Ghazi described his brother Khalid as an enthusiastic capitalist and worried that he had welcomed the overthrow of Saddam Hussein, thinking that it would bring freedom and prosperity. Uncle Khalid remained eager for some kind of normalcy to return to his country and hoped there could be a lucrative rebuilding program paid for by the Americans.

Uncle Khalid, however, was becoming increasingly disappointed with the Americans. He believed that at least some of them meant well, but they were arrogant and impatient. Their commanders thought soldiers could restore order by killing or imprisoning a few radicals and by re-establishing the local Iraqi police. They did not understand anything Islamic or the families, clans, and tribes that had ruled Ar Ramadi for centuries. The shifting alliances and feuds of the clans were old and complicated, and every time the soldiers favored, punished, arrested, or killed one Iraqi, the hearts and minds of a dozen brothers, cousins, sons, and nephews were affected.

"Come in, Haitham," Khalid said. "How is Ghazi doing?"

"He is fine, Uncle Khalid. He gave me permission to come here and ask you if you can help me find work. There are no jobs in Saqlawiyah, and Uncle Ghazi has no extra money. I am getting desperate."

Uncle Khalid did not hesitate. "There are no jobs here either, Haitham. You should go back to Saqlawiyah and stay out of Ramadi. Tell Ghazi that I would help if I could, but there is nothing I can do right now. When things change, I will send word."

It was clear there would be no further discussion of the matter, but Khalid saw the disappointment in Haitham's face.

"I have room here at the hotel for you to stay a few days if you would like to visit the family," Khalid said. "Please come with me for dinner this evening."

Cousin Ahmed took Haitham to a small room on the top floor. It was cold in the lobby but got warmer on each floor as they went to the top. Haitham's room was hot and stuffy. After Haitham looked over the room and put his small duffle bag down, Ahmed asked Haitham a question. "You want to sit with me at the front desk? We can talk and listen to my CDs as long as we don't turn them up too loud."

As the two cousins set at the front desk, Haitham realized that there was not much business at the hotel. Only a couple of people checked in all day, and he didn't see many coming in the front lobby.

Haitham complemented Ahmed. "You are very lucky to work here. Uncle Khalid is a smart man."

"Well, I suppose it is better than living in the street, but there is no money to pay me. I have a room here and can share in the family meals, but that is it. I have no money to do anything."

Haitham looked carefully around and whispered. "Have you thought about working for the Bathists? They say the party has money in Jordan. I bet we could get paid well for helping in the right way without joining the mujahideen."

Ahmed looked scared. "Are you sure you want to try that? It is very dangerous to get involved. You are likely to end up with a bullet in your head, either by the Americans or the mujahideen."

This made Haitham feel cocky. "Yes, for the right money I am available. The danger is everywhere, but to serve God is much better than to be afraid and do nothing."

Ahmed frowned and shook his head. "Well, if you know where to find bombs in Saqlawiyah, I know men who buy them. We might find a taxi driver to take us there and back for part of the money."

"Yes. That might be the way."

CୡEX୦

Ahmed spoke with his friends, explaining that he needed transportation in order to sell bombs to the mujahideen. He needed a taxi driver in Saqlawiyah who could drive them to the location of the bombs, as well as to those who would pay for them.

"It is a dangerous thing you ask," said an old Iraqi who had known Ahmed for many years.

"Haitham needs money to help his Uncle Ghazi finish building his home. He needs a cement mixer. His Uncle Khalid cannot help him."

"Uncle Ghazi is a good man. Are you sure you want to help your cousin?"

"Family is everything."

The old Iraqi nodded. One of his eyes was milky from a cataract. He handed Ahmed a slip of paper with an address while stroking his gray beard. "Be careful, young Ahmed. The mujahideem are dangerous."

"Thank you," Ahmed said. "We shall be careful."

The name of the driver was Nouri Mustafa Saddaq.

Ahmed raced off to the address on the paper—a house on a side street—arriving at a home with a mother tending several young children as she attempted to cook. The mother looked at the paper and then glanced up at Ahmed suspiciously. "You are seeking my husband," she said. "He is not here. He is working."

"May I wait for him?" asked Ahmed.

The woman paused. "You may wait outside. Too many people have been looking for him."

Ahmed waited three hours on the street until the taxi driver arrived. He was in his early 40s, very skinny, and had dark brown skin. Ahmed sprang to his feet and spoke in a whisper. "I was given your name by a friend of the Rasheeds. Can you help us?"

"Help you do what?"

Ahmed explained why he and Haitham needed a taxi.

"Lower your voice," Saddaq said abruptly. "My wife must not know about this. What can you pay me?"

"Five dollars."

"No. Ten dollars."

"Yes, yes. Ten dollars after we get paid."

The taxi driver looked up and down the street. "Very well. I have mouths to feed. Now be off. Tell no one else."

Ahmed walked quickly away to find Haitham. Perhaps they would make money after all.

ᏣᏍᎶ

1530, 13 June 2004
Uncle Ghazi's House
Saqlawiyah, Iraq

Haitham and Ahmed formed the conspiracy before Haitham left Ramadi. Haitham would find the bombs, and Ahmed would send a taxi and sell the bombs to the *mujahideen*.

As soon as Haitham returned home, he began his inquiries. First, he quizzed the fathers, grandfathers, and uncles waiting at the school. Next, he made unexpected visits to family friends and ended up talking about buried bombs. After a couple of days, the whole thing would have been forgotten, and Haitham would have given up on the scheme but for the fact that Uncle Ghazi wanted to resume work on his house. To restart the project, Uncle Ghazi needed the cement mixer running and that meant a trip to the mechanic's shop by Haitham. As Haitham waited and watched the mechanic disassemble the carburetor on the mixer engine, the mechanic asked Haitham a question. "I hear you are looking for bombs. Are you going to attack the Americans?"

The question caused Haitham's heart to race and his legs to tremble with fear, but he answered. "I know where I can sell bombs for a good price in Ramadi."

The mechanic continued to work on the carburetor. "How much are you paying the person who knows where to find the bombs?"

Even though Haitham and Ahmed had spent hours discussing their plan, they never once thought about paying for information. Haitham did not know what to say. "We can pay five dollars after we ourselves get paid."

"That doesn't seem like much money to risk one's life."

"There is no risk. I will be taking the risk by selling the bombs in Ramadi. I won't tell anyone where I get the information."

Haitham was trying to think and talk at the same time.

"Bombs are not easy to find," the mechanic said. "If you have to be shown where to find them, the risk is great."

Haitham was giving up. "Yes. In that case I would pay more."

"How much more?"

"Ten."

The mechanic stopped working and looked at Haitham. "If you pay me twenty dollars, I will take you there tonight. I will keep the mixer until you pay me."

"I don't know if I can arrange the sale that fast. How about tomorrow night?"

The mechanic was agreeable. "Be here after evening prayers tomorrow. God willing, we will find the bombs."

Haitham went straight to the café and paid the owner twenty cents to call Ahmed. The next day, Ahmed showed up in Mustafa's taxi. The mechanic provided directions, and the driver drove to a junkyard east of Fallujah at the point where the city abruptly ended and turned to sand and scrub brush. There was no fence or caretaker, only miles of junk vehicles already stripped of useable parts and metal. The mechanic knew the place like the back of his hand and gave precise directions. The cab drove to an old Soviet-made truck. The mechanic, Haitham, and Ahmed got out of the cab and opened the hood. Inside were four rusted 120mm mortar rounds. The mechanic was proud.

ൽൽ

2000, 15 June 2004
Rasheed Hotel
Ramadi, Iraq

The Iraqi who told Ahmed he would pay for bombs just shook his head and claimed he had no idea who would be interested. Haitham and Ahmed wanted to be careful, but the taxi driver said he had to have his money and came up with an address where the bombs could be sold.

"I have done this before," Nouri Mustafa Saddaq claimed. "But this will cost you more. Twenty dollars. I am providing you with both transportation and information."

"That is agreeable," Ahmed said. "Thank you."

After leaving the hotel, the three headed southwest, speeding along dark dirt roads to the outskirts of the city.

CʒƏɔ

Like most Iraqi cities, Ar Ramadi combined a series of dense neighborhoods of small block and stucco houses with flat roofs laid out on crisscrossing roads. Most of the streets looked the same: rutted sand, garbage heaps, patched fences, on both sides, and intersecting alleys. The taxi driver had trouble finding the address and got stuck in the sand three times.

At around midnight, Saddaq stopped at a dark house surrounded by a fence and insisted that it was the correct address. Haitham and Ahmed did not want to get out.

"Let's come back tomorrow," Haitham said. "You can't go up there at night. We will get shot."

The taxi driver was adamant. "I am tired of you wasting my time. I need my money. I don't even have money to buy gasoline tomorrow. No! This is the right house, and we make the sale tonight."

Haitham and Ahmed begged the driver to leave, but he would not. He got out, walked to the entrance, and banged on the steel gate. Haitham and Ahmed stayed inside the taxi. It looked very dark, but Haitham was able to see someone hit the taxi driver in the stomach, and the driver fell to the ground. One figure picked up Saddaq and shoved him against the gate. Two figures walked to the taxi and one pointed a rifle at Haitham and Ahmed while the other pulled open the door. "You thieves get out before we shoot you."

Ahmed slowly crawled out, followed by Haitham. They put their arms high over their heads, and one of the men shoved Ahmed toward the gate.

"Follow your friend into the house."

There was no light in the entry to the house, and Haitham could see only a dim light in one of the back rooms. The man with the rifle motioned Ahmed into that room. There were four men sitting on mats inside, and each had an AK-47 leaning within reach against the wall. A small middle-aged man with a scar on his face was seated against the far wall and spoke first.

"Who are these assholes?"

The man with the rifle spoke to Haitham. "Well, answer the question."

Haitham was petrified and stood shaking. At that time, the taxi driver spoke. Haitham wondered many times if the taxi driver had spoken out of bravery to save Haitham's life or out of stupidity. "We have mortar rounds in the trunk. We brought them to sell."

The scar-faced man stood up and walked over to the driver. He grabbed his neck, shoved him against the wall, and started choking him. His eyes looked like those of a child on an amusement ride. "What's your name?"

The driver could barely speak but managed to say his name. "Nouri Mustafa

Saddaq."

On hearing the driver's name, the scar-faced man went crazy with rage. "You are a Saddaq coward and you came here to sell bombs to the brave Hadeed heroes? And you bring these little street boys with you?"

The scar-faced man looked around the room at the other men. "The Hadeed family has fought for the protection of Fallujah, Ramadi, and Iraq. Many of my brothers are dead. You Saddaqs do nothing to defend your country. Your sisters are prostitutes! You are betrayers of the faith and worthless cowards. And tonight you have come to my home to insult me by asking for my money! For you cowards it is not enough that we Hadeeds give our blood to defend your whores. You expect us to pay for bombs that you should be using yourself to kill the foreign invaders."

The scar-faced man released the driver's neck and kicked him in the gut, causing the driver to moan with pain. The driver sat back up and tried to speak. "No, no. I mean no disrespect! I don't ask for money. The bombs are not mine. They belong to those two. They hired me to take them to Saqlawiyah. I was only their driver and was paid to bring them here tonight."

Haitham felt cold and clammy. He did not know that life could be so horrible. He looked at the floor and waited to be killed. However, this time the scar-faced man spoke to Ahmed. "What is your name?"

Ahmed could speak and did not even look scared. "My name is Ahmed Rasheed. This is my cousin Haitham from Saqlawiyah. We got the bombs to help the brave freedom fighters, but we didn't know where to take them. We heard this was the place to bring them, and we came to give them to you. We hoped to get some money to pay for the taxi, but we don't want any money for ourselves."

The scar-faced man smiled and looked again at the men still sitting around the room. "Ah, the brave little Rasheeds are the ones bringing us the bombs, but we have to pay their taxi fare."

Scar-face and the other men all laughed, and then he walked over to Haitham.

"Where did you get the mortar rounds?"

Haitham tried to stop shaking and to answer, but he couldn't. "Does your cousin talk?"

Scar-face moved back to Ahmed.

"Yes," said Ahmed. "He talks. He is just scared. The mortar rounds came from the junkyard east of Fallujah. A mechanic from Saqlawiyah showed us where to find them. He also wants money from us for helping."

The scar-faced man appeared to have calmed down and was thinking. "Your father is imam at the Khalid Rasheed Mosque? ..

Ahmed answered quickly. "Yes. Khalid Rasheed is my father."

"Does your father know you are trying to sell bombs to the Hadeeds?"

For the first time, Haitham was thinking that he might survive and was hoping that Ahmed continued to say the right thing. Ahmed looked the scar-faced man in the eye.

"No. My cousin and I wanted to help the freedom fighters, and we have told no one what we are doing. We did not know that asking for money would be an insult. We only wanted money for our expenses, but we see that is not proper, and with your permission we will leave the mortar rounds for you as a gift and a token of our respect and go back to my father's house."

"Oh, but that wouldn't be just," said Scar-face. "You must pay the Saddaq for his taxi."

Ahmed wanted to help. "Yes. My cousin and I will get the money somehow and pay him his fare."

Scar-face walked back over to the driver. "Is that all right with you, Saddaq pig?"

The taxi driver's brown face was wet with tears and contorted with fear when he answered. His skinny body was shaking uncontrollably. "Yes! Yes! Of course! I am very sorry for coming here. I shall never return to your house, and I will tell no one of this night. I am very sorry to have made you angry this evening. May I please leave and take these boys home?"

Haitham could not understand why this made the scar-face man angry, but it did. He stood over the driver and started screaming in anger again. His eyes bore the look of excitement they had earlier. "That is right, you scum of a camel's cock. Beg for your worthless life. I know that you are a spy. You are a traitor to the faith."

The scar-faced man stepped back, pulled out his penis, and started urinating on the driver. "I piss on you. I piss on your father and your entire family."

All the men jumped up. Some started moving their mats to avoid getting urine on them. The driver covered his face and cried.

"No, please," said Saddaq. "Please don't do this. Let me leave."

Haitham tried not to throw up.

In an instant, the scar-faced man grabbed his AK-47 in one hand and pointed it at the driver's head.

"Please!" the Saddaq pleaded. "Don't kill me. I am sorry. Please let me leave."

Haitham could see the scar-faced man's eyes and saw his immense joy from torturing the driver. Finally, the driver shut up. As the scar-face man pulled out a knife in his other hand, he yelled at the men to pick up the driver, but no one did. "I said pick up that pig so I can butcher him!" exclaimed scar-face.

"But Laith, he is covered in piss!" said another. "You can't ask us to soil ourselves like that."

Laith stopped as if in a trance. After a long pause, the AK-47 exploded with a deafening noise, and the driver's head exploded. "Maybe you prefer to clean that up instead."

Laith laughed while the rest of the men frowned.

Even in the dim light, Haitham saw the driver's dead eyes staring at him, the left half of his head gone and his brains and bones scattered everywhere. A pool of blood formed in the middle of the floor and flowed towards Haitham. Laith kept laughing and laughing. Haitham felt sick to his stomach as he thought of the driver's wife and children.

Finally, Laith fell silent and stared at Haitham and Ahmed. He still held the AK-47 in one hand and the knife in the other.

"Now, you little Rasheeds, listen to me. You are going back to Fallujah and bring me every bomb that the mechanic can find. If you do that, I may spare your lives, and I may even give you some money for your trouble. But if you cross me, you will end up just like that piece of shit on the floor, and I don't care if you are Rasheeds or not."

"Saif, you and Abdul are going to work," Scar-face continued. "Bury the bombs in the backyard. Load the body into the taxi and get rid of it on your way to Fallujah. If the little street boys cause you the smallest trouble, you can kill them."

Laith paused and stared at Haitham. "Bring me back more bombs."

Chapter 16

2300, 15 June 2004
Al Asad Air Base
Al Asad, Iraq

At 2300, the temperature held at 115 degrees Fahrenheit inside the concrete hanger built by Sadam Hussein to protect his Russian-made fighters. Mike Beck and the rest of the headquarter Marines sat in rows, sweating and not enjoying their introduction to Iraqi summers. By June of each year, massive hot air masses settled in over central Iraq, fending off any cool air from the north and trapping the occupants in an unmerciful mixture of 120-degree heat and 80 percent humidity.

In an effort to stay cool, most of the Marines took off their flak jackets and battle gear, and some even removed their digital blouses. Beck noticed one exception, a lieutenant colonel that he didn't know. The nametag said "Campbell." He kept his helmet on and remained in full battle gear. In fact, Campbell looked like an advertising poster for high-speed combat gear, with his moisture-wicking T-shirt, extra pouches on his flak jacket, his carrying case for ear-plugs, his hardcover case for sunglasses, extra magazine pouches, an expensive-looking folding knife, a miniature first-aid kit, a GPS, a rappelling rope, a heavy belt, a drop holster with two built-in magazines, his camouflage scarf, handcuffs, old-style bayonet, and digital camouflage camelback. Campbell even wore his gasmask fastened to his left leg, with an elastic band strung around his helmet holding a set of goggles. In addition to the standard issue 9mm Beretta pistol, he had checked out an M-16A2 rifle from the armory and added a personal combat scope, plus a special sling and magazine holder.

Sitting next to Campbell, the Deputy SJA, Maj. Way, looked quite civilized, with only one piece of non-issued gear—a black drop-down holster considered essential by most Marines since the standard holster would not fit comfortably with the flak vest.

A female Marine lance corporal worked the counter. She looked to be about 18 with blond hair, and was five-foot-four and 115 pounds. Because of the heat, she had removed her digital blouse and wore a brown T-shirt that in areas was wet with sweat, revealing her young body and the exact details of her bra. Beck struggled to admire her without getting caught and at the same time marveled at her efficiency in coordinating the arrival and departure of the Marines.

At 2325, she announced the boarding of Beck's flight, and the Marines quickly donned their vests and helmets and headed toward the edge of the flight line.

A Marine wearing a flight helmet and flight suit came running up to him. "Going to TQ?"

"Yes," Beck yelled as loudly as he could.

"Follow me."

Beck paused long enough to give the line of Marines the arm signal to advance and followed the Marine in the flight suit. In less than a minute, all the Marines were on board, a buzzer signaled the raising of the rear ramp, and the aircraft rolled down the runway. In a few more seconds the interior lights were extinguished, rendering the inside of the plane pitch black, making it impossible to see anything. Beck listened and felt for the sounds and forces that indicated a takeoff and climb to altitude and tried to get some rest, relying upon his ability to instantly fall asleep on a plane.

Later, the rapid descent of the C-130 interrupted his nap. He opened his eyes but could see nothing, and the only indication of the flight path was the sound of the engines and the g-forces. Beck assumed that this was a standard maneuver to avoid surface-to-air fire.

The landing went smoothly. As the C-130 slowed to a stop, the interior lights came on, and the ramp started descending. Beck looked over at Way slouched on the canvas bench, mouth open and sound asleep. He looked more like a tourist arriving back at LAX on an overnight from Hawaii than a Marine headed into combat.

In contrast, Lieutenant Colonel Campbell sat straight up in his seat, with his helmet and goggles on, his flak jacket fastened, and his rifle at the ready, as if preparing to jump into a hot landing zone. He looked seriously scary and ready for combat.

Chapter 17

On Laith's orders, Haitham and Ahmed moved the taxi driver's body to the trunk of the taxi and mopped up the blood, guts, and urine using buckets of sand from the backyard. Next, Laith told his third cousins, Saif Malek and Abdul Hamed, to get rid of the body.

Prior to the fall of Saddam, Saif and Abdul had been low-ranking police officers in Ramadi. They were not much different than other police officers. None had any training, and all got their jobs through some family connection. In any event, as far as Saif and Abdul were concerned, police training would be a waste of time. What was the point of investigating a crime or arresting criminals if the judges ignored the facts? They made a living from their salaries, bribes, and what they could steal on the side, and they preferred to spend their time loafing at the police station. Saif and Abdul had one talent: forcing confessions. They didn't have truth serum or sophisticated instruments. Instead, they made their own tools from bicycle chains, rubber hoses, rope, and wood. They did not enjoy hurting people, at least not in the way that Laith Hadeed enjoyed it, but considered it easy work, and to keep their jobs they did what they were told. After the American invasion, Saif and Abdul reported to the police station every day for two months, but there was no one to pay them, and eventually they gave up and went to work for Laith Hadeed.

Starting the Toyota required great skill. Saif and Abdul argued violently over what to do—pump the accelerator once, pump it twice, or just let the Toyota sit for awhile?

Haitham expected Saif and Abdul to fight, but they just cussed each other and the old car. Eventually, Abdul agreed that the carburetor had flooded, and they fell asleep waiting to try to start it again. Ahmed also fell asleep, but Haitham felt too scared and stayed up listening to the sound of dogs barking and Saif and Abdul snoring. Haitham prayed all night that nothing would happen to him.

When the sun came up, Abdul awoke and tried the starter switch. The Toyota started, and Abdul drove 20 miles straight east from Ramadi down a canal bank to a house next to a date grove. Saif got out, spoke to a middle-aged man who answered the door, and returned with a shovel. Haitham and Ahmed took turns digging the taxi driver's grave at the far edge of the date grove. The taxi driver stank horribly, a smell unlike anything Haitham experienced before—sweet and sickening—and it seemed to stick inside Haitham's nostrils.

Moving the taxi driver without touching blood or guts was impossible, and by the time Haitham and Ahmed dropped him in the grave, Haitham had the smelly fluid on his hands, waist, and legs. Haitham tried to wipe some of the stench off with sand, but the horrible smell remained.

An hour later, Abdul pulled the Toyota into the long line at the Saqlawiyah fueling station. The car reached the gas pump two hours later, and they arrived at the mechanic's garage at about four o'clock. The mechanic worked under the hood of an old Mercedes while the owner waited.

Saif and Abdul walked over to the owner of the Mercedes. "We are police. You come back tomorrow."

The owner of the Mercedes left, and Saif and Abdul then cornered the mechanic. "You are under arrest for trafficking in explosives. Step inside with us."

They shoved the mechanic inside his shop and told Haitham and Ahmed to close the overhead door. In the dim light, Abdul held the mechanic, and Saif spoke close to the mechanic's ear. "We don't have a lot of time. We caught these street boys in Ramadi with your bombs. We want to know where the rest are, and if you tell us now, we take the bombs and leave you alone. If we have to beat it out of you, we may forget to stop beating. After you're dead, we will beat your family."

Even in the darkness, the mechanic could see the terrified look in Haitham and Ahmed's eyes and made a quick decision to talk. "I am an honest and godly man. I didn't ask for trouble. I only tried to help. I know there are more bombs in the junkyard because I have seen them when getting parts. They are in trucks and cars. It would bc better if I take you there after dark."

Saif and Abdul looked at each other. "All right," Saif said. "Open the door and go back to work. After evening prayers, we will go for the bombs."

ⱌ৪ʓ

At the junkyard, the mechanic had trouble finding the right truck, and Abdul had to drive up and down the rows of vehicles several times, shinning a flashlight out the window. Finally, the mechanic yelled to Abdul to stop beside an old dump truck, and they found four 122mm anti-aircraft shells stacked inside the vehicle. Next, the mechanic stopped at a truck that had the hood and fenders removed and found three mortar shells hidden under the back seat. The last stop was at a Soviet-made six-wheel truck, but this time no bombs were found. The mechanic claimed that he had seen bombs there and insisted that someone must have taken them. Regardless, Saif and Abdul seemed pleased with the haul and, since the Toyota was already weighted down near the axles, decided to call it a night and drove to the mechanic's garage.

"What do we do with the street boys?" Abdul asked Saif.

Saif felt tired and did not like doing so much work in one day. "If we take them back with us, Laith Hadeed may give them money. Or we can just leave them here."

Again, Ahmed bravely spoke. "Can you take us to the Rasheed Hotel on Zuba Street?"

Abdul liked that idea. "Yes. We can leave you there tonight and easily get you tomorrow if Laith wants you."

Abdul knew all the checkpoints between Saqlawiyah and Ramadi and how to get around them. He drove the Toyota cross-country—through fields, on canal banks, and down farm roads. The dawn light guided them as they finally drove into Ramadi.

At the hotel, Saif spoke to Haitham and Ahmed. "You don't tell anyone about anything, and you don't leave the hotel. We will come back tomorrow. Say nothing to Khalid Rasheed."

ೞೞ

0600, 16 June 2004
Rasheed Hotel
Ramadi, Iraq

Saif and Abdul drove away, and Haitham burst into tears, shaking and sobbing. As Ahmed led him inside the hotel, he was afraid the loud wailing would wake the guests.

Ahmed did all the things he had seen his mother do to quiet a baby. He held Haitham, squeezed him tightly, talked softly to him, patted him on the back, told him he was safe, and tried to reason with him. Eventually, Ahmed gave up, found an empty room, and put Haitham in bed. Ahmed then removed Haitham's stinking man-dress, washed it in the bathroom sink, and hung it to dry in Haitham's room. Haitham sobbed face down on the sleeping mat.

Haitham woke in the morning with an intense sick feeling in his stomach. He felt terrified and expected Laith Hadeed to open his door at any moment. He sat on the sleeping mat, staring at the memory of the horrible events.

Haitham tried to pray. He desperately wanted to communicate with God, to ask for his protection and to feel safe, but as usual Haitham received no comfort in prayer. He kept trying.

At 8:00 a.m., Ahmed returned to Haitham's room and found him saying his prayers. He remained naked, and Ahmed tried to help him into the man-dress; however, when

Haitham saw the bloodstains he refused to wear it. Haitham sat naked on the sleeping mat and said nothing.

Haitham stayed in the room all day. He could not eat or drink. He did not even need the restroom. He just waited for Laith to come get him. But no one came the first day.

After a week, the sick feeling in Haitham's stomach would sometimes go away, but it would quickly come back. Each day, Ahmed brought Haitham food and tea, tried to talk to him, and kept telling Haitham that the Hadeeds had forgotten all about them and that they were safe.

On the 20th day, Haitham left the hotel to help Ahmed carry supplies from the market. He watched for anyone who looked like a terrorist and avoided getting close to anyone.

After a month, Haitham made up his mind. "I am going back to Saqlawiyah. If Laith Hadeed wants to kill me, he will have to come get me. I will never return to Ar Ramadi."

CRED

0900, 17 July 2004
Uncle Ghazi's House
Saqlawiyah, Iraq

The sick feeling in Haitham's stomach occurred less frequently at Uncle Ghazi's house. On some days it would go away for hours.

Haitham never left the yard and would no longer go to the mosque for Friday prayers. Haitham's aunt didn't complain because Haitham proved useful around the house. He cleaned, picked up trash, irrigated the garden, and repaired anything that was broken. He nagged Uncle Ghazi to buy more bricks and mortar so that he could start building again.

On Friday afternoon, Haitham told Uncle Ghazi the story about the scheme to sell bombs, as well as the killing of the taxi driver. Haitham expected the worst, but Uncle Ghazi offered his support. "You are not to blame for the death of the Saddaq. He should not have been so impatient. The Hadeeds are a dangerous family. No one should go to their house at night."

Over the weeks, Haitham had thought of only Laith Hadeed, and he continued to explain the situation to Uncle Ghazi.

"The taxi driver was stupid, but he did not deserve to die," Haitham claimed. "The Hadeeds love killing. I have seen that now. It is wrong that a man can be killed and nothing is done about it."

Uncle Ghazi answered. "Yes. What you say is true, but this is something for the Saddaq Tribe to deal with. The Saddaqs will have their revenge. Remember that only one's family can protect a person. You must act to protect your family, the Rasheeds. This is above all else."

"What will happen if the Hadeeds come for me? Who will stop them? When they want, they will come and kill me. Our family can do nothing to stop the Hadeeds."

Uncle Ghazi tried to explain. "Haitham, your family has already protected you. We have more than guns. We have our friends. You are alive now because you are Rasheed. They have not come for you because you are Rasheed, and they will not come for you because they fear our friends."

There was a long period of silence before Haitham delivered startling news. "I want to join the police. I will protect all families from killers. Uncle Ghazi, our family will never be safe as long as the Hadeeds do what they want."

"It is good that you want to be a policeman, but what police will you join? The Saqlawiyah Police? The Ramadi Police? The Hadeeds control the Ramadi police."

"I will join the Iraqi police. The National Police in Baghdad."

Uncle Ghazi stopped to think. "If you want to join the National Police, I won't try to stop you. But don't be impatient like the taxi driver! They say the National Police work for the Americans. You should wait until we have Iraqi police controlled by the Iraqi people." Uncle Ghazi paused. "You are right not to leave this house. This is a time of uncertainty.

Please wait to see if the Americans leave, and then you should join the National Police."

Haitham voiced his agreement.

Chapter 18

The 4th Division headquarters at Camp Baharia sat three miles from the headquarters of the 1st Marine Expeditionary Force at Camp Fallujah in the center of the Division's area of operation. The convenient location facilitated the Division's mission of mentoring the Iraqi Security Forces and providing security for the civil affairs teams, contractors, and government workers.

Built by the British at the end of World War I, Camp Baharia used many of the buildings that housed the Iraqi Army prior to Operation Iraqi Freedom in 2003. Unfortunately for the members of the 4th Division, when the Iraqi Army left, the looters moved in to take anything of value, including air conditioners, windows, doors, plumbing fixtures, and everything made of wood. The Seabees of the Marine Engineer Group immediately went to work to replace these things, but much still needed to be done when Beck arrived.

Beck, as Staff Judge Advocate, was supported by his deputy, Maj. Way—Legal Chief—Gunnery Sergeant Ryan, and a legal clerk, Lance Corporal Martinez. They all moved into a small office in the 4th Division headquarters building.

Beck considered Gunny Ryan an impressive Marine. At age 43, Ryan maintained one of the highest physical fitness test scores in the Division. He worked out so much, running ten miles a day, doing push-ups, sit-ups, and chin-ups, that the young Marines regarded him as some sort of god. Naturally good looking, women frequently approached him in bars, wanting to know if he was an actor. He served four years as a grunt, but tired of the long deployments and barracks life, and changed his military occupational specialty to 4400, legal services. He excelled in the legal field, keeping young Marines motivated and out of trouble, dealing with the senior staff non-commissioned officers, and keeping senior JAG officers happy. By this point in his career, his main source of job satisfaction became occasionally influencing the disposition of charges against a Marine by tactfully making suggestions to the Staff Judge Advocate.

Martinez had the build of a bulldog and seemed equally impressive—smart, obedient, and hard-working. Like the prize pupil in a class trying to please the teacher, he looked for things to do in the office. He constantly challenged Gunny Ryan to find enough work to keep him busy.

The first week revealed that, for Beck and Way, life at Camp Baharia would be hectic. LtCol. Carter and the other staff officers had lots of legal questions. They both worked 18-hour days, but it didn't matter because without booze or women, there seemed little else to do but work.

ध्य

0900, 15 July 2004
Public Affairs Office
Camp Baharia, Iraq

Anne Merrill and two reporters flew from Camp Victory to Camp Baharia aboard an Army Blackhawk helicopter. The pilot frequently gazed back at Anne, noticed that she enjoyed the ride, and flew closer to the ground than was normal. The more she smiled, the faster he flew.

A gunnery sergeant met the reporters at the landing zone and drove them to a tent surrounded by sandbags for briefing by the Public Affairs Officer, First Lieutenant Carol Copeland. During the brief, Copeland informed Anne that four journalists had previously arrived at Camp Baharia and were waiting for assignments. A field assignment would require at a minimum two weeks' delay.

A few days later, Lt. Copeland started receiving reports that the male Marines at Camp Baharia were going crazy over Anne Merrill. The reports were confirmed when she overheard a wisecrack by the Logistics Officer that the arrival of Anne Merrill in her blue jeans and T-shirt had done more for his morale than any Morale, Welfare, and Recreation program. Another officer made the comment that the vision of Anne strolling around the camp, attending the briefings, and dining at the chow hall brightened his day.

First Lieutenant Copeland resolved to protect Anne and prevent the male Marines from getting into trouble. She organized her own makeshift security detail of enlisted women Marines. A member of the security detail accompanied Anne everywhere and shielded her from any contact with male Marines, regardless of rank. Copeland personally escorted Anne to the chow hall for every meal.

Next, Copeland moved Anne to a trailer within an all-female area of the camp and assigned her a not-so-good-looking roommate, a female reporter from Phoenix, Arizona named Mary Seabear. Copeland prohibited Anne from going to the shower trailer, or anywhere else, alone.

After a week Copeland drove Anne and Mary Seabear to a guard tower atop the concrete block fence surrounding Camp Baharia. The guard shack had large sliding windows, and an air conditioner had been installed near the floor. As the three entered the guard shack, Lt. Copeland announced the purpose of the visit to the guard. "Good morning, Marine. I am the Public Affairs Officer, and these ladies are reporters."

"Good morning, Lieutenant."

"May I use your binoculars for a moment?" Copeland asked.

The Marine nodded and continued to scan the horizon.

"Ladies, you are looking at the city of Fallujah, Iraq. It's a savage place. Everything of value has been looted or destroyed. No one is in charge. We estimate that there are at least six thousand terrorists in the city. If captured, you can expect to be raped, tortured, and beheaded."

Copeland paused to let Anne and Mary have a chance to look through the binoculars.

"There have been attempts by the terrorists to infiltrate other camps in Iraq. We do the best we can, but no security system is perfect. If a terrorist gets over this wall, you two would be targets."

There was another long pause.

"That is why we assign battle buddies. If something happens, there is someone to help or at least report it. Let me make this clear. This is not just a suggestion. It is mandatory. From this point forward, the two of you will be together at all times while you are aboard this camp. You may not like it. You may end up hating each other, but while you are here, you will eat, sleep, shower, and move about together. If I hear that you are running around camp alone, I will send you back to Baghdad and you won't come back. I hope you understand it is for your own good. Do we understand each other?"

After seeing how close the camp lay to the city, Anne Merrill welcomed Mary Seabear as her battle buddy. However, Anne did not like her next conversation with Copeland, who tried to convince Anne to remain inside the wall at Camp Baharia and not accept a combat assignment.

"The Marine Corps does not tolerate any form of sexual harassment, but I'm concerned that the grunts will be thinking too much about you. They are young men and, at best, they will be overly protective, and, at worst, half the unit will be infatuated with you. Either way, it could get someone killed."

Over the next two weeks, Copeland increased her efforts to dissuade Anne from embedding with a combat unit. She offered Anne special treatment, including a first shot at important stories and photographs, but the offers were not acceptable to Anne Merrill. She insisted on going in the field with a Marine combat unit.

Chapter 19

Saif and Abdul wandered into the Rasheed Hotel and approached the front desk, where Ahmed sat reading a book.

"Where's your cousin?" Saif asked.

"He waited many weeks," Ahmed answered. "When you didn't come, he went home."

Saif handed Ahmed 50 American dollars.

"Make sure your cousin gets half," Saif said. "We have a job for both of you tomorrow. You better be here in the morning. And tell your cousin he better not make us find him."

Ahmed immediately called Uncle Ghazi. "Uncle Ghazi, will you have Haitham call me? It is very urgent."

"Have the Hadeeds done something?"

Ahmed hesitated because he didn't know if Haitham had told Uncle Ghazi about what happened.

"Ahmed!" Uncle Ghazi exclaimed. "We don't have family secrets. What has happened?"

"Yes. The Hadeeds were here. They were very polite, and they left money. But they want to see Haitham and me tomorrow. They said they have work for us."

"This could be bad. Ahmed, you must tell your father right away. I will call him tonight."

Uncle Ghazi, Uncle Khalid, Haitham, and Ahmed debated the problem with the Hadeeds. After six phone calls, they decided that the Rasheeds should at all costs avoid trouble with the Hadeeds. Haitham must go back to Ramadi, and he and Ahmed must do whatever the Hadeeds asked.

Uncle Ghazi awakened Haitham at dawn, and after prayers walked Haitham to the café to catch a cab to Ramadi. Haitham arrived at the hotel at nine o'clock, and he and Ahmed waited for the Hadeeds. Saif and Abdul entered at noon.

"Good," said Saif. "Both of the street boys are here. Let's go."

০৪৪০

1000, 5 August 2004
National Islamic Resistance Center
Fallujah, Iraq

At 10:00 a.m. Haitham Rasheed, Ahmed Rasheed, Saif Malek, and Abdul Hamed climbed the narrow steps to the third floor of the National Islamic Resistance Center in Fallujah and tromped into the waiting room of the new office of Laith Hadeed. The waiting room had no windows and no furnishings except a dozen plastic chairs. Middle-aged men with lazy, insolent looks filled most of the chairs. Haitham recognized some of the faces as Hadeeds. No one spoke. Haitham sat down and listened to the conversation in the other room through the thin door. The talk concerned an Iraqi from Karbala working for the Marines at Camp Fallujah.

Haitham soon recognized the voice of Laith Hadeed and got an overpowering sick feeling in his stomach. Someone wanted $100 for information about where the Iraqi could be picked up, but Laith Hadeed sounded skeptical. "Does he have U.S. ID?"

"I don't know," answered a voice.

"Has anyone seen him at the gate?"

"No."

"Why do you accuse this man?"

"He has new American dollars. He is just a brick layer, but he always has money!"

The confabulation carried on for a long time, but after an hour, Laith Hadeed ended the discussion by shouting, "I will pay you twenty dollars and you will take my men to get him! If he doesn't work for the Marines, they will cut your tongue out!"

The door opened, and Laith Hadeed stepped into the waiting room. Haitham tried to remain calm, but Laith terrified him. This time the sensation felt more intense than ever and was centered deep in his gut, somewhere below his stomach and above his balls. His penis felt limp and his palms sweaty. Haitham sensed danger and that any mistake would be his last. He knew everyone in the waiting room felt the same way. Laith Hadeed knew it also. Laith smirked in the pleasure that, as the leader of this pack of thieves, he controlled their every move.

Laith Hadeed carefully scanned the room and spoke. "Saif, take Abdul and get me the bricklayer in Karbala. This Fallujahan will take you there."

The informer looked faint. To Haitham's astonishment, Abdul interrupted Laith Hadeed. "We need help. Ahmed Rasheed from Ramadi and his cousin Haitham from Saqlawiyah are here."

Laith Hadeed shrugged. "Take them with you."

The four trudged down Andolusa Street, picking their way through the discarded tires and other trash for two blocks, turned, and then hiked another three blocks to the old white Toyota. Haitham hurried into the front seat, knowing that it was broken. He did not want to guard the informer placed in the middle of the back seat.

It took three adjustments to the carburetor to get the old Toyota started and an hour to find a street vendor selling gasoline in five-gallon containers. They then headed south across desert roads to avoid the American vehicle checkpoint outside Fallujah's east side. After heading south, they circled around the old *mujahedeen khalq* training base, where Saddam Hussein trained his Special Forces to infiltrate Iran—which was now the American Marines' base—and back up to Karbala. The trip took an extra three hours this way, but it was worth avoiding the terrorist thieves at the checkpoints and the Marines.

They arrived in Karbala at 3:00 p.m. and proceeded to the commercial district adjacent to the canal. Boys getting out of school and heading home to their families filled the market street. Karbala merchants used small stalls with steel overhead garage doors as shops, but only about a third of the shops were open for business. Even for the four Iraqis, the street smelled horrible. Soon, Haitham realized that the local butchers used the ditch behind the shops to dispose of bones, hides, and guts. The ditch also contained human and animal feces. The odor assailed Haitham's senses and made him sick to his stomach.

The group got out of the Toyota and slogged through the market to the first side street, maneuvering their way through open sewage and ankle-deep mud that stuck to their sandals like sand-colored glue. Many of the residents stood in the doorways of their homes, looking out into the street. No one made a gesture. Strangers from Fallujah and Ramadi were becoming frequent visitors to Karbala and were not welcome. The informer pointed at a small, windowless brick shack identified as the home of the bricklayer.

No one in the group cared enough to check for a back door. If the four had anything in common, it was laziness. Saif returned to the Toyota while the rest waited. When Saif came back, he parked the car a hundred feet up the street, opened the trunk, and passed out the four rusted AK-47s.

The informant moved down the street while the four kidnappers took out black wool caps and pulled the facemasks down. The armed group then approached the bricklayer's home. They found the door locked but the bottom hinge broken, and Abdul plowed in, followed by Saif, Ahmed, and Haitham. The little shack had one room, and the bricklayer sat on a rug reading the Koran. The back door stood open, and Haitham saw the bricklayer's wife cooking on a stove in the backyard. His two children played in the corner of the yard.

Saif hit the bricklayer high on the side of his head with the stock of the AK-47, and Abdul pointed the muzzle of his weapon at the man's face. Haitham looked the other way. He did not like the violence.

Abdul searched the room for anything he could steal. The wife started screaming. It took Haitham only seconds to determine that the bricklayer was very poor, with no TV, cell phone, furniture—not even a radio. There would be nothing of value and probably no money.

Saif motioned for everyone to leave, and as they dragged the bricklayer back into the street, Abdul stole the only thing he could find to steal—an old blanket probably worth only a few cents in Fallujah. He rolled the blanket around his AK-47 so it would look like he was hiding his weapon.

The group climbed into the Toyota, put the bricklayer in the informer's place, and drove off, speeding by the informer, who tried to wave them down for his $20. It took another three hours for Abdul to retrace the dusty route back to Fallujah, and they returned to the National Islamic Resistance Center at 7:00 p.m. Once there, they took the bricklayer to the basement. Haitham started to recover, but the damp and filthy smell of the basement made him sick again.

Saif ordered Haitham and Ahmed to guard the bricklayer, who squatted in the corner and said nothing. Haitham felt that he was about to throw up but was afraid to go upstairs. He sat contemplating how he could someday get away from the Hadeeds. Finally, Saif came back down.

"We have to take the bricklayer to Kamis Hadeed's house," Saif said.

ଓଞ୍ଜେ

0730, 06 August 2004
Staff Judge Advocate's Office
Camp Baharia, Iraq

Beck usually returned to the Staff Judge Advocate's office after the morning brief, enjoyed a cup of coffee, and brought Maj. Way up to speed. LtCol. Campbell also started showing up every morning.

Beck heard lots of rumors about Edward Campbell. He held the military occupational specialty of infantry officer, with the numerical designation of 0302, but had a license as a civilian lawyer in Dallas, Texas. He had not been certified as a Marine Corps judge advocate. He looked a few years younger than Beck, and was six feet tall, skinny, and nervous. He acted like he must have been beaten up daily in high school.

At the beginning of his military career, Campbell had been forced out of the Marine Corps for failure to be selected for augmentation to the regular officer corps. He had terrible fitness reports, so bad that he couldn't even get into the active reserves. No commanding officer would accept him in his unit. Most officers would have quit and dropped to the Individual Ready Reserve, but not Campbell. He never gave up trying to be a Marine, and he joined all the Marine Corps auxiliary organizations in Dallas.

Through the years, Campbell became an expert at locating obscure billets, and he volunteered for assignments that no one else wanted, including Watch Officer, Investigating Officer, and Administrative Discharge Boards. Also, Campbell was lucky enough to come up for promotion to major when the Marine Corps Reserve was promoting everyone.

He had pulled all strings to get on active duty during the Gulf War and managed to get activated at the Dallas Mobilization Center. He also did everything possible to get activated for Operation Iraqi Freedom, but was not successful until the first round of reservists went home and the Marine Corps needed more officers. Someone must have thought that an infantry lieutenant colonel would be an asset in a combat zone, and Campbell was activated with the 1st Marine Augmentation Command Element and sent to Iraq. The Chief of Staff tried Campbell in several billets, and he failed within a week each time. In desperation, the Chief of Staff transferred him to the 4th Division.

The Chief of Staff at 4th Division, LtCol. Carter, knew trouble when he saw it.

"Sir, there is nothing going on at the command deck," Campbell said. "Do you need an Investigating Officer?"

Usually it made no sense to appoint a lieutenant colonel as an Investigating Officer. However, after listening to Campbell for three weeks, Beck decided he would walk down and discuss the issue with the Chief of Staff.

"Vic," Beck began, "Lieutenant Colonel Campbell says he doesn't have enough work to keep busy, and he's volunteering to complete one of our pending investigations. What do you think?"

"Mike, he'll drive you fucking crazy, but if you're willing to keep him under control, you can use him anytime you want."

Chapter 20

S aif and Abdul thought the hours had turned out to be another long day's work—too long for them. Haitham thought that this time he would throw up for sure, and he silently prayed that God would save the bricklayer or at least forgive Haitham for doing nothing to help him.

Saif made Haitham and Ahmed take the bricklayer outside, and after the 30 minutes necessary to start the Toyota, they headed for Kamis Hadeed's house, located in the Dolan Heights District of Fallujah—about a 20-minute drive from the National Islamic Resistance Center. The large house included many rooms, a basement, and a large open area that served as both a workshop and storage area for weapons, including 122mm mortars, AA guns, 57mm recoilless rifles, detonation cord, and explosives.

Haitham and Ahmed had never been to Kamis Hadeed's house, but Saif and Abdul had been there many times through the years. Although Saif and Abdul were considered topnotch torturers, Kamis Hadeed was the best in all of Al Ambar Province, and he was Laith Hadeed's first cousin. He worked the cases as a sort of freelance artist. He was so good that Saif and Abdul were employed as his assistants to help torture many in Kamis Hadeed's house. At first, the house was mainly used to get information or confessions, but since the fall of Saddam it had become the Hadeed family's killing factory.

Most of the work was done in the basement, and one wall had the black banner of the Islamic Jihid Movement for filming beheadings. Other furnishings included a wheelchair, white plastic chairs, and various torture instruments, such as rubber hoses, bicycle chains, ropes, wooden clubs, and small electrical generators. Saif and Abdul had assisted in four beheadings filmed on DVD photographs, with copies produced on five computers located on the ground floor. Saif and Abdul were sure that Laith and Kamis Hadeed were making good money selling the DVDs in Baghdad, but they never offered to share.

The bricklayer had been quiet and emotionless on the trip, but when they got to the basement, he became agitated. He pleaded with Saif, yelling and waiving his hands. "I have done nothing!" He made all the pleas Saif and Abdul had heard before.

Haitham knew deep down that the bricklayer had done nothing, and it was a terrible thing that he would be tortured and probably killed. That night, Haitham tried to think of a way to help the bricklayer but couldn't. It was going to be another night in hell for Haitham.

The bricklayer pleaded, shouted, and cried. He did not want to die that night. He made such a commotion that, despite Haitham's desire to help him, Haitham was glad when Abdul made the poor man be quiet by smashing his mouth shut with a wooden club.

After an hour, Kamis Hadeed himself came down to the basement. He looked about 40 years old. He was skinny and had the look of a madman, with wild eyes and inappropriate expressions. Saif later said he was only half as crazy as he looked, but that was enough.

"Give me the name of who you work for," Khamis said.

"I work for anyone that hires me," the bricklayer replied. "I have not worked in many days."

"Where do you get your money?"

"I don't have any money."

"Yes you do. You get paid good money for working for the Americans. We have seen you go to the base."

"That's not true. I am just a bricklayer. I don't have any money and I don't work for the soldiers. You have the wrong person."

At that, Kamis Hadeed went back upstairs and returned a half-hour later with a two-foot length of motorcycle chain wrapped in electrical tape. "You are going to tell me the names of the traitors," he said, "or I am going to beat you until you do."

Kamis Hadeed suddenly hit the bricklayer over the shoulder with the chain, and the man went down on his back. The second blow was across the chest, and the victim doubled. The next blow was over the bricklayer's head. The next ten blows tore the man's face apart. Kamis Hadeed smiled all the time he was beating the bricklayer.

The severely injured victim stopped moving, and Kamis Hadeed went upstairs again.

Saif and Abdul sat in the white plastic chairs, trying to get some sleep. Haitham and Ahmed stood, looking at the bricklayer on the floor and trying to decide what to do.

Kamis Hadeed returned in 30 minutes. "Pick him up!"

Haitham and Ahmed grabbed the bricklayer by the arm-pits and lifted him up. It looked like he was still unconscious. Kamis Hadeed slapped the bricklayer in the face, but he didn't move. Next, Kamis Hadeed pulled the bricklayer's eyelid back and poked him in the eye. The man didn't move.

"He is dead," Khamis proclaimed. "Bury him in the back-yard."

Kamis Hadeed went upstairs for the last time. Abdul went outside to get the buckets of sand to clean up the blood while Haitham and Ahmed carried the body to the backyard.

Standing in the dark, Haitham started crying. This alarmed Ahmed. "Haitham, you must be quiet! They will kill us if you start this again. I feel bad for the bricklayer, but we must think of ourselves and our family."

Haitham couldn't answer, but he tried not to cry. Ahmed told Haitham to stay in the yard and went for the shovel. When he returned, Haitham was still sobbing, so Ahmed started digging, hoping that Haitham would stop before Saif came out of the house. Haitham cried and cried, even after Ahmed had finished burying the bricklayer. Ahmed then sat next to Haitham and talked softly. "Haitham, you must stop until we get home. Saif will be out any minute."

Suddenly, Haitham stopped. He looked angry and started toward the house. Ahmed was afraid that Haitham was going to do something stupid but could not catch him. When Ahmed got to the door of the house, he heard Haitham speak. "The traitor is buried."

Chapter 21

1700, 09 September 2004
Camp Baharia
Fallujah, Iraq

After chow, Corporal Nelson, Lance Corporal Case, and PFC Goldman headed back to the 3rd Battalion area and observed PFC Hale running after them, yelling.

"The platoon sergeant has been looking for you. We're going on a mission tonight. The confirmation brief is scheduled at 1900 at the COC tent. The STA team is being attached to the QRF!"

The four hurried back to the tent and started surveying their gear. As always, Case had everything laid out and ready to roll according to the STA team checklist: helmet, desert cover, desert cammie—top and bottom—desert boots, interceptor vest, SAPI plates, dog tags—neck and left boot—magazine pouches, magazines, pistol magazines, first-aid kit, camelback, molle frog pouches, peanut light, weapon sling, pressure dressings, ID card, knee pads, and night-vision goggles.

The mission excited all the members of the STA team. The QRF, or Quick Reaction Force, existed as an elite organization set up by the battalion to react to emergency situations, including aiding Marines in a firefight, reinforcing security at Camp Baharia, and responding to any insurgent attack on Iraqi Security Forces. The QRF Marines had the reputation of being highly motivated, and some had special training, such as the Special Operations Training Group or Survive, Evade, Resist, and Escape. For young, hard-charging Marines, the successful completion of these schools represented a notch on the handle and a lot of time spent discussing living off the land, special killing techniques, and the week in a mock prisoner of war camp.

When the STA team arrived at the COC, their excitement increased. The QRF Marines appeared fully decked out in their special battle gear, with determined looks on their faces. Cpl. Nelson got so fired up that he could hardly sit still.

The QFR leader presented a detailed and extensive patrol brief, and Case learned that, for the mission, the QRF would be task-organized into three teams: headquarters led by the platoon commander, and two tactical teams. The headquarters team included a platoon sergeant, air officer, radio operator, translator, corpsman, and intelligence specialist. The other teams had a team leader, assistant team leader, radio operator, point man, driver, scout, slackmen—extra gear carriers—machine gunners, and riflemen.

The platoon commander explained that 3rd Battalion had received Human Intelligence Report that insurgents had kidnapped an Iraqi contractor working for the MEF Engineering Group and were holding him at a house south of Iskandariya. The QRF would rescue the Iraqi contractor and capture or kill the kidnappers.

Due to the importance of the mission, no time was available for coordination with other units, and the distance to the kidnapping site from Camp Baharia meant that if the QRF got into trouble, they would have to depend upon themselves. The STA team would serve as last-minute reinforcements for the Marines.

The QRF convoy departed Camp Baharia at 2200, with 20 personnel-carrying combat packs in five vehicles. The STA team climbed aboard vehicle number five, a high back Humvee with a cargo bed protected by high-armored steel plates. The convoy moved out at dark, and Case noticed that it remained hot and that the fine sand caked in his eyes, nose, and ears.

cs80

As the QRF rolled out of Camp Baharia, Haitham sat in the Toyota with Saif, Abdul, and Ahmed, intending to leave Laith Hadeed's house in Ramadi for Saqlawiyah to pick up a load of mortar rounds and deliver them to the farm house on the road to Hit.

As usual, it took Abdul half an hour to get the Toyota started. Haitham and Ahmed sat in the back seat, Abdul drove, and Saif occupied the front passenger seat. They stuck the AK-47s in the trunk. No one talked as Abdul expertly drove the back roads toward Saqlawiyah.

 CRBO

The planned route for the QRF convoy went through the main roads—MSR Aluminum to MSR Red—however, just outside of Camp Abu Ghraib, the convoy received radioed instructions from the Regimental Operations Center at Camp Baharia to change course. An F-18D jet had observed a vehicle leaving the target house, and the task force needed to intercept the vehicle. Therefore, the task force turned off MSR Aluminum and proceeded to the intersection of two farm roads to set up a roadblock.

CRBO

Abdul, Saif, Haitham, and Ahmed approached the intersection from the east, circling Fallujah to get to Saqlawiyah. Haitham instantly knew they were in trouble when the headlights of the Toyota illuminated the Humvee blocking the farm roads.

"Oh no!" Abdul screamed as the Humvee blocking the road came into view.

"Just keep driving and don't slow down!" Saif yelled at Abdul.

"We are dead now!" Abdul exclaimed.

"Go around it," Saif commanded.

"I can't. They will shoot us."

Abdul brought the Toyota to a stop.

As the Toyota slowed, one of the QRF Marines put a spotlight on Abdul, Saif, Haitham, and Ahmed. An interpreter using a bullhorn told them to get out of the vehicle with their hands in the air. Haitham had trouble breathing.

"Move slowly," the interpreter said. "Don't anyone do anything stupid."

The QRF Marines did the takedown and search of Abdul, Saif, Haitham, and Ahmed. Case watched from the high-back Humvee. The Iraqis were quickly flex-cuffed and put into the Humvee with the STA team. Case felt a rush of adrenaline as Nelson motioned for the detainees to assume sitting positions next to the gun mount and issued orders to Hale. This was the kind of action Case had envisioned for so long. His training had paid off. He wasn't scared, but rather pumped, excited, and eager to continue.

"Don't take your eyes off these four for one second, Hale," said the team leader.

Hale braced himself against the tailgate, pointed his SAW—squad automatic weapon—at the detainees, and stared intently at them while they waited for the QRF to search the Toyota. The search party quickly found the four AK-47s in the trunk, and the rifles were unloaded and put in one of the other vehicles. The stop, search, and capture of Abdul, Saif, Haitham, and Ahmed took less ten minutes, and the task force continued the roadblock operation. After 30 minutes, the QRF convoy resumed the tactical march to the kidnapping site.

It was so dark riding in the back of the Humvee that Haitham couldn't see a thing, so he just listened for movement. At one point Haitham heard Saif start to speak, but an American soldier kicked him on the foot, and he shut up. Haitham prayed that the Americans would not shoot them.

After traveling ten kilometers, the QRF convoy headed cross-country over a river bottomland that had not been farmed for several years. The ride got rough. The old plowed fields had grown up with tall weeds, and the drivers had difficulty seeing the irrigation ditches and many times drove directly over them. The STA team and the Iraqis bounced around in the back of the Humvee and were thrown against the sides of the high-back.

Case looked at the detainees. He wondered how people could be hostile to the soldiers who sought to give them freedom. Anger briefly tensed his muscles.

Haitham kept hitting his back against the gun mount. While crossing one ditch, an American fell on top of him and bent his knee sideways. Haitham screamed in pain.

At the rally point, the QRF convoy stopped and split into two teams: a reaction element, which was to remain stationary; and an assault element, which was to proceed to the house. The STA team was assigned to the reaction element, but Nelson approached the commander.

"Sir," said Nelson, "I know we're not a regular part of the QRF, but I think my STA team could set up on the canal bank and provide cover for the extraction in case the enemy engages from the roof."

The platoon commander didn't have time to consider the offer. "Thanks, Devil Dog, but that won't be necessary. I want your people with the reaction team."

Nelson responded. "Aye aye, sir."

Since the STA team was part of the reaction element, they stayed with the vehicles. After a couple of minutes, Nelson ordered the detainees removed from the vehicles and had them sit in an open area with Case, Goldman, and Hale as guards. Hale checked to make certain that the flex-cuffs were not too tight. Case thought the caution to be unnecessary, and couldn't care less if they were too tight or not.

"Goldman," Nelson barked. "Stay with the SWA in vehicle three. Your field of fire is from that tree on your left to ninety degrees on your right. Got it?"

"Got it."

"Case," said Nelson, "You man the Two-Forty Golf in vehicle five."

Case climbed on top of the Humvee and set himself down in the turret behind the machine gun. He then hung his rifle over his back and checked the machine gun to make sure it was in condition one—round in chamber and weapon on safe. He felt a surge of power and adrenaline coursing through his veins.

From the turret position, Case could hear the radio traffic, and a few minutes after the assault force left, word came over the radio that the F-18D had detected up to ten enemy personnel outside the target house. This message was relayed to the platoon commander.

Case wondered whether he would see real action. A bead of sweat ran down his forehead. He was eager. He sighed heavily. But was he too eager? He shook off his doubt. No, he was more than ready. He recalled his excellent scores from target practice on the rifle range. He thought that there wasn't anything he couldn't do. There were real targets in Iraq—unpredictable targets—and if he was ordered to take them out, he would.

The platoon commander led the assault element and moved out in team order across the same terrain that the vehicles had crossed getting to the rally point. Case continued to monitor what was happening by listening to the radio traffic. The assault element approached from the south, and when they reached the objective at approximately 2245, they stopped to tighten up the formation with the first two teams forming into stacks to breach the target house while Team Three and Team Four went to the east and west sides of the house to block off the objective and provide security.

The south side of the house had two entrances, and the plan was for Team One to enter the east entrance and Team Two to enter the west entrance. The platoon commander was leading Team One. When everyone was set, he raised his arm, and both stacks entered the target house.

The house was empty.

The platoon commander then gave the order that the reaction force was to move up to the target house, and the STA team Marines grabbed Haitham and the other Iraqis and put them back in the Humvee.

The route between the rally point and the target house was over the same rough terrain, and there were berms, ditches, mounds, rocks, and crop furrows. The STA team was thrown rudely from side to side in the back of the Humvee.

It seemed to Haitham that the Marines were driving as fast as possible, and he tried to brace himself against the gun mount but kept sliding on the floor. A soldier fell on top of him three or four times, and at one point the rear door flew open and Haitham almost fell out. About 300 meters from the target house, the Humvee hit an irrigation ditch, and the door slammed shut, knocking Haitham forward on the floor as the side of his face smashed against the gun mount. Case and Hale looked at the youth but said nothing. Their faces were expressionless.

At the target house, Haitham and the other Iraqis were again taken out of the Humvee. This time, Cpl. Nelson ordered Case and Hale to have the detainees lay face-down in a line, heel-to-toe. Nelson had been told that this was the best method to prevent detainees trying to talk to one another.

After the house was secured, the Marines took Saif, Haitham, Abdul, and Ahmed back to the Detention Facility at Camp Baharia. Haitham's fear did not abate. He perspired as his stomach churned with uncertainty. Laith Hadeed would surely be displeased, depending on what the Americans did—and he had no idea what the Americans planned to do with him and Ahmed. He tried to pray but couldn't.

❦

0500, 10 September 2004
Detention Facility
Camp Baharia, Iraq

Haitham watched the sun come up and tried to recollect what happened the night before. He remembered arriving at the detention facility and sitting on the ground for an hour before someone removed the duck tape over his eyes. He was moved to a pit with banks too steep to climb and concertina wire at the top. A soldier with a rifle stood guard in the front and with an easy shot at anyone who dared head for the top. He remembered that Abdul, Saif, and Ahmed had also stayed in the pit.

A large guard came inside the pit and handed Haitham, Abdul, Saif, and Ahmed bottles of water and plastic sacks with food. The sacks contained crackers, jelly, cheese, and a pound cake, the best meal Haitham had eaten in months.

After they finished eating, another guard motioned for the four to follow him to a building near the gate where Iraqis stood in line. Haitham moved slowly towards the front door. Inside, soldiers sat behind a counter just like the one at Uncle Khalid's hotel, except that yellow footprints were painted on the concrete floor. Haitham reached the front, and the interpreter told him to look straight ahead while a camera took his photograph. Haitham realized that his fingers were being photographed at the same time, and the interpreter began questioning Haitham, while the soldier at the counter typed Haitham's answers into a laptop computer: name, family names, address, occupation, place of birth, and other basic information.

Next, Haitham was moved into a large room with an air conditioner, wooden benches, and steel bars on the windows. Haitham sat next to Ahmed, and the air conditioner felt good. Haitham and Ahmed remained in the room for a long time until a guard came for Haitham, who was taken to a separate room, this one without windows. He was left in the room alone for about an hour. Then three people came in.

Haitham guessed that one was a doctor, because he examined Haitham's black eye and wrote something on a piece of paper. The Arab translator had a weird accent that Haitham had never heard before. Later, an American wearing jeans and a t-shirt asked the same questions regarding his name and address. Because Haitham had lied at the counter, he could not remember what he said the first time, and he was scared. The questions came fast: "Who are the other Iraqis? Where were you going? Why did you have rifles?"

The questions were non-stop. "How did you bruise your face? Did anyone hit you? Were you beaten by the Americans?"

Haitham could not think fast enough and usually answered that he could not remember.

After an hour, the three men left and Haitham was given a plastic mat and a blanket and taken outside to another pit that had steel fence in the front, dirt sides, and a tin roof. Inside the pit were ten Iraqis sitting on similar plastic mats or squatting on the dirt floor. Haitham could not find Ahmed, Abdul, or Saif, so he laid out the plastic mat and blanket and sat down. In a few minutes, two of the Iraqis came over and squatted next to Haitham. They wore dirty man-dresses and sandals, and one looked very old.

"What happened to your eye?" asked an old Iraqi.

"I hit my face on the side of the truck," Haitham replied.

Another Iraqi, younger, joined the conversation. "You should say that the guards hit you. They may pay you money."

The old Iraqi disagreed. "I would not do that. If you do, they will keep you in prison for a long time and probably take you to Baghdad. It could be months before you get back to your family."

The young Iraqi asked a question. "What were you doing when they brought you here?"

"I was just riding in a car. There was a truck in the road. The Americans stopped us and brought us here."

"Did you have anything in the car?"

"Just four rifles in the trunk."

"That doesn't sound too bad. If you don't say anything, they might let you go."

Chapter 22

The door to the SJA office opened and Lieutenant Colonel Campbell came in with a serious look on his face. "Sir," he said, "I hear they brought in some detainees that look like they may have been roughed up by the 3rd Battalion's Quick Reaction Force."

Even though Campbell had completed several investigations, Beck still considered him to be a pain in the ass. Everyone knew Campbell's ultimate goal was to get himself a Combat Action Ribbon, and the Division investigations gave him the opportunity to travel to just about every camp in Iraq.

The criterion for award of a Combat Action Ribbon included receiving hostile fire and returning it in an effective manner. No matter how hard he tried, Campbell could not get into combat action. He represented the best protection available for a Marine unit. A convoy that included Campbell could go anywhere without fear of attack. The Chief of Staff described him as a "one-man fucking St. Christopher's medal."

⚮

After hearing Campbell's request, Beck agreed to appoint him to investigate the alleged detainee abuse by the QFR and walked over to the command deck to make the courtesy call on the Chief of Staff. When Beck returned to the SJA office, Way was sitting at his desk drinking a cup of coffee from a stainless steel mug.

"Need to make a PX run?" Way asked.

"Sure," Beck replied.

It felt relaxing to be outside in the middle of the morning, almost like being on vacation, and Beck used the time to discuss some of the items on the SJA to-do-list with Way. As they had walked out of the office, they'd passed a set of four generators and a row of Porta-Johns. That symbolized Camp Baharia: the sound of generators and the smell of Porta-Johns.

A large portable building, looking like an oversized mobile home encircled by blast barriers, housed the Post Exchange. Barriers provided protection form mortar or rocket shrapnel. At Camp Baharia there were four types of blast barriers: Hesco, Jersey, Texas, and Alaska. The Iraqis manufactured the barriers somewhere off-base, and the ones enclosing the PX looked about four feet wide at the bottom, two feet thick, and twelve feet tall. In addition to the blast barriers, sandbag bunkers ringed the PX so that Marines could quickly dive into them in the event of a mortar attack.

Today, Beck and Way felt lucky because no one waited in line to get in the PX. When the two men approached the door, Way instinctively opened it and stepped aside to allow Beck to enter first. As Beck entered the doorway, two civilian women stepped out and he ran smack into one of them, knocking a package out of her hands. Without looking, Beck bent over and picked up the package, and when he straightened up he was stunned by her good looks.

"I'm very sorry, sir," said the woman.

Beck could barely talk, but after a second responded. "No. It was my fault."

Anne Merrill smiled and continued out the PX.

ଔଚ

1100, 10 September 2004
Post Exchange
Camp Baharia, Iraq

Anne was bored to death sitting in her living quarters, editing and re-editing the story she would file with DNS by satellite that afternoon. The beautiful day made it worse and gave Anne an excuse to get out of her trailer. She easily convinced Mary Seabear to walk to the exchange to purchase pens and paper.

The unexpected good weather also caused the Morale, Welfare, and Recreation Manager to make a rare executive decision to hold an impromptu volleyball game. Notices were quickly posted at the chow hall, post office, and on other bulletin boards around Camp Baharia, and were sent out by email to all the units around the camp. Next, the manager set up four volleyball nets in a vacant sand lot across from the PX and even produced T-shirts for prizes, coolers of soda, and some snack food from the chow hall.

After bumping into the lieutenant colonel, Anne and Mary heard the rock music and the MWR employee doing his best to be a disc jockey. In broken English he announced, "Let's party, Baharia! Come on out for a good time. We are rocking at MWR."

Anne noticed that the players had unique suntan patterns. Their faces, necks, and hands were darkly tanned—almost black—but the rest of their bodies remained perfectly white. There appeared to be only two body types in the Marine Corps: skin and bones or bodybuilder. No one in combat appeared to have a medium build—neither the young Marines nor the older staff NCOs.

Anne and Mary went over and joined the small crowd of spectators sitting on the sidelines, enjoying the weather and being amused by the game. Anne quickly noticed, however, that her presence reduced the teams' skill. Players started missing easy returns and not concentrating on the game.

Soon, she heard one yell, "Watson, stop looking at the babe and start playing ball!"

Anne and Mary headed back to the trailer. What would be lame in California seemed like fun in Camp Baharia.

෴

1400, 10 September 2004
3rd Battalion Area
Camp Baharia, Iraq

Lance Corporal Case sensed bad news when he saw the QRF platoon commander talking to the captain at the Detention Facility. The first lieutenant looked scared, and the only words that Case could hear the lieutenant say were, "Yes, sir," over and over.

After dropping off the detainees, the QRF Marines drove straight to the chow hall, parked across the street, and headed inside. Although he had been up all night, Case didn't feel tired. He removed his body armor, web belt, and helmet and put on his soft cover to walk to the chow hall. He ate a huge breakfast, returned to the 3rd Battalion area, and went to sleep in his rack.

At around 1400, Cpl. Nelson squeezed his arm. "Wake up, Case. I hear we're in a world of shit!"

The words seemed like a dream until Nelson started shaking the cot.

"What's up, man?" Case asked groggily. "I'm trying to get some fucking sleep."

"Dude, I just got news from Lance Corporal Brooster at the S-3. They're doing an investigation, and they're going to nail our asses because one of those fucking Iraqis got a black eye."

"That sounds like bullshit to me," Case asserted.

"It is bullshit all right, but you know that they have to hang someone."

Case sat up on the cot, rubbed his eyes, and sat thinking for a minute. "We were with the QRF the whole time. No one hit the detainees, and there are plenty of witnesses to back us up."

"I hope you're right, Case," Nelson said, "but we better get our stories straight before the investigating officer gets here."

"What do you mean—stories? Just tell the truth. There aren't any stories."

"OK. OK. I don't mean it like that. I'm just saying that lawyers can get you to say the wrong things. Brooster says that the S-3 and the CO are talking about it right now. At least we should talk to Hale and Goldman. You know what fucking morons they are."

Nelson and Case headed over to the smoking pit, but Hale and Goldman weren't there.

"Well, where in the fuck do you think they went to?" Nelson asked.

The two men walked around the area, asking everyone if they had seen Hale or Goldman. Finally, a Marine said he'd seen Hale in his shorts and running shoes, so he'd probably gone to the gym.

Nelson and Case headed straight for the 3rd Battalion gym. The tent was air conditioned and had an assortment of weights, stationary bicycles, rowing machines, and treadmills, and there was a refrigerator with cold bottles of water. Hale and Goldman stood in the back, lifting weights with three other Marines. Nelson headed straight for them.

Nelson cornered Hale and Goldman. "I need to talk to you outside."

As they walked outside, Hale had a look on his face like he had screwed the pooch. "What's up, Corporal Nelson? I thought we had the day off."

"Don't worry, you ain't done anything yet, Hale," Nelson said. "We just want to let you know that some shit is coming down. The S-3 is doing an investigation on the condition of one of the detainees last night. I want to make sure you idiots tell the fucking truth and don't go freaking on us. It's not our fault that the QRF was going cross-country at ninety miles an hour."

Hale looked confused, but Nelson looked disgusted.

"Look, Hale," Nelson admonished, "just tell the truth, but don't fucking volunteer anything. I hear that's what the lawyers always say."

The three headed back to the STA team tent, expecting the worst.

ೞ

0800, 11 September 2004
3rd Battalion Area
Camp Baharia, Iraq

In the aftermath of Abu Ghraib, an allegation of detainee abuse was a big issue for the 4th Division, and Beck immediately sent emails to the commanding general, the battle staff, and the Staff Judge Advocate at I MEF, Colonel Ray Moore, to report the incident. He ordered Campbell to complete the investigation as quickly as possible and assigned Way as Campbell's legal advisor to assist in the investigation.

Campbell started by requiring every member of the QRF, excluding the STA team, to write out sworn statements. He and Way reviewed each statement and interviewed each member, asking additional questions and adding details to the statements. The QRF statements were consistent. The detainees had been injured by riding in the back of the Humvee while crossing rough ground as part of a tactical movement.

Next, Campbell obtained satellite photographs, maps, and PowerPoint slides from the 4th Division S-3 shop to show the exact route of the QRF convoy and the condition of the route. One map identified the convoy's location at all times.

At the motorpool, Way discovered that the STA team's Humvee had been extensively damaged, with the front tie rod bent so badly that it had to be replaced. He took photographs and obtained a sworn statement from the mechanic, explaining that crossing rough terrain at high speed had caused the damage.

Campbell acquired Haitham's medical file and then interviewed the medical officer, who testified that Haitham's injuries were consistent with the testimony of the QRF members. He also discovered that several of the Marines riding in the convoy had similar injuries caused by bouncing around in the back of the Humvees.

At 1000, Campbell and Way started the interviews with the STA team. Campbell instructed each to write out a sworn statement. This was followed by separate interviews.

Nelson, Case, Goldman, and Hale all said they had read the 4th Division order on detainee procedures and attended Captain Pascal's lecture at Camp Victory. They'd done their best to follow the procedures. No one had struck a detainee. A detainee had been accidentally injured because the door on the Humvee jarred loose and hit him, pushing his face into the gun mount. During the STA team interviews, Hale was extremely nervous, but his testimony never changed.

At 1400, Campbell and Way went to the Detention Facility and took one of the Iraqi Security Force officers with them. At the Detention Facility, the two officers took statements from the guards and the interrogator and obtained copies of the interviews. Campbell noted the discrepancies in Haitham's answers. He then asked to interview Haitham.

Campbell interviewed Haitham in one of the interrogation rooms at the Detention Facility. Haitham had already decided to take the old Iraqi's advice and not claim that he'd been beaten, but when he entered the room, he started shaking. He thought that Campbell was a general in the American Army, and he was also afraid of the Iraqi officer. Haitham continued to lie about most things and told Campbell that he was 25 years old and lived in Ramadi and was a bricklayer. He claimed he was traveling to Najaf with the other Iraqis to look for work and that the rifles were for personal protection. Campbell, with the Iraqi officer acting as a translator, tried to get to the truth.

"Which Marine hit you in the eye?" asked Campbell.

"No. I fell down in the back of the truck. It was a very rough road. I hate Saddam Hussein and I like Americans."

The Iraqi officer then intervened. "It is all right for you to tell us the truth. No one will hurt you. We need to know the truth so that we can stop soldiers from hitting Iraqis."

Haitham thought about getting paid money by the Americans by claiming to have been hit, but the old Iraqi's advice seemed sound. "No. The soldiers did not hurt me. It was a mistake. They made a mistake, and I want to go. But no one hit me."

The interview with Haitham lasted an hour. Haitham never changed his story.

ଔଚ

At the same time, Way interviewed Saif in a separate interrogation room. Saif had the same plan as Haitham: say nothing and get out of prison as quickly as possible. Of course, Saif's explanation of what he was doing the night before was totally different than Haitham's. Saif told Way that they were headed to Baghdad to stay with family and had gotten lost. Abdul, Haitham, and Ahmed were his cousins, and the rifles belonged to Haitham and Ahmed. Like Haitham, Saif described how rough the ground was and how they were all bounced around in the back of the truck. Saif asked if he could get paid money for his bruised leg, and Way explained how to file a claim at the Fallujah Liaison Center.

Campbell and Way were not surprised when Abdul and Ahmed had different explanations about what they were doing on the road. Abdul was mainly interested in getting the Toyota back and was allegedly told that it had been left at the roadblock site.

The two investigating officers left the Detention Facility at 1800 and returned to the Staff Judge Advocate's office, where they started typing out the investigation report and organizing the attachments.

The JAG manual required separate findings of fact supported by a witness statement or document. The findings of fact were followed by conclusions and recommendations. Like most things in the military, the format had been used for

over 50 years and was time-consuming to complete. Campbell and Way stayed up all night finishing the report. They
handed the report to Beck the next morning at 0600.

Chapter 23

C aptain Loper motioned with his hand, and Ismaeel Latif moved to the front of the desk, placed the claim form, receipts, and photographs down, and glanced toward the attractive young Iraqi woman interpreter. Loper investigated and settled claims for battle damage in Fallujah. The payments symbolized an expression of sympathy and remorse for damage caused during the fighting in April following the attack on the Blackwater security contractors.

Captain Loper agreed that something needed to be done to assist the people in Fallujah. Without a source of employment, nothing replaced the monthly payments made by Saddam Hussein. The mission of the 1st Marine Expeditionary Force included the support of the local population, and, in fact, the Marine Corps judge advocates were proud that only the Marines obtained approval to make the *solatia* payments in Iraq. This, in turn, boiled down to an obscure legal issue of whether it was part of the customs and traditions of the Iraqi culture to avoid hard feelings by making a payment of blood money. Because the Marine Corps leadership wanted to make solatia payments, the Marine Corps judge advocates established, to the satisfaction of CENTCOM, that there was a tradition in Arab culture to avoid conflict by making payments of money.

Captain Loper compared Ismaeel Latif's receipts with a list of addresses on his laptop and frowned at the interpreter. "Do you own this house?" he asked.

Ismaeel Latif nodded his head. "Yes, Yes! This is my house."

"Who lives there?"

"My family. My wife, my sons, and my daughters. My brother and his family, too."

Loper studied the information on the laptop again. Mr. Latif represented the thirty-fifth Iraqi to submit a claim using this same address. Captain Loper knew that the receipts and photographs were phony, but he also recognized that Mr. Latif had stood in line for the last four hours and probably had no way to feed his family. As a bright young attorney, Loper figured that the whole process existed as a scam, but he followed the orders of his superiors to win the hearts and minds of the Iraqis. This afternoon, he felt generous and decided that $200 was worth keeping Mr. Latif happy.

Loper did not know that his interpreter acted as a member of Lakeeb Saddaq's terrorist cell. After work, she provided Saddaq with a list of Iraqis who received solatia payments, including Ismaeel Latif's name. Saddaq's thugs promptly paid Mr. Latif a visit, accused him of cooperating with the Americans, and gave him the chance to rectify his mistake by turning the money over to Saddaq.

∞

2300, 20 September 2004
Nazal District
Fallujah, Iraq

Lakeeb Saddaq sat on the floor of an abandoned house in the Nazal District of Fallujah, waiting for the mortar crew to arrive. He pulled out the money taken from Ismaeel Latif and separated it into four $50 piles. He needed to move quickly because sometimes the American planes spotted the mortar crews, and a house might explode instantly after the firing of a mortar.

When the crew arrived, Lakeeb Saddaq handed out each $50 pile and raced out the front door. The crew sprinted out the back, set up the mortar, and fired one round toward Camp Baharia.

CRRO

2301, 20 September 2004
Officer's Quarters
Camp Baharia, Iraq

At 2301 Beck woke in a panic with his heart pounding. He could see nothing in the pitch-black room but heard the air conditioner running at full blast. In a split second, he heard the deafening explosions, one after another. He felt the walls shake and smelled the rooms as they filled with dust. Soon he recognized the explosions as outgoing—Marine artillery firing a counter-battery mission into Fallujah.

Airborne radar instantly acquired the mortar round fired from the Al-Jaleel 82mm mortar towards Camp Baharia by Lakeeb Saddaq's crew. The radar identified the point of origin and projected the point of impact. Upon establishing the acquisition, the radar team called in the counter-fire missions to the TCP, or targeting processing center, at the fire support coordination center—the FSCC—and within seconds the computers at the FSCC calculated the firing data and initiated a counter-fire mission. It took only seconds for the artillery crew to get off the first round.

As a result of this technology, training, and teamwork, the blast Beck heard was the first round fired by the Marine artillery. The Marines returned fire before the insurgent mortar round even exploded. Tonight, the insurgent round would impact in the desert outside the wire and cause no damage. Marine artillery obliterated the house in Fallujah.

CRRO

0800, 21 September 2004
3rd Battalion Area
Camp Baharia, Iraq

Pending the commanding general's action on Campbell's investigation, the 3rd Battalion Commanding Officer took Nelson, Case, Goldman, and Hale off field duty and gave them assignments at Camp Baharia. It annoyed the men, but at least the 3rd Battalion Commanding Officer took the time to personally explain his reasons. "You Marines know that back home, if a cop has to shoot someone, then he's put on administrative leave. It doesn't mean the cop is guilty or that the police department wants to punish him. It's for the cop's own good. From what I've seen, you followed the detainee handling procedures and did nothing wrong. I expect that as soon as the investigation gets to General Scott, this thing will be over with."

Corporal Nelson found the waiting difficult. In his view, doing anything except leading the Marines assigned to his STA team was degrading to his rank. He absolutely hated Case, Goldman, and Hale working for other corporals, and the first three days he walked over to complain to the sergeant major. By the fourth day, the sergeant major had enough. "Corporal Nelson, I don't care if you sit in your tent all day with your thumb up your ass. Don't come back here pissing and moaning again."

No matter how many times the sergeant major explained the situation to Hale and Goldman, they remained certain that, in a short period of time, they would be hauled off to the brig and court-martialed.

⊛

1300, 21 September 2004
Detention Facility
Camp Baharia, Iraq

As the Division Staff Judge Advocate, Mike Beck had the authority to make the decisions in each case, such as whether an Iraqi should be released, held, or turned over to the Iraqi Criminal Court. There existed two legal grounds to detain Iraqis. First, United Nations Resolution 1546 granted to the United States authority to take "all necessary measures" to contribute to the maintenance of security and stability in Iraq. Under this authority, the Marines could detain for imperative reasons of security any person that threatened force protection or attempted to overthrow the government through violence. These security detainees were held in the custody of multi-national forces. Second, the Marines could detain persons who committed crimes under Iraqi law. The criminal detainees were turned over to the Iraqi Government and tried before an Iraqi Criminal Court in Baghdad.

Campbell's investigation cleared the 3rd Battalion STA team of wrongdoing, and Gen. Scott approved the report and forwarded it to the I MEF Staff Judge Advocate, Colonel Ray Moore, for review and approval by the Commanding General of I MEF, Lieutenant General Bailey.

In Beck's opinion, the possession of the AK-47 rifles in the trunk of the Toyota by Abdul, Saif, Haitham, and Ahmed amounted to insufficient evidence to conduct a hearing or hold them past 14 days, and he ordered their release.

Therefore, on the 14th day after their confinement, a guard came for the four detainees, loaded them in the back of a Humvee, and drove them to the Fallujah Liaison Center. An officer made a long speech translated by a pretty Iraqi girl, explaining that the Marines came to Iraq to help the Iraqi people escape the brutalities of Saddam Hussein and that they were being released in accordance with Iraqi law. He said they would not get the rifles back, apologized on behalf of the American government for their detention, and gave each a $20 bill. Saif could not help himself, grinned, and thanked the officer when he was handed the money. The four were then escorted to the front gate of the Fallujah Liaison Center, where a taxi waited. Abdul gave the driver directions to the Toyota.

When they arrived at the crossroads, the Toyota was still there.

CB80

1620, 2 October 2004
4th Division Headquarters
Camp Baharia, Iraq

Beck gasped when he saw the note from the Operations Officer at the bottom of a string of emails asking him to attend a targeting meeting with the general at 1630. Beck cussed because he had not read his emails earlier. He hoped that Way had received a copy and prepared for the meeting.

Since arriving in Iraq, Way seemed a different man. With the prohibition of alcohol, he stayed sober and worked hard 16 hours a day. When not working on an assignment, he read everything he could get his hands on and studied constantly. He edited, proofread, and re-edited everything he wrote, and his writing improved dramatically. After three months, he knew more about the rules of engagement than anyone in Iraq, and Beck relied on him to answer the most difficult questions.

"Steve, did you get the email from the G-3 on the target meeting at 1630?"

Way stared at Beck with a blank expression. "No. What targeting meeting?"

A feeling of panic shot through Beck when he realized that he would have to go to the targeting meeting completely unprepared.

The G-3 Officer located the target cell in a tent of modern design and upgraded construction across from the headquarters building about ten minutes from the SJA office. The perforated plastic floor worked perfectly for boots and sand, and the double-lined walls with thick rubber inserts provided extra insulation. The Seabees constructed an entrance out of plywood, with a solid door and a flap to keep in the cool air so that the portable air conditioner kept the temperature in the seventies.

When Beck walked in the tent, a staff sergeant met him. "Sir, we have a seat reserved for you here."

Beck sat to the left rear of the general's seat.

Soon, the tent filled with officers, mostly lieutenant colonels and majors who did not know each other. Soon afterwards, Gen. Scott arrived with the G-3 Officer.

The Assistant G-3 Effects Officer commenced the brief on a proposed air strike on a target house in Fallujah. The Effects Officer followed standard military procedure. He spent all of his time preparing PowerPoint slides and very little time thinking about what he would say. The result was that Gen. Scott ended up reading about a dozen fancy slides but received little information, and this caused him to start firing off questions. The first question caught Beck by surprise.

"Mike, I don't have the authority to approve this target, do I?"

Beck strained to remember the massive number of orders and regulations applicable to the issue and cussed himself again for not reading his emails that morning. He waited as long as he could with out appearing awkward.

"Yes, you do, General. You are the approval authority."

Scott looked surprised, but automatically accepted Beck's advice as being correct. As Beck glanced around the room, he noticed the Chief of Staff giving him looks of approval.

General Scott demanded to know the specifics on the intelligence reports, credibility of the informants, and attempts to verify the information. He wanted all the information on the type of weapon that would be employed and the possible collateral damage. The issue that he kept driving home was positive identification that the men in the target house were hostile.

"They're dirty," the Effects Officer claimed. "We know that they are connected to the Omar Hadeed cell."

"I know you would not push a target up to me unless you honestly believed it was a good target," Scott said. "But you just don't have enough solid intelligence on this one for me to feel comfortable with the decision to kill these men. The target is not approved. If you get better intelligence, you can bring it back to me."

At that, Gen. Scott paused and stood up. The Effects Officer called everyone to attention, and the general walked out.

The Effects Officer looked devastated. "What does he want? I just don't know what more I can give him!"

The G-3 looked sympathetic. "We'll have to verify the statements someway."

Chapter 24

Anne Merrill and Mary Seabear opened the door to their trailer at 0810 and headed to the 3rd Battalion area chow hall. Fortunately, the Division chow hall stayed open until 0830, and so they hurried.

After eating, they walked out the door and discovered they were on the wrong side of the building. Standing outside and trying to figure the way back, they saw about a dozen trucks parked in a dirt field, with a group of men standing around a small fire. At least a half a dozen looked to be Americans, and the rest were East Indians or Arabs. Anne could see the surprised look on the trucker's faces as they walked up. "How's it going, guys?" the ladies asked.

One of the truckers answered in English. "Well, howdy, good lookin'! What are a couple of beautiful girls like you doing in a godforsaken place like this?"

"We're news reporters," Anne answered.

Wilburn Johnson loved to talk, and he jumped at the chance to tell Anne his life story. He claimed to be 58 years old and a Vietnam veteran from Weatherford, Texas. He'd served three years in the Army and 20 years as a deputy sheriff. After that he drove long-haul trucks in the winter and spent his summers as a fishing guide in Alaska. He wore a cowboy hat, a bulletproof vest, two Colt .45 cal. pistols, blue jeans, cowboy boots, and had ugly tattoos up and down both arms. Most of his teeth were missing, but it didn't bother him, and so he grinned constantly.

Wilburn Johnson and the American truckers were damn proud that they hauled food for the Marines, and they were making good money doing it. They loved the fact that some of the money was tax-free. Wilburn Johnson explained that the rest of the drivers were from Jordan or India, were paid almost nothing, and were just trying to survive.

Johnson showed Anne the bullet holes in his truck's trailer and explained how Iraqis tried to hijack the trucks to steal the food. These were not insurgents, just criminals looking to sell the cargo. Johnson bragged that he had a truck blown out from under him by an improvised explosive device and also claimed to have killed at least three Iraqis with his pistols.

"We got to stop running away all the time," Johnson said. "You have to let people know you're not going to put up with it. I would take on these bastards and kill everyone within ten miles of a hijack attempt."

Johnson liked the shocked look on Mary Seabear's face. "If you did that, the tribal chiefs would take control and keep out the criminals. There wouldn't be any more hijackings. You know, if you don't have the stomach for that, then all you have to do is bribe the damn sheiks. Just like the old Barbary Coast, these sons of bitches will do anything for a little cold hard cash. Pay for protection."

Johnson turned and looked at two Humvees and three black Chevrolet Suburbans headed toward the dirt field at high speed. "It looks like Corporal Evans is ready to roll!"

"Can I get a photo?" Anne asked.

"Why, sure you can, darlin'."

Wilburn Johnson climbed up the side of his truck, tipped his cowboy hat, and smiled a big toothless smile. Anne snapped the photographs as the other truckers ran to their trucks and started the engines. Black smoke filled the air, and the ground shook.

As Anne watched the big trucks move out, she got the feeling that Wilburn Johnson didn't want to see the conflict end. He loved driving his wagon through Indian country. But she was a bit put off by his cowboy mentality—anything goes in the Old West, or in this case, the Middle East. He was a colorful character, the kind she loved to cover and photograph, but he seemed to have a total disregard for life.

Anne checked her camera, wiping off dust and grit that always seemed to accumulate on its exterior. Taking pictures of buffoons like Johnson was all well and good, but she was here to get the news, to take not just any picture, but the big picture she'd always dreamed would make the front page of a major newspaper. At heart, she was still a photojournalist, and she wanted some meaningful pictures. Wilburn Johnson was mere window dressing.

Chapter 25

0600, 27 October 2004
Laith Hadeed's House
Ar Ramadi, Iraq

Early in the morning, Saif and Abdul picked up Haitham and Ahmed at the hotel and drove them to Laith Hadeed's house in Ramadi. Haitham and Ahmed wore their new clothes: western-style black pants, silk shirts, and sandals. When they arrived at Laith Hadeed's house, they were each handed a shovel and told where to dig in the backyard. With the numerous rocks in the hard desert soil, it took an hour to dig down two feet. They found nothing.

Saif went inside and came back with Laith. "You all are idiots," Laith said. "Can't you see that is hard dirt? You dig only where it is soft. That's where something has been buried."

Laith took the shovel and started sticking it in the ground near the hole Haitham had dug and quickly located a soft spot. He kept poking until he had identified the boundary of the soft dirt and handed the shovel to Saif. "Dig there, you fool. And hurry! The mortars must be placed in the roads and carefully concealed before the Americans come."

Haitham easily dug through the soft dirt and within minutes his shovel caught on a plastic bag containing the two mortar rounds buried the night the taxi driver was killed. Haitham and Ahmed loaded the rounds into the Toyota, and they headed out of Ramadi towards Hit. Twenty miles outside of town, where the highway crossed the river, Abdul turned down a steep bank onto a dirt farm road. The houses along the river had gardens, fruit trees, and livestock, and Haitham had to jump out of the Toyota to open gates blocking the road. Abdul eventually stopped at a tiny house with no glass in the windows, went inside, and returned with a farm boy about Haitham's age.

Abdul then returned to the highway and turned back towards Hit. Just past the intersection with the Baghdad Road, the farm boy yelled, "There they are." He pointed at large potholes on a mile-long stretch of road.

Abdul kept driving for three miles, pulled a U-turn, and circled back toward the pothole, soon turning off the main road onto a farm road leading south. The ease with which Abdul could find his way around on the farm roads amazed Haitham. This time he did a huge circle and ended up behind a farmhouse about half a mile from the potholes.

Haitham and Ahmed each took the mortar rounds out of the trunk. It took Saif 45 minutes to move past the farmhouse and get into position to act as a lookout for the northern approach. Saif called Abdul on his cell phone and informed him that it was all clear. Haitham, Ahmed, and the farm boy slogged through the field toward the potholes, carrying the mortar rounds. As they got close to the potholes, the farm boy took the lead and guided the group to a large green bush, where the rounds were carefully hidden under leaves and a plastic bottle placed on top. The three trudged back to the Toyota, and Abdul drove around to pick up Saif. He then took the farm boy home.

At the farmhouse, Abdul told Haitham and Ahmed to get some sleep and that at dark they would return and move the mortar rounds to the potholes. The detonators would be set once the rounds had been placed.

When the sun had set, Abdul and Saif woke Ahmed and Haitham. It was time to retrieve the mortar rounds, place them in the potholes, and set the detonators.

Haitham rubbed the sleep from his eyes. He had only wanted to sell bombs and earn money for Uncle Ghazi. He could not disobey Laith Hadeed, however. He and Ahmed moved into the night, carrying mortar rounds.

⋐⋑

1430, 27 October 2004
3rd Battalion Area
Camp Baharia, Iraq

"Pack your shit! We have a mission, and we have fifteen minutes to get ready!" Corporal Nelson screamed at the STA Team as he ran into the tent.

Case needed only five minutes because he had everything set, with his rifles and pistol clean and gear all packed. All he needed was to grab his newest pair of sunglasses, and transfer his cross and St. Christopher metal to his neck chain. In less than a minute, Case was standing at the hatch waiting on Nelson and the rest of the team, and in minutes they were all headed towards the S-3 tent.

At the S-3 tent, they were told to standby outside. That really annoyed Nelson and he seemed fit to be tied after 30 minutes when a sergeant finally came out and escorted them inside.

"I am Sergeant Harrison with S-3; I am going to give the brief for tonight's mission. Sign this receipt for the radio."

Nelson acted angry and stared at the sergeant as he continued.

"An IED initiated ambush occurred at the intersection of MSR Copper and MSR Purple two nights ago resulting in one death and three wounded. IEDs have been regularly placed on this stretch of MSR Copper. In the last three months, four IEDs have been found within a quarter of a mile of the intersection. The mission is to set up a twenty-four-hour over watch position to prevent the emplacement of any further IEDs at the intersection."

At that point, the 3rd Battalion S-2 intelligence officer took over and briefed the STA Team on methods insurgents used to emplace improvised explosive devices.

"The most common IED emplacement method at this time is a multiphase operation. It starts with site selection and ends with placement of the initiator. The insurgents take their time. They first send out scouts who locate the spot for the IED. The scouts have no contraband or weapons on them. Once they have identified the spot for the IED, the scouts leave the area. The IED materials are staged in a safe location, near where the IED will be placed. Insurgents who carry no weapons or other contraband place these materials in that location. If the insurgents are compromised, they simply drop what they are carrying and walk away. As a separate stage, a hole is dug or other concealment prepared. Again, by men who are carrying no weapons or contraband. Once the hole or concealment is prepared, unarmed men place the explosive. They are followed by the initiator, a time fuse, long range cordless phone, slash wire, or monofilament line trip wire. Each of the insurgents spends only a short amount of time at the IED site. You know what IED materials look like, so in addition to weapons watch for any kind of ordinance, wire, or fuses."

As the brief continued, the STA Team learned that two members would be inserted into the area by a tactical convoy every 12 hours. The over watch position was an abandoned house overlooking the intersection.

Nelson planned to take Case out the first 12 hours and then go back out with PFCs Goldman and Hale. Until everyone knew the drill, he wanted to be with the team if anything happened and figured he could get some sleep during the Goldman/Hale watch. For the mission, Nelson ordered the STA Team to each bring an M-16 5.56mm rifle, an M-40A4 7.62mm sniper rifle, a Beretta 9mm pistol, and two frag grenades. One team member would carry in a spotting scope and the other would carry the radio.

Two hours after the briefing a small convoy of four up-armored Humvees dropped Case and Nelson off at the back yard fence of a house across the street from a mosque on the road to Hit, one mile from the intersection of the Baghdad road. The men quickly secured their gear and ran for the mosque wall. Case packed in the spotting scope and Nelson carried the radio. From there, they ran down a ditch to a fence line overgrown with trees and brush, and then along the fence line to an abandoned house about 200 meters off MSR Red.

The stucco was flaked off the sides of the house and the windows and doors were busted out. Case followed Nelson around the side of the house. They ran along a dirt path between overgrown bushes and an ancient block fence and eventually emerged in a small court yard surrounded by an overgrown hedge.

Case hated entering abandoned houses, and applauded the fact that Nelson kept the lead, first entering the back door and searching the kitchen on the ground floor and then moving up the stairs. The dark interior of the house made it difficult to see anything but Case took a deep breath and followed Nelson inside. The place smelled of mold, old wood and rotting garbage. He took cautious steps, careful to not make a sound and searched the remaining rooms on the ground floor. Fortunately, they found the house clear and they proceeded to the roof and set up their position.

The roof parapet was small, forcing Nelson and Case to stay low. This meant they were forced to lie in the prone position for hours, and soon, Case started to shiver on the cold concrete roof. At 1900, Nelson spotted two Iraqis in a field north of the mosque. He identified them as military-aged males, and confirmed that they wore western style black pants, silk shirts, and sandals. He motioned for Case to have a look.

Nelson watched the two Iraqis through the rifle scope for a long time. Case watched through the spotting scope. The Iraqis moved west through the field and then south to the bushes that paralleled MSR Copper.

ೞಿ

Haitham did not like this part of the job. The Americans shot Iraqis at night. It would be easy to get killed looking for that dammed plastic jug the stupid farm boy used to mark the location of the mortar rounds. They should have put the mortar rounds in the pothole on the first trip. Now, Haitham thought they should just wait until the morning and pleaded with Ahmed, "If we are seen walking around, we will be shot for sure. Let's get out of here."

As usual, Ahmed had no fear.

"Laith Hadeed will be angry if we don't finish. He may beat us or kill us. We have to find the bottle."

Ahmed moved back and forth with his head down, but could not find the plastic bottle or mortar rounds. After 30 minutes, even Ahmed decided to give up. The two slowly crossed over to the opposite side of the road. A minute later they walked north, constantly watching the road for cars, and eventually reaching a large cluster of trees.

⊛

The entire time Nelson and Case were watching Haitham and Ahmed, and when they entered the cluster of trees, Nelson motioned for Case to move next to him and whispered in his ear, "What do you think?"

Case ignored the question for several minutes, continuing to study the two Iraqis with his spotting scope. Eventually, he whispered back.

"I can't see what they are carrying, but they are up to no good. I think I have seen that tall fucker somewhere before. You recognize him?"

Nelson stared in the rifle scope for another ten minutes.

"No. I don't recognize either one. I don't think we have enough for hostile intent."

Case disagreed.

"I know that one son-of-a-bitch and I can tell that they are looking for something in that field. What would an innocent civilian be doing at night hiding in the bushes and staring at the roadway? These guys are looking for a place to hide an IED. I say we take them out."

"Well, I don't know—what do you call the range?" Nelson whispered.

It was Case's job to provide the range to the shooter.

"Three seven five, maybe four hundred."

"I have the cross hairs on the one to the left."

"Take the shot," Case answered

Nelson held the cross hairs on Haitham for a long time, and then whispered, "They're not moving now. I can always take the shot if they move. I'll cover them while you radio it in. Tell the staff sergeant that I have them in the crosshairs and if the fuckers make a move they are dead."

"Roger."

Case radioed the platoon sergeant that the team had identified a possible target at RT 039478003 and relayed all the facts regarding the Iraqis actions. The platoon sergeant ordered him to standby and shortly got back on the net asking questions about what the Iraqis were wearing, what they were carrying, had they picked anything up or dropped anything off, and a dozen other details. Case relayed all available information, and the platoon sergeant ordered him to stand by again.

Finally, the staff sergeant radioed instructions.

"The Battalion S-3 Officer says to observe but do not take the shot without positive identification on a weapon, IED materials, digging or placement. You copy, Night Hawk?"

"Copy all. Out."

Case crawled back to Nelson and whispered in his ear.

 "S-3 says no shot without PID on weapon, IED materials, digging or placement."

Without moving Nelson whispered back, "Got it."

C3&0

Haitham and Ahmed stayed hidden in the trees for another two hours and finally decided it was safe to leave. They headed north and away from the MSR without getting killed.

0900, 6 November 2004
SJA Office
Camp Baharia, Iraq

The Outlook Reminder appeared on Beck's screen at 0900: "I MEF Confirmation Brief-I MEF Commanding General's Conference Room, Camp Fallujah." The confirmation brief was the final briefing by the 4th Division staff to its superior unit, the 1st Marine Expeditionary Force, before commencement of the Second Battle of Fallujah. It was intended to make certain that Major General Scott's boss, the Commanding General of I MEF, Lieutenant General Bailey, understood and approved all aspects of the Fourth Division's battle plan.

Before leaving the office, Beck did a quick check of his uniform: felt for his rank insignia, re-bloused his trousers, and brushed the dust off his desert boots. He then picked up his green notebook, stuck a pen down the inside of his blouse buttons so that it could not be seen and headed to command deck for transportation to Camp Fallujah.

On arrival at I MEF Headquarters, he took an inconspicuous seat and looked around. The conference room was well furnished, even better than the 4th Division Conference room back in New Orleans. It had a massive table surrounded by 20 black leather chairs. Gen. Scott entered the room followed by the I MEF Commanding General, LtGen. Bailey.

"At ease, ladies and gentlemen. Please take your seats."

Each section in the 4th Division Battle Staff presented briefs using PowerPoint slides delivered to the S-3 the night before. Beck had four slides and briefed the generals on the rules of engagement for the upcoming Second Battle of Fallujah. The rules had been approved by the I MEF Staff Judge Advocate, Colonel Ray Moore, and by the MNC-I Staff Judge Advocate in Baghdad.

The briefs lasted less than an hour, and at the conclusion Gen. Bailey told everyone that he wanted to say a few things.

"Ladies and gentlemen, thank you for a professional brief. I am honored to be here. It is obvious to me that this operation will be a success, and it has to be. This is a proactive campaign.

Our profession is all about calculating risks. Nothing worth accomplishing can be done without risk. The Marine or soldier clearing a house in Fallujah with nothing but his body armor and rife takes an extreme risk.

"As commanders and staff officers, we also must be willing to take risks, including the risk of failure. I am willing to take that risk and to give you the top-cover you need.

"Let me say that I was in Washington, D.C. last week and that the American people support what we are doing here. The political debates are just that, politics. Don't let your Marines, soldiers, sailors, and airmen think for one second that a politician doing his or her job of asking questions means that what we do here is not appreciated. It is, and it will be, as long as all of us do the right thing.

"America is watching you. I believe that historians will record the Second Battle of Fallujah as the turning point in this conflict.

"Good luck and God Bless."

General Bailey stood up, the aide barked, "Attention on deck," and all stood at attention while the generals walked out.

The briefing was concluded. The battle was about to start.

೮೩৪৹

Anne and Mary had been ordered to stay together at all times, but for the coming mission into Fallujah, Anne would be going this one alone. She'd asked for an embed position, and after a lot of lobbying and waiting, she'd gotten the assignment. She could handle a couple of cowboy truckers, but the Marines were different. Sure, they had a certain cowboy mentality at times, and some seemed so young and naïve that she thought of them as her children.

But they were disciplined. They had protocols that were far different than any rules followed by truckers moving supplies and food. These were the men that people back in Chicago watched on the evening news as they engaged in street fighting. They were the soldiers who were injured by IEDs as they patrolled the streets in Humvees. They lived on orders and adrenaline and courage as much as any bravado they might display.

Now she had to step up to the plate. Being proactive about stateside news stories was one thing—old women getting eviction notices from con artists—but riding with soldiers fighting terrorists capable of killing Americans and committing unspeakable acts of terrorism was altogether different.

She was ready, and she knew it. She'd been hungry to advance her career and make a difference. In a few hours, she would bring her A-game to the streets of Iraq and take her place with other journalists who risked their lives to let Americans know what battle was like.

She packed her gear: rations, a medical kit, a blanket, water, cameras, and a dozen rolls of film. She was certain she would be given more when her convoy moved out.

She hugged Mary and said goodbye before moving into the dim, dreary evening. The sky reminded her of a November evening in Chicago: dark and, in a strange way, ominous.

Chapter 26

Saif, Abdul, Haitham, and Ahmed exchanged terrified glances as they hastened out of the National Islamic Resistance Center while pondering Laith Hadeed's order that they go with Kamis Hadeed to a school building to join the mujahideen in the defense of Fallujah. How would they get away from the Hadeeds before the fighting started?

Kamis Hadeed turned south and tore down Jubail Avenue. The group strolled past abandoned shops, empty houses, and vacant lots. Haitham tried to keep up, but the extra 30-round magazines given to him for his AK-47 rifle kept falling out of his pocket.

At the intersection of Jubail Avenue and Hey al Sinala Street, Haitham recognized a tea shop he used to frequent. The windows had been knocked out by an explosion, and the furniture and contents looted. Obviously, this part of the city had been taken over by the *mujahideen*.

At the next intersection, Kamis Hadeed turned right and headed west on Nazal Street along an ugly row of cinderblock houses, with clumps of cactus, scraggly palm trees, and rubble-strewn yards. Soon they reached a small school, walked in the front door, and entered a classroom. The room smelled of stale cigarette smoke and sweating bodies, and six young Arabs sat on dirty blankets in a corner, smoking cigarettes and talking. Kamis Hadeed ignored the Arabs and walked to a small room at the rear of the building. Two of the Arabs got up quickly and followed him. Kamis Hadeed stopped at the door. "I have brought you more martyrs."

The man sitting in the room was a Syrian with a dark complexion, shoulder-length black hair, and glaring green eyes. The room had no furniture, but Haitham noticed a bedroll, water bottles, and empty Pepsi cans. The Syrian wore a dirty white *dishdasha* and spoke to Kamis with an air of authority. "Tell Laith that we are being treated like pigs here. We have no food, only Pepsi and bread. No one came yesterday. How am I supposed to feed these four?"

Kamis and the Syrian stared at each other while the other terrorists looked nervous. Finally, Kamis Hadeed's eyes brightened as he leered at the Syrian. "Hey, we all will die soon. No need to get fat eating bread."

Kamis turned and walked out of the school. The Syrian glared at Haitham, Saif, Ahmed, and Abdul with his crazy green eyes.

"Samir, take these Fallujahans to the teacher's office. They cannot die with Jihadists. They will defend the west building."

Samir took the group outside to a two-story building in the southwest corner of the schoolyard. He then walked over to the small building that served as the school's toilet and returned with a single shovel, studied the yard and the teacher's building for several minutes, and then carefully made four Xs on the ground.

"You must each dig yourself a fighting hole," Samir told the group. "When the Americans come they will blow up the buildings, and you will defend our backs. To survive to kill Americans, you must make the holes deep so that you can hide until the time is right."

Samir laid the shovel down and sauntered back into the school. Haitham, Saif, Ahmed, and Abdul gaped at each other while slowly moving to the wall. They each squatted down to smoke cigarettes. No one planned on sticking around to fight the Americans.

"How will we escape?" Haitham openly asked Saif.

Saif carefully studied the situation and rolled his eyes up to convey that they were being watched. After a few minutes, Haitham casually looked around and saw one of the jihadists on the roof of the school. He also could see that the jihadist had a Dragunov sniper rifle.

Haitham looked back at Saif. "We will have to wait until it is dark. Even if we got out of here, there is no way we could make it to the river in the daylight."

After a couple of hours, Ahmed felt so bored that, to everyone's astonishment, he picked up the shovel and started digging. The rest of the group enjoyed watching Ahmed dig. At least they had something to do, and after half an hour Abdul asked Ahmed for the shovel, and he started digging as well. Abdul, Saif, Haitham, and Ahmed spent the rest of the afternoon in this fashion—digging or watching.

⊂🙰🙵⊃

At around 4:30 p.m., the Syrian sent a young Saudi named Sdeek to them with cans of Pepsi. He was 19 years old, thin, and full of energy. He seemed to be looking for a friend. "Are you mujahideen?" he asked.

Saif answered for the group. "No. We are Fallujahans. We only want our city back from the Americans, but we will fight like lions when the time comes."

"I come from my home in Saudi Arabia for jihad," Sdeek remarked. "I want only to be a martyr."

Sdeek then spent an hour talking non-stop to the group. "My father is very religious, and he sent me to the school in Riyadh when I was sixteen. When I returned to Diriyah, my father said I must go to Fallujah to kill kafir. He gave me the telephone number of a man in Jordan who could arrange my transportation. He took me to a safe house in a poor part of the city. Other jihadists also came to the house. There were twelve of us living in the house, but no one came to get me. Finally, I was sent to this school two weeks ago and given this rifle and told to kill Americans. I have never shot a rifle but, God willing, I will shoot straight. I can only hope that my bullets kill Americans."

At dusk, Sdeek led the group back to the classroom for evening prayers and a meal of Pepsi, stale bread, and hummus. After the meal, Sdeek escorted the four to a vacant room on the second floor of the Al Hareery School. Saif, Abdul, Haitham, and Ahmed made their beds with dirty blankets in a corner. The Hadeeds slept in the classroom while the jihadists camped on the first floor of the office building.

"We will wait until the jihadists go to sleep and then we will sneak out the front door," Saif whispered to the group. "It will be easy. When we get out, we will head to the river."

The blankets smelled of sweat, but Haitham curled up and pretended to sleep. When the sun went down, the school became very dark. Haitham felt certain that they would be able to get out of Fallujah. He could not sleep and lay awake on the floor for hours, listening to Saif and Abdul snore. Finally, he decided to wake Saif, and quietly moved over to shake his shoulder.

"Saif," Haitham said. "We must leave. The jihadists are asleep."

Saif and Haitham woke Abdul and Ahmed, and the four lined up with Saif in front and headed down the stairs. Haitham kept his hand on the extra magazine to make certain that it didn't fall out of his pocket. They had to feel their way as Saif moved very slowly. Saif thought he could see the floor below. He stopped and put his head near the steps. Suddenly, he could see a man standing at the front door. He jumped and started back up the stairs. At the top he spoke. "The Hadeeds are guarding the door. They will kill us if they see us try and run. We must wait for a better chance."

Chapter 27

The sun glared inside the school when Haitham Rasheed opened his eyes. Abdul, Saif, and Ahmed still slept. The second floor of the Al Hareery School existed as a partial floor, and Haitham picked up an empty Abraaj water bottle and walked out the door leading onto the roof. Haitham ambled to the southeast corner, unscrewed the lid, pulled down his pants, and carefully urinated in the bottle. It seemed very efficient. You drank the water, and then you filled the bottle with urine.

As Haitham started to return to the room, he noticed that paper leaflets covered the roof. Recently, it seemed, the Americans dropped leaflets every other night. Haitham bent over and picked up one to read. It started by saying that the Prime Minister, under the Iraqi National Security Law, had issued an emergency decree. All citizens of Fallujah were ordered to immediately leave the city, and any person that did not leave would be subject to a 24-hour curfew, starting tomorrow. All government offices were closed. The Fallujah Police were disbanded and were no longer authorized to wear uniforms or carry weapons, which were now prohibited. In large bold letters, the leaflet warned that, starting tomorrow, anyone seen with a weapon would be shot on sight.

Haitham got that sick feeling in his stomach and ran to the sleeping room. "Wake up! It is too late! We are going to be slaughtered!"

Ahmed looked up, terrified, and Haitham handed him the leaflet. In a second, Saif jumped up and grabbed the leaflet out of Ahmed's hand, read it, and handed it to Abdul. Saif let Abdul read the leaflet and started speaking. Haitham noticed that, for the first time, Saif looked scared and his voice trembled.

"Laith should not have left us here," Saif claimed. "There is no money here. I am not dying for nothing. It is time for us to get out of Fallujah."

Abdul answered in a slow and determined voice. "We will head for the river and find a boat."

Haitham looked at Saif. "Will you take us with you?"

"Yes. Don't worry, street boys. Saif will get you out of this alive."

ᘓᔑᘔ

0400, 8 November 2004
3rd Battalion Area
Camp Baharia, Iraq

At 0400, under a cloudy sky and misting rain, the STA team climbed in the back of a high-back HMMWV with a cargo bed for protection against small arms fire, with sandbags on the floor to shield against improvised explosive devises. Hale climbed up first and Goldberg handed up the gear—four MOLLE packs, followed by the SAW. Case and Nelson strapped their M-40A1 sniper rifles over their backs. Case climbed up next, and Nelson handed up both M-16A1s.

The STA team moved to the front of the Humvee directly behind the ring-mounted .50 caliber machine gun. They found places to kneel or sit and positioned themselves so that when the convoy moved out, they would be able to return fire if attacked. They had done this dozens of times without difficulty, in practice and on the STA team's previous missions. This time was different. They believed they were headed for a major battle, and they were excited to be a part of it.

Corporal Nelson felt terribly nervous. He rehearsed every scenario in his mind. He kept telling himself, *Don't fuck this up.*

Case thought about the thousands of Marines who had enlisted after Vietnam. Many served 20 years and had retired without the opportunity to engage in a real battle. But here he sat, bristling with grenades, ammunition, and weapons. His mind raced with excitement and dread. The rest of the STA team felt the same. They ran through last-minute mental checklists, said prayers, and triple-checked their weapons. They all believed that the battle would be a tough one.

It was pitch dark, but Case could see that the person sitting to the rear of the driver didn't have a helmet cover. He was holding a small backpack. Case suspected that the person was not a Marine and guessed that it was one of the interpreters.

The convoy moved out exactly on time. The first hour involved a series of stops and starts in order to exit the east gate of Camp Baharia. Military police and officers remained posted at intersections, directing some units to stop and others to proceed. As the convoy wound its way around Camp Baharia, Case could hear the sound of air strikes in Fallujah, and every so often there was a huge explosion. He imagined that these were the GBU-12s—two-thousand pounders—being dropped on pre-designated targets.

When the truck arrived at the east gate, he recognized the location and realized that the road would head north, past the Fallujah Liaison Center and onto the freeway designated MSR Aluminum. At MSR Aluminum, the convoy turned left into the right two lanes and picked up speed past the Jordanian hospital and the potato factory, again turning north at vehicle checkpoint one. At this point, the convoy came within small arms range of the houses on the outskirts of Fallujah, and Case knew these were sometimes used by insurgent snipers. Case didn't know if the insurgents had night vision capability, but he kept his head down to be safe and yelled at Nelson, Goldman, and Hale to get down behind the armor plating.

At vehicle checkpoint one, Case gave up predicting the convoy's route. The trucks proceeded in the darkness for several miles, turning off the freeway and winding along dirt roads kicking up large clouds of dust. When the convoy stopped, Case checked his watch. It was 0600. The STA team followed standard procedure, quickly disembarked, and knelt down at the rear of the vehicle. In ten minutes, the platoon commander came back and opened the A-driver's door, and Case could see that the passenger was a woman. She got out and left with the Executive Officer of Kilo Company.

૭૪৪

As Case knelt behind the vehicle, he thought of killing the whitetail buck. The animal had disappeared for a moment before reappearing. He curled his finger tighter around the trigger of the Redfield, his mind focused. The deer was in his scope. He squeezed the trigger, and the buck went down. He'd done his job.

"What are you smiling at?" Hale asked him.

"What?" Case said. "Smiling? Nothing. Mind was wandering."

Hale rolled his eyes. "I don't think this is a good time to take a mental trip."

Case nodded. "Say, who's the woman?"

Hale shrugged. "Don't know. Probably a reporter. Ain't that shit?"

"With a capital S," Case said.

૭૪৪

Anne walked around the Humvee, staring into the darkness.

"I told you to stay in the vehicle, Ms. Merrill," said Captain Chris Douglas.

Anne smiled and walked back to the vehicle. "Sorry. Didn't think we were in combat conditions yet."

Douglas sighed in exasperation. "Ma'am, snipers are everywhere Some places may be safer than others, but here is the rule of thumb that you will follow. *No place* is safe in Iraq. Do I make myself clear?"

"Perfectly," Anne replied.

She checked the digital Nikon slung over her shoulder and looked about her a second time.

"Now, Ms. Merrill!" Douglas reiterated.

Anne returned to the Humvee and again climbed into the seat behind the driver. She scribbled some notes in a small notebook, after which she spoke quietly into a digital recorder in the breast pocket of the light khaki vest she wore. Working with Frank Tobolski had given her a thick skin. Frank was a tough, no nonsense kind of guy.

She'd had to push men like Tobolski and O'Daniel back in Chicago to get the assignments she wanted, and she intended to push Douglas a bit. She intended to follow the embed rules for reporters, but it never hurt to let men know she wasn't going to get steamrolled.

※

The convoy proceeded into the streets of Fallujah. When it stopped a second time, Douglas again exited the vehicle while the men knelt at its rear.

Five minutes passed.

"Where's Merrill?" Douglas barked. The first sergeant shrugged his shoulders.

Anne was next to a row of shops selling wares—cloth, vegetables, and used electronics.

"Merrill!" Douglas called.

Anne made no reply. She was totally absorbed in snapping pictures of Iraqi shops, although most were now closed. She was about to take another photo when a hand clamped down on her shoulder and spun her around. She inhaled sharply, her eyes wide with fright.

"I told you to stay in the damned Humvee!" Douglas said. He rubbed the hands of his right fingers over the short hair on top of his head.

"But I was in plain sight," Anne protested. "These people are civilians, and they—"

"Sometimes, Ms. Merrill," Douglas said, interrupting, "the distinction between civilians and insurgents is pretty damn thin. We take nothing for granted, and neither should you."

Anne returned to her seat in the Humvee. She'd been ecstatic to finally be embedded, and the enthusiasm of the STA team had been infectious. But she had to admit that she wasn't a soldier and knew little of the streets of Fallujah. She was naïve. But she also knew that a good journalist took risks. That's the way it was on the streets of Chicago.

She rested her head sideways against her right hand. Yes, risks, but she had to choose her moments. Douglas was right, and she knew it. She decided to try and restrain her impulsivity.

She wondered if she could do it. If an opportunity came...

ભ૮૪૭

Case thought of his life at Stateline. It seemed a thousand years ago that he'd driven a forklift, gone to bars, and lived with his parents. Was he even the same person?

He also thought of waiting in the stand to shoot the buck. He'd felt great pride when he'd hit the target. It was shortly after that when he decided he could do something useful. But he no longer waited in the rural bush for an animal to get clear so that he could take a clean shot. This was street fighting. His targets were human, but he was proud to be a Marine. He was making a difference. He looked briefly at his weapon and suppressed a grin.

He would do whatever he had to do. The recruiter had been right. Being a Marine was more than just a job, and Case was glad that he'd been turned away on that first day.

He understood that he was not just doing a job, but rather he was fulfilling a mission.

It was his destiny, and the gun felt good in his hands. Very good. It was an extension of his body and his mind. He could squeeze off a round without even thinking, the same as he'd done on the rifle range.

CRBO

0030, 8 November 2004
Al Hareery School
Fallujah, Iraq

Haitham and Ahmed remembered standing on top of the National Islamic Resistance Center when the Marines launched the feint attack three weeks earlier. On another night they stood within half a mile of an American air strike. But those experiences were nothing like what was happening tonight. This time there were multiple air strikes occurring within minutes of each other. The bombs could be heard all over Fallujah.

Haitham also recognized the "buzrrr, buzrrr, buzrrr" of the C-130 gun ships. He knew this was the main attack and prayed that it would not be the end of his life.

At least there was a chance that the Americans wouldn't bomb the school. Everyone knew that the safest places were hospitals, mosques, and schools. In fact, that is why the jihadists had been staying at Al Hareery School in the first place.

Haitham asked Saif a question. "What do we do now?"

Saif still looked scared. "We can't leave the school. We will have to wait for the soldiers. When they get here, we will give ourselves up. Just keep your mouth shut like last time and the Americans will let us go in a few days."

At about midnight, Haitham heard several large explosions on the north side of the city. The Marines were battling their way into Fallujah.

Part III

Chapter 28

0700, 8 November 2004
Fallujah Train Station
Fallujah, Iraq

F ive minutes after dismounting the truck, the STA team
moved out behind the 3rd Platoon heading south into
Fallujah. They marched for 15 minutes before stopping and assuming a hasty defensive position. It started to
rain, and Nelson gave the order to don the raingear. One at a
time, each member of the STA team removed their body
armor, put the Gore-tex parkas on underneath, replaced
their gear, and resumed their defensive positions.

Without warning, the team felt a mammoth explosion,
much greater than a 122mm Katyusha rocket, a 120mm Al-
Jaleel, or a 155mm artillery round. It was unlike anything
they had ever experienced. It shook the earth, deafening the
men. Case surmised that the air strike had hit an ammunition dump, especially since the first explosion was followed
in seconds by two similar explosions, and the three repeated
after 15 minutes. One of the grunts said that the explosions
were the destruction of the railroad berms and that four
holes were blown in the embankment to allow the 1st Division and 4th Division to simultaneously attack the city from
the north. The soldiers and Marines were streaming through
the breaches, led by Army armored battalions with Abram
tanks and Bradley Fighting Vehicles. The armored battalions
had punched through the roadblocks and headed into the
heart of the city, overwhelming the few insurgents on the
north end of the city. Case's unit, 3rd Platoon, Kilo Company,
3rd Battalion, had orders to follow in trace. Soon the unit was
moving again.

The STA team slogged down the deserted Fallujah streets, assisting the 3rd Platoon in clearing the two-story homes hidden behind block walls and metal gates. As they fanned out, they observed the small orange fireball from an AK-47 erupt from a rooftop two blocks away, with Marines ahead returning fire. Although the troops were issued night-vision goggles, it would be difficult to see the enemy at night. The insurgents had the advantage of not having to move and could wait for an opportunity to ambush the Marines.

Corporal Nelson put himself in the front of the team and used hand signals to increase speed, shift right, shift left, or decrease speed. It was nearly impossible for the STA team to keep up with the 3rd Platoon. The STA team always carried more gear than infantry Marines, and for Operation *Al Fajar* the team carried one M-16A1, one M-203 rifle and grenade launcher, three M-16A1s, three M-40A1 sniper rifles, one SAW, four 9mm Beretta pistols, and a dozen frag and smoke grenades. Case felt he carried an extra 20 pounds of gear, but his enthusiasm hadn't waned.

There were no stops and no talking for the next three hours. It proved the most physically demanding task of Case's life, but he was up for it. Finally, the 3rd Platoon halted and Nelson came over to speak to Case, Goldman, and Hale. Shortly, Case saw the platoon commander coming back to issue new orders. "We're taking fire from two houses up front. Time for you to go to work, Corporal Nelson. Can you get your team into position to take one out?"

Nelson scanned the sky. A scintilla of light glimmered in the east. "Sir, if you can break here until daylight, we can get into position on the roof of the house over there. We may get a shot."

The platoon commander studied the horizon. "It will be daylight in ten minutes. You better get moving, Corporal."

Nelson charged straight for the house across the street, with his team following as fast as they could run. The four had rehearsed the procedure of stacking outside the door, entering the house, clearing the first floor, and then moving up one floor at a time. This morning, Nelson shocked the team by busting inside the house and running straight up to the roof, leaving everyone else standing outside. Case prayed that no insurgents were in the house and moved behind Nelson up the stairs. Goldman and Hale came after Case.

ৎৎ৪৩

When the STA team reached the top floor, Nelson cracked open the door leading to the balcony and scanned the two houses on the next block. He then slid back into the darkness to talk to Case, Goldman, and Hale. "Here's the plan. I'll spot using the window. Case, you take the shot through the door. Hale, you cover our backsides in case we left enemy down there. Goldman, you watch the other side of the street."

In a second, the four Marines assumed their assigned positions, and Nelson scanned the two houses up the street. Although it exposed him to any enemy sniper, Case chose the sitting position just inside the doorway. He always shot best from the sitting position, and it gave him the best field of fire for the two houses. The light of the sun coming up that morning in Fallujah had the same crystal clarity as the morning when he'd shot the deer in the Missouri bottoms. Things seemed to jump out of his scope. The adrenaline once again surged through his system.

Before long, Case spotted an Iraqi looking out a window down the street, but couldn't see a weapon. In a second, the man stepped back out of sight, and Case motioned to Nelson to watch the location.

Suddenly, three Iraqis burst out into the street, and Nelson yelled louder than ever before: "Take the shot!"

In less than a millisecond, Case placed the crosshairs of the scope on one man's back and pulled the trigger. The insurgent went down. He squeezed off a second, and another insurgent went down. He felt as energized as when he'd shot the deer in Missouri. His training was paying off.

The third Iraqi made it to the side of the house and was turning when Case shot him in the left hip. He went down with the other two.

"Yessss!" Case muttered.

Case didn't move. He continued to peer through the scope at the house for more insurgents. Looking through the scope, the rifle moved excessively up and down. He could see no other movement, but observed that one of the insurgents had a large blood spot on his back. The other two lay still without visible injuries. Case tried to spot a weapon, but couldn't see one.

After ten minutes, the grunts moved up, rolled one of the insurgents over, and pulled him to the side of the road. They repeated the procedure for the second and third insurgents. 3rd Platoon was moving out and headed south down the street.

Nelson barked an order. "Let's get down before we get left behind."

He headed to the house where the insurgents were first seen and plowed inside the doorway. Before Case got there, he saw Nelson exiting the house, carrying three AK-47 rifles. Nelson removed the magazines and cleared the weapons and then handed one to Case.

"You think you got the strength to carry this until we catch up with the grunts?"

"Yeah. No problem at all."

Since taking out the sniper, Case was in the zone. It was a good place to be.

 CRWO

0800, 8 November 2004
Al Hareery School
Fallujah, Iraq

Haitham gazed out the window of the school. He saw no one on the street, and the city looked abandoned. It sounded like the fighting to the north had died down, and he heard fewer explosions.

The rest of the jihadists and insurgents started to wake, and Haitham could hear them talking among themselves.

They debated what to do. Some wanted to leave the school and head north toward the fighting, while others wanted to stay at the school. Kamis Hadeed stopped the debate. He said that he would go and receive their orders. He left Samir in charge. As soon as Kamis Hadeed exited the school, the group started looking for something to eat for breakfast, but as usual found only warm Pepsi and stale bread.

In the last four months, Haitham had been shocked many times, but nothing shocked him as much as seeing Laith Hadeed walk into the school 30 minutes later, accompanied by a half-dozen Hadeeds carrying AK-47s. Laith had the same excited look on his face that he got when he tortured or killed someone. "The Americans will be here soon!" he said. He said this like he expected to hear the group cheer, but everyone remained silent. "Last night we killed many of them. Our brothers in Baghdad are demanding that the Americans leave Fallujah. All we have to do is kill enough of them today and they will leave."

The jihadists looked serious, and some started their morning prayers without letting Laith Hadeed finish. Hadeed, his scarred face showing contempt, walked around the room, giving orders to everyone. He sent the jihadists to the office building. The Hadeeds were assigned the classroom building, and some insurgents from Hadithah were sent to the west wall, where Haitham and Ahmed had dug the holes. When Hadeed got to Abdul, Saif, Haitham, and Ahmed, he smiled his crazy smile. "My brave torturers and little street boys, what should you do for the people of Fallujah? I know! You shall have the place of honor. You will guard the north building, and you shall have the first chance to kill Americans."

Haitham thought to himself that Laith Hadeed wanted them dead. The Americans would destroy the small building within minutes.

The group had no choice but to head to the north building, which appeared to be about ten feet wide and twelve feet long. It had a door on each end and a window in the middle. It looked like it had served as the teacher's residence.

Haitham led as the four stepped inside the building. He wanted to get inside fast and talk to Saif without the terrorist present. Haitham, of course, did not really care what the others decided; he planned on leaving—and leaving right now. He and Ahmed would sneak out and run away. When Haitham stepped through the door to the building, he received his second shock of the day. An Iraqi family now occupied the building. Haitham just stood at the doorway until Saif got there.

"Who are you people and what are you doing here?" Haitham asked.

An old man spoke. "I am Khalil Saddaq. We stayed to protect our homes, but the bombs came last night and we moved here. We want to leave Fallujah."

While the old man spoke, Haitham stared at two middle-aged women, two girls about Haitham's age, and a young boy. Haitham wondered how the old man could have been so stupid. How could one protect one's home in these circumstances?

Haitham made his declaration. "Ahmed and I will take them to the Americans."

Saif stopped and looked at Haitham. "We will all take them to the Americans. I will go tell Laith. He will let us go."

Saif went back to the school building and remained inside for ten minutes. When he returned, Laith Hadeed walked with him. They were followed by the four Hadithans.

Laith Hadeed entered the teacher's quarters and looked at the family with a wild look in his eyes. "So the torturers and street boys want to be heroes by taking these Saddaq to the Americans?"

Laith glared at Haitham. "Nobody is going anywhere."

Laith Hadeed enjoyed scaring everyone. "Saif," he said, "you and Abdul stay here. The street boys will come with me."

⋘⋙

1300, 8 November 2004
Al Hareery School
Fallujah, Iraq

When they returned to the classroom building, Laith Hadeed sent Haitham and Ahmed to the office building at the southwest corner of the schoolyard. Being with the jihadists scared Haitham, but the office building sat on the west side toward the river. The Americans would come from the north.

Haitham heard the Americans coming down Jubail Avenue about one mile west of the school, and soon he made out the sounds of the main tank guns, the 25mm Bradley guns, .50 caliber machine guns, and small-arms fire. He pretended to guard the front door of the school building and even asked the jihadists for more ammunition, which they didn't have.

Like Haitham, each jihadist had only two magazines, or 60 rounds. It made Haitham angry to think the jihadists sacrificed their lives with just two magazines. But, of course, Haitham had no intention of fighting the Americans. At the right time, he and Ahmed would run to the river. In the meantime, Haitham pretended to be anxious for a fight.

Sdeek came over to offer Haitham a cigarette. While the two smoked, Sdeek handed Haitham a wad of money and a piece of paper. "Will you remember my story? Please call my father at this number. He must know of my martyrdom."

Haitham thought about asking Sdeek to go with him, but knew that he would not, so he just nodded and spoke. "If God wills that I survive, I swear I shall call your father and proclaim your heroism."

When Sdeek walked back to his position, Haitham noticed that the jihadists were looking at him, and he wondered if they suspected anything. From the front door, Haitham had a view of the street. Moments later, he saw mujahideen running down the street headed south, and he could hear the engines and tracks on the M-1A1 tanks and Bradley Personnel Carriers on Jubail Avenue.

The machine guns shot constantly—*thud, thud, thud, thud, thud, thud*—pause—*thud, thud, thud, thud, thud, thud*. Even worse was the sound of the tank guns blasting into the houses. Every time the tanks fired, the earth shook, and Haitham's ears hurt.

Haitham stood next to the door and watched the gate closely, hoping that neither the Americans nor the mujahideen would enter. He tried to get his courage up. He planned to run away as soon as the jihadists were not looking.

Then, Haitham heard the sound of an AK-47 firing from the roof of the office building. As always, he knew what to do but waited too long. He should have just run. God was punishing him again.

Ahmed watched him from the other end of the classroom. Neither could decide what to do. Was it safe to run?

Haitham thought about moving to the roof. He could act like he was going to join in the fight. He thought about running out the door and into the street with his hands up, but was afraid the jihadists would shoot him in the back.

Haitham again decided to run when the bullets started hitting the office building. The wall prevented the Americans from shooting at ground level, but rounds were striking the top of the building. Dust, dirt, plaster, and broken bricks flew everywhere. Haitham saw that the .50 caliber machine gun fire pierced the walls of the office building, and he froze in fear.

Soon the AK-47 rifle fire stopped. Maybe the Americans would leave. Haitham lay flat on the marble floor, looking out the door, waiting for a chance to put up his hands and surrender. Suddenly, he could see an American tank through the gate, and Haitham scrambled to the corner and curled up on the floor.

The tank fired only one round into the building. The 120mm HE round pierced the south wall and exploded inside the north wall. The jihadists on the roof were all killed from the concussion. Four of the jihadists inside died instantly from shrapnel. Sdeek was hit in the groin and legs with four pieces of shrapnel and was bleeding, but the shrapnel missed his arteries.

The terrorist next to Haitham took a spoon-shaped piece of shrapnel in the face, splitting his head open so that his brains spilled out onto his chest. He died in seconds.

Haitham and Ahmed were hit with large and small pieces of the brick wall, and Ahmed's right arm and leg were severely bruised. A large brick hit Haitham in the left knee, and he had shallow cuts on his face and arms.

CRSO

When the American soldiers entered the office building, all of the insurgents except Sdeek, Haitham, and Ahmed were dead. Haitham and Ahmed were in shock from the concussion and could not comprehend what had happened. The soldiers quickly gathered up the AK-47s, magazines, and ammunition, and these were taken outside. The soldiers moved Haitham and Ahmed to the southwest corner of the office building and laid them next to Sdeek along the east wall so that the medics could examine and treat them.

From the start, the Division ordered 1st Battalion to move quickly through the city, and at that time the battalion was three hours behind schedule, seriously jeopardizing the entire operation. The brigade commander therefore issued additional orders that the battalion commander do whatever was necessary to reach phase line green as soon as possible. This meant that the battalion could not take the time to search the other two buildings or pursue the enemy. Instead, the battalion had to keep moving down the street. Speed had become essential for the concept of battle, and the battalion commander had to keep going.

During this time, the Hadeeds had not fired a shot and gave no reason to the American soldiers to think that the other two buildings were occupied.

The medics finished their work on Haitham, Ahmed, and Sdeek in two minutes. They were assessed as having non-life threatening injuries, and their wounds were cleaned and bandaged. Antibiotics were injected, and they were made comfortable and given water, MREs, and pain relievers.

Of course, the battalion took a risk leaving the wounded behind in the office building because they might easily recover and re-arm themselves. However, the battalion commander had to take this risk if he wanted to reach his objective on schedule. Also, the battalion commander expected that Haitham, Ahmed, and Sdeek would soon be picked up by the Marine battalion following in trace of 1st Battalion. In less than five minutes after the attack, 1st Battalion was out of sight, headed south down Jabail Avenue.

ೞೞ

The pain medicine made Haitham feel drowsy, and after 1st Battalion left, he tried to understand what had happened. He heard Sdeek speak. "God has willed that we survive."

Haitham started to think about that. Maybe Uncle Ghazi had been right. Everything that happens does so because God has willed it.

Suddenly, Haitham heard the voice he hated. Laith Hadeed. "Where are your weapons?"

Sdeek answered.   "The Americans took them. They left us here and said they would be back."

"How many were they?" Hadeed asked.

"I could not tell. There was a tank."

Laith Hadeed did not worry about Sdeek. "Others will be here soon. Can you still fight? We have killed many Americans. They will soon give up and run. There are many mujahedeen here, all willing to die. The Americans cannot come back here. We control this area."

Laith Hadeed looked at the bodies of the terrorists and told Saif and Abdul to search them. Saif and Abdul naturally looked forward to the opportunity to strip the dead of any valuables. There might be some money in this thing after all.

One of the dead jihadists had 2,000 American dollars in his pocketbook. That would be more than enough for a new Toyota. To Saif's surprise, almost all the jihadists had money, and it looked like each carried everything they owned. One had $1,000, another $800, and the others similar amounts.

The total take for the Hadeeds totaled nearly $6,000, a small fortune in Iraq.

Haitham, Ahmed, and Sdeek were taken back to the classroom and each was given another AK-47 rifle.

1900, 8 November 2004
Al Hareery School
Fallujah, Iraq

As soon as he returned to the classroom, the pain medicine caused Haitham to fall asleep. When he woke, the sun had gone down and he could hear rain falling outside. The classroom felt cold. Haitham slowly stood up and went in search of blankets.

The Iraqi family moved inside the classroom building and had needed the blankets, so Haitham could find only a dirty one in the opposite corner. He carried it back to his spot, lay down, closed his eyes, and tried to huddle next to Ahmed. Something startled him. One of the Iraqi girls placed a blanket on top of Haitham and Ahmed. Haitham protested. "No, no. We have plenty. You keep your blanket."

The girl just smiled and wandered back to her family. As Haitham lay curled up in the blanket, the sounds of the battle gradually died out.

0530, 9 November 2004
Al Hareery School
Fallujah, Iraq

The sun had fully risen, and the classroom felt warm when Haitham opened his eyes. Everyone else appeared to be awake. Haitham had recovered from the blast, and it felt good to stand up and walk outside to relieve himself. Ahmed went with him. One of the Hadeeds kept a careful eye on them, and Haitham assumed this was to make sure they didn't run away. Outside, they would have a chance to talk.

Ahmed spoke first. "God has saved our lives for some purpose, and God will protect us from both the Hadeeds and the Americans."

"It sounds like you have been talking to Sdeek all night," Haitham said.

"Sdeek is going home to Saudi Arabia. He believes it is God's will that he live. I believe that also."

Haitham looked at Ahmed. He had a serious expression that Haitham hadn't seen before. "You talk like Uncle Ghazi. It is always God or family that protects us. Ahmed, we must protect ourselves and get out of here."

Haitham glanced at the Hadeed watching them from inside the school. "This time when the Americans come, I am running out the back door," Haitham proclaimed. "If you are smart, you better come with me."

When they went back, Haitham searched for food but found none. Haitham then remembered the plastic bags the Americans left and the meal he'd eaten at the Camp Baharia prison. He strolled past the Hadeed that had been watching them and spoke to Saif. "The Americans left food in the office. Come with me so we can eat."

Laith Hadeed sat at the far end of the classroom, talking in a low voice to another Hadeed. When he heard Haitham speak of the food, he ordered one of the other Hadeeds to go with Haitham and Saif. Laith no longer trusted Saif.

Haitham returned with the MREs, passed them around to the Saddaq family, the Hadeeds, and sat on the blanket to eat.

Chapter 29

After his morning brief, Corporal Nelson ordered the STA team to assume the counter-sniper mission for lead elements of Kilo Company. A sniper had shot a BCT-9 soldier the day before, and the commanding officer expressed concern that enemy snipers might infiltrate the Kilo area of operation. Case was tired and sore but also felt excited. The anti-sniper mission represented the primary mission of the STA team, something the team had studied and frequently practiced at Camp Pendleton, California.

Kilo Company headed south towards Phase Line Yellow, and the STA team followed in trace. After six blocks, Nelson motioned for the STA team to enter one of the houses. Doctrine required the STA team to clear the entire house before moving up to the roof. On the first day, Nelson just dashed straight to the roof in every house, and Case now considered him a tactical genius. Case very much preferred the straight-up-the-stairs method, but as the team approached the first house, Nelson hesitated and seemed to have second thoughts about his new technique. He ordered the team to form a stack, with Hale in the lead, followed by Goldman, Case, and himself. Case's heart beat steadily as he stood in the doorway, waiting for the signal to enter. After a minute, Nelson gave the signal and the team surged inside the house.

The buck had disappeared for a moment, but then it had reappeared in the scope of the Redfield. Case squeezed the trigger.

Inside, the team moved from room to room, with Hale in the lead, and Goldman and Case providing security. It took ten minutes to clear the kitchen, prayer room, and two bedrooms. The occupants had left in a hurry, leaving food on plates on the kitchen table. They found no one and stood by to move to the second floor when Nelson motioned for the others to wait at the foot of the stairs. Hale gave Case a look and whispered in his ear. "What's up? Has he lost his mind?"

Nelson returned with a three-foot-long stick, and the team raced up the stairs, cleared all rooms, and stacked at the door leading out to the balcony. Nelson slowly opened the door and crawled out on the roof, looking over his shoulder every few seconds. After working his way to the edge, he peered over the top of the wall and motioned for Case to come out.

Looking over the balcony wall, Case observed two M-1A1 tanks and four Amtracs moving down the street. Nelson then pointed toward the second floor roof, took off his gear, and handed Case both his rifles. He then carefully crawled to the top of the second story. On top, he dropped a det-cord and hoisted his gear to the top. Case and Goldman repeated the maneuver and pulled up their gear.

They found a 20-inch hole in the wall near the corner. It was large enough to cover the area, and Nelson carefully assumed the prone position, with his sniper rifle pointed through the hole. Case moved to the opposite corner, took out his spotting scope, and looked for a way to conceal it so that he could peer over the wall and scan for enemy snipers. After ten minutes he spoke in Nelson's ear. "I don't see a setup here."

Nelson agreed. "I hate to do it, Case, but we're going to have to split up. There's a spot for you and Goldman to set up down on the balcony. Keep the radio on, and if you see something, radio me up here. If you can't radio, do your best solo."

Case and Hale crawled back down to the balcony and lowered their gear using the det-cord. They soon discovered a great spot to set up in a shadow four feet back from the edge. The location provided Case a good field of fire. He lay on his stomach, peering through his riflescope, studying the view of Fallujah, and listening to the sound of numerous firefights, mortar rounds, and artillery and air strikes. He listened for single shots and scanned the locations that an insurgent sniper might occupy.

Case thought about the higher elevation of Nelson's position but figured he had a good view of most of the buildings. He identified a dozen spots that he would use if he were an enemy sniper. He concentrated on watching the likely sniper locations. He was once again in the zone.

Case's mother smiled warmly. "I'm so proud of you, Jeremy."

After an hour, Nelson radioed Case that he had decided to try the oldest sniper trick in the book. He ordered Hale to put his helmet on the stick carried up from the first floor and to carefully move it near the top of the wall. "Don't make it obvious, Hale. Just move it a tiny bit above the wall. Don't do it except once every half hour."

At 0700, Hale edged the helmet towards the top of the wall. He didn't do it again until 0725, and again at 0740. At 0755 he repeated the maneuver and the helmet went flying down to the ground. It was an impressive shot by the insurgent sniper since the helmet had been less than half an inch above the wall. Case instinctively crouched closer to the balcony floor.

He couldn't spot the sniper, but thought he could identify his location from the sound inside a house about 600 yards to the south. Case started his calculations. He counted the blocks and thought about the wind, the temperature, and the difference in height between himself and the sniper. As he stared through his scope at the suspected location, he heard Nelson shoot. He then saw blood splatter on a wall near the roof he was watching He still couldn't see the sniper.

He kept his eye glued to the blood location for another 30 minutes. Finally,

Nelson called on the radio. "Can you confirm, Case?"

"I can see blood, but not the body."

"I can see the body, and he hasn't moved," Nelson said. "Let's get over and take a look."

It took the team 30 minutes to reach the sniper's location, to clear the house, and to reach the roof. They found a dead insurgent sniper.

Chapter 30

Inside the Al Hareery School, the Iraqis finished eating the last of the MREs and sat around listening to the battlefield sounds. Laith Hadeed didn't post a lookout and no one inside saw the Marines approaching from the north.

CRESO

During the night, the Battalion Intelligence Officer had analyzed situation reports from the first day and determined that insurgents had fortified every mosque and school in Fallujah as strongholds. Therefore, the Intelligence Officer identified the Al Hareery School as a Kilo Company objective, and he prepared a pre-planned attack for the school, which included use of the STA team for protecting the infantry from enemy snipers. Kilo Company paused two blocks from the Al Hareery School, and the commanding officer sent the STA team forward to take up an over-watch position.

Corporal Nelson seemed overly excited about the mission. He motioned for Case, Hale, and Goldman to follow as he raced through the backyards of the houses on the west side of Nazal Street. Case realized that this unnecessarily exposed the STA team to enemy fire, but without time to do anything about it, he simply pushed on and tried to keep up with Nelson.

In minutes, the STA team reached a house north of the school, and the team members started to stack up for the entry. As the team pressed against the wall, panting for breath, Nelson reverted to the straight-up-the-stairs method and just charged inside and scrambled up the stairs.

Hale grabbed Case's pack and shouted. "He's definitely lost his fucking mind!"

Case struggled loose from Hale's grip and ran up the stairs. Hale and Goldman followed.

෩෨

Inside the school, Haitham sat next to Saif, Abdul, and Ahmed. He noticed Abdul glance out the window but didn't know that Abdul saw the Marines moving down Nazal Street. Abdul said nothing. He calmly propped his rifle against the wall, ambled across the classroom, and darted out the back door. He moved fast for a fat man.

෩෨

From the position on the roof, Case watched Abdul run, but he didn't shoot. He told Hale to radio the information to the platoon commander. Abdul fled a block west, turned north, and walked down the street with his hands in the air. The Kilo Company Marines immediately took him as a prisoner and sent him to the rear.

෩෨

Inside, it took Laith Hadeed a moment to realize what had happened. He jumped up and screamed, "Shoot that coward!"

He dashed to the back door, looked out, and saw the Marines moving down Nazal Street. He bellowed his warning. "The Americans are here! Kill them!"

No one inside the school moved toward the windows to fire their weapons. Instead, everyone hunkered down and tried to take cover. Haitham and Ahmed curled up on the floor next to one of the concrete pillars. Haitham observed

Saif doing the same thing, and he also glanced quickly at the back door. The Hadeeds also kept their heads down and didn't fire their weapons.

CREP

Outside, Nelson remained agitated. "Case, this spot sucks. I can't see shit. We've got to find someplace better." Nelson pointed to a house closer to the school. "Let's go. Now!"

The move violated all of the STA team's training and tactical instructions. Again, Nelson exposed the team's position and put the members at extreme risk, but no one questioned his decision. The team raced out the house toward the next one.

As they ran between houses, Case observed insurgents looking out the school windows and heard them open fire. Fortunately for the Marines, the insurgents didn't bother to aim their weapons, but rather squatted down behind the wall, held their AK-47s over their heads, and fired them on automatic. The insurgents put a lot of lead in the air but failed to hit any member of the team.

As soon as the insurgents started firing, Case heard the unit in front of the school open up. The firing sent dust and smoke into the air. The grunts fired for five minutes and only ceased when the insurgents stopped.

CREP

Inside the classroom, the Hadeeds squatted, trying to see through the smoke and dust. Laith Hadeed's eyes seemed on fire, and he had a grotesque grin on his face. He rushed over and yelled at the Saddaq family. "Turn around and face the wall!"

Everyone in the classroom stared at each other. No one guessed what Laith Hadeed intended to do. "I am not going to tell you again. You better get your faces against that wall."

The Saddaq family members gazed at Laith Hadeed and at the rest of the men in the room. The old Saddaq man gently guided the women and children over to the wall, and each knelt down facing the wall, as if to pray.

Laith Hadeed roared at Kamis Hadeed. "Use your pistol. Shoot them in the back of the heads. It will look like an American atrocity, and the soldiers will leave Fallujah."

Haitham sat stunned, unable comprehend what he thought he'd heard. No one, not even Laith Hadeed, could be that evil. Haitham kept telling himself that Laith had said something different. Then Haitham watched Kamis Hadeed pull out a pistol.

Haitham stood up. "Stop!"

Haitham's mind raced. He saw things before they happened. Ahmed and Sdeek stood next to him. Laith Hadeed turned to face Haitham with his rifle held in his right hand.

Haitham sensed what would happen next. He held his AK-47 in both hands, his finger on the trigger, and slowly pointed the barrel at Laith Hadeed. Laith's scarred face leered at Haitham. "You think you can stop me, street boy?"

Haitham didn't answer. His legs trembled, but he didn't feel scared. He detected the Hadeeds slowly moving their rifles in position to shoot, but he knew that he would kill Laith Hadeed.

Haitham pulled the trigger. Eight 7.62mm rounds spewed out of Haitham's AK-47 and hit Laith Hadeed squarely in the middle of his chest. The bullets tore Laith's heart, lungs, and arteries into a hundred pieces and knocked him on his back to the marble floor. Laith's body lay there with dead eyes staring at the ceiling.

Next, Haitham pointed his AK-47 rifle at Kamis Hadeed. "You leave these people alone."

Kamis glanced around the room but did not speak or move.

Finally, Saif strolled over to Laith's body. Haitham knew Laith was dead but assumed that Saif would try to help. Instead, Saif simply reached inside Laith's pocket and took out the money from the jihadists and counted it.

"There is money here for everyone," Saif said calmly. "Let's not fight anymore."

Kamis stared at the Hadeeds and spoke. "No, we do what Laith said."

Haitham felt the pain of the bullet strike his chest and saw his rifle crash into the floor. He sensed that he was falling backwards. He heard the Saddaq family screaming. As he went down, Haitham saw Ahmed standing near the front door, firing his rifle at the Hadeeds. Sdeek stood near the door, also shooting. In seconds, Ahmed and Sdeek went down.

Haitham's back hit the floor. He couldn't move, but he could hear. Kamis Hadeed screamed at the Saddaq family. "Shut up and put your faces against the wall."

Haitham's breath was suspended in his chest. He wasn't sure what would happen next. Kamis Hadeed held his weapon firmly, his gaze fixed on the Saddaq family. Haitham struggled to move, but he lost consciousness.

ଔଡ଼

Captain Douglas had paused the Company two blocks from the Al Hareery School in order to plan the attack. Anne sensed that this was her chance to get closer to the action. She'd advance, but she'd still be with Marines. It was a risk, but it was the one she'd been looking for. She bolted ahead towards the school.

Crouching, she walked to the front of the Company and joined the lead platoon, which was making its way along a cinderblock fence. The school complex ahead looked like a small prison, with three stucco buildings surrounded by another fence. There was a large classroom building with windows, flanked by a small two-story building and a shed. The smaller building had sustained extensive damage.

The .50 caliber machine guns on the Humvees blasted the buildings further, the rounds sending dust, plaster, and smoke into the air.

She ceased taking pictures as the steady *pop pop pop* of insurgents' bullets flew over her head. Suddenly, she bumped into the back of a corporal and fell into the mud. A hand quickly grabbed her and pulled her back to her feet behind Marines forming a stack line next to the wall.

She put her hands over her ears momentarily when she spied a squad of Marines forming a stack line along the wall next to the front gate.

She took a deep breath. She was going in. It had all come down to this moment.

03⃝80

When the insurgents opened fire, Nelson, using the run-up-the-stairs technique, had already made it to the balcony of the second house, leaving Case and the team in the court-yard. Fortunately, the insurgent attack returned Nelson to his senses, and he instantly yelled down at Case, ordering the team to take cover and return fire. When the shooting stopped, Nelson motioned from the roof for Case and the others to enter the school.

The three men rushed to the wall of the classroom building and carefully looked in the window. They observed no movement inside, so Case threw his M-16A1 over his shoulder, pulled out his Beretta pistol, and yelled at Hale to follow. They charged into the classroom, Case holding the pistol in front with both hands. He had no idea what he would find, but his nerves were steady. Goldman and Hale ran into an adjoining room to make sure the entire area was clear.

Case was alone in the classroom.

03⃝80

Anne followed the stack through the gate of the school. After that, she'd stayed a few feet behind the grunts as they charged into the school. Clutching her camera, she tried to take a photograph several times, but things were happening too quickly, and her hands trembled. The Marines were pointing their rifles from side to side.

The dust and smoke were thick, and Anne couldn't see clearly. The squad turned right, but Anne veered left, tricked by shadows in the chaos.

She inhaled, but choked on the dust. She'd thought that the mean streets of Chicago could have prepared a brave reporter for just about anything. She'd been wrong.

"Steady yourself," she said to herself. "You can do this."

Her heart pounded against her ribs. She swallowed hard and realized that she'd gotten separated from the squad. She'd have to retrace her steps.

The dust and smoke had settled somewhat, and she moved back to the right and entered a classroom. She stopped and gasped. She wasn't sure what she was looking at. She nevertheless raised her camera.

CঞৎD

Suddenly, Case detected movement to his side. He wheeled around and faced an American woman pointing a camera at him.

"Don't shoot!" Anne screamed as she pressed the button on her Nikon, taking a picture of Case.

Case instantly raised the pistol toward the ceiling. Anne stared at the dead bodies on the floor. Hale and Goldman entered and knelt next to the bodies in the center of the room, checking for a pulse in each. Several bodies lay in the center of the room, some twisted grotesquely. Against the wall, several people lay slumped on the floor. All had been shot in the back of the head. Hale and Goldman glanced up at Case, who said nothing.

Anne quickly pivoted, snapping several pictures of the dead bodies near the wall.

Case looked from the bodies to Anne, his mouth hanging open. His entire body began trembling. "I...I..." He stammered, jerking his head sharply around, surveying everything in the room a second time. His steady nerves had disappeared.

Anne took a step back. "Did you..."

Case swallowed hard. "I...I mean we... "

Anne persisted. "Tell me what you..."

She was interrupted by the sound of approaching boots on the concrete floor. A second later, the platoon commander walked in and shouted an order to the sergeant. Soon, Capt. Douglas was inside the school, asking what happened.

Nelson had descended from the roof.

"What happened here?" Douglas barked.

"Sir," said Nelson, "I don't know. I wasn't here."

"What do you mean you weren't here?" Douglas countered. "Your team was here, but *you* weren't?"

Nelson stood silently, a painful look on his face.

"Who else is on the STA team?" Douglas asked.

"Sir, the other members are Lance Corporal Case, PFC Goldman, and PFC Hale."

"Get them in here!" Douglas ordered.

Goldman and Hale joined Case.

A massive explosion shook the school, followed quickly by a second mortar round, knocking those in the schoolroom to the floor.

"I better call this in to Battalion!" Douglas shouted. "We'll have to come back for the bodies later!"

CASO

Anne was again seated in the Humvee. Her stomach knotted up as she thought about what she had just seen. The dead bodies and bloodshed, as well as the loud concussions, were quite different from any television report she'd viewed on the war. There were moments at the school when she thought she might retch. She had recovered, however, and her reporter's instincts had now taken over as the convoy raced away from the Al Hareery School.

She had a story that would be on the front pages of newspapers around the world. And DNS would certainly ask her to do a TV spot once she filed the story. She had the photographic evidence of an atrocity commited by a U.S. Marine. It was an ugly story, but it was one that she was compelled to write. People deserved to know the truth.

The Humvee bumped along the uneven streets as the convoy exited Fallujah. Capt. Douglas occasionally glanced at her out the corner of his eye. "You could have compromised this mission," Douglas said disdainfully.

Anne made no reply. To her way of thinking, the Marines themselves had compromised the mission. Indeed, one in particular had gone off the reservation.

1800, 9 November 2004
Al Hareery School
Fallujah, Iraq

Haitham Rasheed had the sensation of being awakened, but he couldn't open his eyes. A throbbing pain in his skull beat in time with his heart. His mouth felt dry, and he tasted blood. It took a long time for him to comprehend that he lay flat on his back on a hard floor in a pool of dried blood. He lay like that for hours.

Haitham desperately wanted to open his eyes, but they were frozen shut. He wanted to use a finger to push open an eye, but his hands felt like they were tied behind his back. Haitham concentrated on his left eye and tried to force it open. It started to come up slowly, like a Venetian blind. His mouth hurt, and he realized that he had a hole though his tongue. Finally, he forced his eye open and could see a ceiling, but he remembered nothing. He tried to sit up, but something held him down. He wanted to move his body—any part of it in any direction—but he was too weak. No part of his body moved.

At least he could think, and he tried to figure out how he'd ended up on the floor and why he couldn't move. Then he remembered Laith Hadeed's scarred, bloody face. He felt the old tightness in his stomach. This time the feeling quickly passed because Haitham remembered killing Laith Hadeed.

Haitham didn't know it, but he'd been shot in the shoulder, the side of the face, and twice in his right leg. He passed out.

Chapter 31

Mike Beck reached for his watch to turn off the alarm and cursed the sharp pain in his shoulder. The pain got worse each day, and he started to worry that it might be serious. He remembered the date, November 10, the Marine Corps Birthday, but no one at 4th Division would be celebrating.

When he crawled out of the rack, the room remained clouded with dust from the rocket attack two hours earlier. He slipped on a pair of gym shorts, t-shirt, and shower thongs. Next, he put on his flak jacket, attached his 9mm pistol, grabbed his helmet, and started the five-minute walk to the showers in the dark. As he walked, he remembered that he was here on the seven-month rotation plan: arrive, learn a little, and leave.

At 0400, he opened the door to the SJA Office. Without light he could see nothing, but he could hear the fronds from the date palm outside the window swatting the stucco walls of the headquarters building. The office differed from his office in Chicago. At roughly one-fourth the size, it served as work space for the equivalent of two lawyers, one office manager, and a secretary. In the Marine Corps that meant a lieutenant colonel, major, gunnery sergeant, and lance corporal. It smelled like a dusty garage.

The furnishings included four desks, five chairs, a work-table, two filing cabinets, three bookshelves, three printers, five laptop computers, a safe, three telephones, a television set, a radio, a coffee maker, a mini-refrigerator, and a micro-wave. Beck used a high-back swivel chair and the rest of the legal staff sat on folding chairs. Even without windows, a layer of fine white dust covered everything. Beck felt depressed just looking inside, and it seemed intolerable to spend 16 hours a day in this room with four other people. At least no one would be in the room until after he left for the morning brief at 0630. That meant he had several hours to get some work done without interruption.

He unlocked the safe to take out his SIPER—secret—hard drive. He inserted it into one of the two laptops on his desk and turned both on. He then turned on the television set and tuned in Fox News. Next, he typed in the passwords to the computers and started checking his emails on both the SIPER and NIPER, or unclassified. Since hitting the rack at 2100 he had received eleven emails on the SIPER and five on the NIPER.

He started with two emails from his boss, Major General Scott. These required no work and were just thank-you-type replies to emails sent within the last week.

The door opened and First Lieutenant Lewis, the 4th Division Aide-de-Camp, walked in. "Hey, sir, isn't it a little early for television?"

"It's never too early for the news," Beck replied. "What's up?"

Lewis mouthed the words he repeated a dozen times each day. "The General needs to see you, sir."

The two started down the marble-floored hallway towards the commanding general's office. When they arrived, Gen. Scott sat at his desk in PT gear—green shorts, t-shirt, and running shoes—staring at his computer screen. The general's office was about as large as Beck's civilian office in Chicago and had a sitting area and conference table.

"You better get the Assistant Division Commander and Division Chief of Staff," Scott instructed Lt. Lewis.

"Yes, sir," Lewis replied

Scott got up and started toward the sitting area. "Mike, how about a cup of coffee?"

"Thank you, General."

The two walked out of the general's office into the aide's office, poured themselves a cup of strong coffee, and returned to the sitting area.

Beck liked working for Gen. Scott. He had worked for a lot of clients in 25 years as a trial lawyer and had a unique opportunity to observe the human character. In simple terms, trial lawyers know that most people are selfishly immoral, and when push comes to shove, nine out of ten people will lie, steal, and cheat. Trial lawyers also know that a small number of people are honest and moral creatures. Every now and then they see a client tell the truth or do the right thing even if it costs the client dearly. Mike was certain that Gen. Scott was in the latter one-percent category. He would in all cases do the right thing, regardless of the personal consequences.

Within a few minutes, the Assistant Division Commander, Colonel Rob Hall, and the Chief of Staff, Lieutenant Colonel Carter, came into General Scott's office. They both had serious and questioning looks on their faces and gazed sternly at Beck, as if to say, "Why didn't I know about this meeting? Did you go to the general without going through me first?"

General Scott maintained his relaxed demeanor. "I got a message through the Senior Watch Officer that women and children were massacred in Fallujah last night. One of the embedded reporters has photographs of the Marine pointing his pistol at a line of dead bodies. Mike, I need you to run this to ground, find out what happened, and get back to me as soon as possible."

Scott and the Chief of Staff looked at Beck like he should have an immediate solution.

"I'll hook up with the reporter as soon as possible," Beck said. "I know that the rules for embedded reporters prohibit photographs of dead or wounded Iraqis. Maybe the reporter will wait to hear the Marine's side of the story."

Lieutenant Colonel Carter chimed in at that point. "Let me go talk to him. He's an American. We can't let those photographs get out until we have time to investigate the facts. We would have every radical Arab in the Middle East coming to Fallujah. We have to talk him out of those fucking photographs before they show up on Al Jezeera. That reporter has to know that we're talking about saving lives here. This ain't a fucking high school journalism contest."

General Scott had served with Carter for years and knew he was more bark than bite. "I agree Vic, but we're not going to interfere with the press. We have to know the facts first, and I think Mike is the best person to get that done in a hurry. Mike, I'm giving you front-of-the-line privileges on this one. When you can get things under control here, you take my personal security detachment into Fallujah. Let's make sure the Public Affairs Officer has a contingency plan in case the story and the photographs get published. Mike, I want to have the anti-venom ready."

"Yes, General." Beck replied.

"Also, Mike, make sure you let Lieutenant General Bailey's Staff Judge Advocate know what we're doing. If he has any different ideas, let me know."

"Yes, sir," Beck replied. "I plan to keep Colonel Moore in the loop."

ঙ৪৩

As Beck headed down the command deck hallway, he passed the Chief of Staff's office. "Mike, come in," Vic Carter called out.

Carter directed Beck to a small round conference table and closed the door.

"What the fuck are you going to do, Mike?" Carter asked in an intense voice. "Don't we have the right to seize the camera as evidence or keep it because the reporter violated the embed rules? Why do we have fucking rules if the cock suckers can just ignore them? I don't understand this shit, Mike."

"I can't answer that, Vic. No one asked for my opinion on the embedded reporters. That's all handled by the I MEF Staff Judge Advocate."

Carter roared back, "Just a bunch of assholes trying to get political top-cover instead of making the tough call for the Marine on the ground. Mike, we need to get the truth about the shooting out there before that reporter goes public. If there's one thing I know, it's that the public will believe the first thing they hear, no matter if it's bullshit or not. If they see gory photographs, this thing will get uglier than a bag of elbows."

Carter looked at Beck like he was going to be the first man out of a landing craft. "There has to be some way to put this reporter on ice until you complete the investigation. Can't we get a fucking injunction, lock his ass up, or some shit like that?"

Beck felt powerless. "Vic, I think there's a snowball's chance in hell that the Marine Corps would seek an injunction under these circumstances."

Beck could tell that Carter didn't like the answer.

"Mike, let me give you a short history lesson. I was here for the first attempt to take control of Fallujah in April. After our Marines fought and died, that operation was stopped by Prime Minister Allawi. That disaster happened because of the public outcry that was the result of Al Jeezera's exaggerated claims of civilian deaths and battle damage. I'm an infantryman, and I can tell you from a tactical standpoint that the young Marines on the ground performed brilliantly in April."

Beck listened intently as Carter continued. "The tactical victory won on the ground in April was thrown away by the Iraqi government and the senior generals. I just want to kick someone's ass every time I think about the Marines being ordered to turn the city over to a so-called Iraqi National Guard unit, the Fallujah Brigade. The Fallujah Brigade lost control to the insurgents in two weeks! You see, Mike, notwithstanding the professionalism of the Marines, I MEF was stopped in its tracks by Paul Brenner yielding to the requests of Prime Minister Allawi. I learned a long time ago that a Marine officer doesn't blame others for failures, but I know that the outcome could have been different with better information and public relation operations."

Carter stopped talking and waited for Beck's response.

"Vic, I agree with everything you said. I want you to know that I'll do whatever it takes."

"If you get the reporter back here and I talk to him, do you think we can convince him to hold off on the story until the investigation is complete?" Carter asked.

"First, Vic, I guess no one told you that the reporter's name is Anne Merrill. Second, from the little I know about reporters, it's going to be tough to get her to agree to delay the story."

"You've got to be shitting me! We have women reporters in the middle of Fallujah? Oh, that's fucking great! I need another woman here like Custer needed more fucking Indians." Carter paused briefly and sighed. "All right, Mike. You need to get going. I'm here if you need anything. I'm counting on you to pull this thing out of the shitter."

೮೩೪

Beck walked from the Chief's office to the Combat Operations Center. It took about ten minutes for the Senior Watch Officer to get the Commanding Officer of the 4th Marines on the radio and confirm that a convoy with the reporter and the wounded insurgent departed Fallujah for regimental headquarters at Camp Baharia, with an estimated time of arrival of 0500.

Mike Beck returned to the Staff Judge Advocate's office and telephoned the S-3 Alpha at the regimental headquarters and made it clear that the insurgent should remain under guard and that the reporter needed to be brought directly to the Staff Judge Advocate's office.

Next, he telephoned Colonel Ray Moore, now serving as the Staff Judge Advocate for the 1st Marine Expeditionary Force at Camp Fallujah. "Sir, this is Mike Beck. We have a potential law of war violation, and I wanted to get you up to speed."

Beck briefed Moore on the information he had and the planned course of action. Moore sounded pleased to get the information and said he would immediately pass it further up the chain to the Staff Judge Advocate at Multi-National Corps Iraq in Baghdad and to the Staff Judge Advocates for Marine Corps Central Command—MARCENT—and for the Commandant of the Marine Corps.

"Mike, I appreciate the call," Moore said, "and if there's anything I can do for you here, let me know."

Beck then telephoned the senior Naval Criminal Investi-gation Services agent, Rusty Davis, at his living quarters in Camp Baharia. They'd already worked together, and Beck knew Rusty to be a 47-year-old senior agent who looked 67. He had white hair and looked like skin and bones. His chain smoking gave him a deep, gravely voice. But Beck found Rusty to be hardworking and easy to get along with. He explained what had happened and asked Rusty to be at the NCIS office to interview the reporter at 0500.

挃所

Anne sat in her quarters, alone. In her absence, Mary Seabar had been embedded with another unit. She'd showered, toweled off, and put on a pair of shorts, T-shirt, and sneakers.

She'd looked at the pictures she'd taken at the Al Hareery School again and again. She'd taken her risk, and it had paid off. Anne didn't just have a story—she had a scandal. Her piece would rock the world. A Marine had killed an Iraqi family execution-style. The wounds in the back of the heads, coupled with the bodies lined against the wall, made it clear what had happened. She'd heard stories of soldiers simply losing it, of how they opened fire on civilians because sometimes the action was too intense and there wasn't much time to think. But there were other stories as well, stories of soldiers who hated the Iraqis and killed them as if for sport. When she'd arrived at Camp Baharia, she'd concluded that such stories were quite likely exaggerated, but she'd actually been on the scene where LCpl. Case had obviously gunned down the family.

It had been a massacre, and it was her duty to bring it to light.

လ၆၈

0515, 10 November 2004
Staff Judge Advocate's Office
Camp Baharia, Iraq

The lock on the door to the Staff Judge Advocate's office could be tricky, and Beck stood outside the door jiggling his key on his way to breakfast before the morning brief. He looked up and saw a lieutenant and a civilian. He immediately recognized the civilian as the woman with the package at the PX. He stopped trying to lock the door and instead opened it and motioned for them to follow him inside.

"I'm Lieutenant Colonel Beck, the Staff Judge Advocate for the Fourth Division. You look like you might be Anne Merrill?"

While asking the question, Beck quickly checked out the reporter. She wore a jacket, hiking boots, blue jeans, and a black ballistic cloth backpack. She tied her blond hair in a ponytail and appeared full of energy. Her good looks were a little intimidating.

The lieutenant thought he might pass out from exhaustion at any moment and could barely focus. Beck addressed him first. "I can take it from here, Lieutenant. I'm sure you need to secure your men."

"Thank you, sir. I'll be leaving then."

Beck then smiled at Anne Merrill. "Thanks for coming over and meeting with me."

Anne extended her hand. She immediately recognized Mike Beck's name and his role in the Oliver Case. "Nice to meet you, Colonel. Anne Merrill with Dearborn News Service."

"Would you like a cup of coffee?"

Anne accepted, and Beck filled one of his insulated cups and handed it to her.

"Anne, I hope I'm not rushing you, but when you finish your coffee I'd like to walk you over to the Naval Criminal Investigative Service. They need to start their investigation as soon as possible. Also, General Scott would like to meet with you at 0800. We're hoping that you'll give us a chance to investigate before you release a story."

"I'll be happy to meet with the general, but I'm not sure I can agree to delay releasing the story."

Anne gulped down the last swallows of coffee, and they headed for the NCIS office. Again, locking the office door proved difficult. As the two turned to head down the hallway, Beck realized that Anne had left her pack inside the office but decided not to say anything.

NCIS located its office at Camp Baharia inside a metal shipping container with doors and an air conditioner. Beck used his key-light to navigate the steps, curbs, ditches, and blast barriers that had to be crossed to reach the office. He was thinking about Anne's pack inside his office, and since Anne appeared not to carry a camera, he guessed that it was inside the pack. By the time they arrived at the NCIS office, he'd made up his mind.

"Rusty, this is Anne Merrill. I need to stick my head in the operations brief for a second. I'll be right back."

Without giving anyone a chance to say anything, Beck turned, dashed outside, and headed back to the Staff Judge Advocate's office. He ducked around the corner of the office and started running as fast as possible. In the morning darkness, he immediately tripped on the curb and fell head first onto the sidewalk. Next, he stumbled on the stairs leading towards the headquarters building, crashed forward, and stopped his fall by grabbing the side of the building, wrenching his shoulder backwards. The pain was intense, and he screamed—but didn't slow down. He figured that Anne Merrill would be right behind him, and he kept running as fast as possible.

Ten seconds after he'd left, Anne realized that she didn't have her pack. She cussed and ran out the door.

While running, Beck decided on his hiding place. When 4th Division had moved into Camp Baharia, the air conditioner systems had been stripped since it was easier for the Seabees to install room air conditioners than replace the central system. One of the old systems was lying between the Staff Judge Advocate's office and the COC building.

On arrival at the command deck, he saw no one in sight. He cursed out loud when at first the lock wouldn't open but quickly managed to open the door. He found Anne's pack under the worktable next to the chair where she'd been sitting, opened it, and took out the camera. He left the door wide open and headed down the hall and out the door towards the COC building, stopping at the old air conditioner. He pulled on one of the panels and tossed the camera inside, quickly re-positioned the panel, and ran to the COC.

He stopped a moment to catch his breath before walking in the back door of the COC. All the ramifications of stealing the camera raced through his mind as he stood at the rear, listening to the morning brief. At the first opportunity, he sneaked over to his chair, sat down hard, and continued his effort to get his breathing under control.

Within a minute, Gen. Scott stood up and looked at the back of the COC toward Beck's chair. "Is the judge here?"

Beck jumped up and hurried to the microphone. "I'm right here, General."

"What authority do the courts in Ramadi have over Iraqis that commit crimes against Coalition Forces?" Scott asked.

Beck took a deep breath and answered. "In theory, the local courts would have authority to punish an Iraqi for violation of the transitional administrative law, but practically, that isn't going to happen. The judges no longer show up at the court and are too intimidated to punish insurgents."

"All right. Thanks, Mike."

Beck went to the back of the room again.

In the dark, Anne Merrill made a wrong turn at the chaplain's office, ran for about five minutes, and concluded that nothing looked familiar. She turned and went back to the NCIS office and arrived out of breath.

"Please!" she cried. "Help me find Colonel Beck's office. I left my camera there!"

Rusty Davis jumped up. "Don't worry. I'm sure it will be there."

Davis and Anne headed to the office at a fast pace. Around the same time, Major Way, having finished breakfast early, arrived at the office and thought it strange that the door stood open, but he didn't notice Anne's pack under the worktable. He was installing his SIPER drive on his laptop when they rushed in the door.

Anne Merrill went straight for her pack, opened it, and discovered the camera missing. She instantly realized that Beck had taken it. She had never before been this mad at another human being, and she turned and yelled at the top of her voice at Maj. Way. "Where is Colonel Beck?"

Anne startled Way so badly that he dropped his laptop on the floor. He remained in a state of shock when he answered, "I don't know for sure, but he should be at the operations brief."

Anne Merrill screamed again. "That son of a bitch stole my camera!"

Chapter 32

Anne needed to talk to her boss, Joe O'Daniel. Unfortunately, her satellite phone had stopped working and she needed to borrow the one at PAO or use the public phone. There would be no privacy at the PAO building, so she decided to use the public phone.

At Camp Baharia, a mobile home served as an oversized phone booth. It had no windows, but two air conditioners connected to a diesel generator that in the summer blew cold air from each end. Inside the trailer, two banks of phones faced each wall.

There always seemed to be a line of Marines standing outside the trailer waiting to call their loved ones. There were no signs or attendants, but the callers seemed to follow an unwritten rule that as one came out, another walked inside. When Anne turned the corner at the Post Exchange, she saw that the line had grown longer than usual. The young men standing in line all had on their flak vests, helmets, and other fighting gear. They were filthy, gaunt, and tired.

"Damn it," Anne said to herself as a bolt of anger hit her. "I'll be in this line for an hour."

Anne soon realized that most of the Marines were watching her, and she quickly checked her clothing, thinking that, in her anger, something may have come undone. Fortunately, her clothes were in place. She hurried to the safety of the end of the line, hoping that the men would stop gawking. The lance corporal at the end of the line was young, skinny, sunburned, and wiry. "Good morning, ma'am," he said. "Please go in front of me."

Soon, everyone in line repeated the same thing. They just kept smiling at her and asking her to go in front until she ended up at the head of the line. When a caller came out, Anne hurried inside the trailer. She almost gagged on the strong odor of sweat, dirt, and diesel fuel. It was hard to breathe. She sat down and dialed the number for Joe O'Daniel, Vice President of DNS.

Joe O'Daniell's voice was hoarse. "Hello?"

"Joe, this is Anne."

"Christ almighty. Do you know what time it is here?"

"You said to wake you anytime I had something important. This is important, Joe."

Anne told him about the school, the photographs, the trip back to Camp Baharia, and her meeting with Mike Beck. She then tried to explain that Beck had left her very suspiciously at the NCIS office.

"Joe, I'm certain Lieutenant Colonel Beck has my camera."

Joe O'Daniel took several minutes to digest the information. "And you're sure that this Marine Corps judge who is a colonel stole your camera?"

"You think I'm making this up?" Anne was yelling into the phone.

"Calm down, Anne. This is a pretty wild story." Joe O'Daniel paused for several minutes. "What is a Marine judge doing in a combat zone?"

"Damn it, Joe! He's not a judge. H's a staff judge advocate. He's just another lawyer!"

"OK, OK." There was another long pause. "He took your camera from your pack that you left in his office?"

"No. Well, yes. I left my pack and camera in his office because he took me to be interviewed at the Naval Criminal Investigation Services Office. I know he saw me leave it there, and he went back for the camera." Anne pleaded, with hurt and impatience building in her voice.

Joe O'Daniel tried to sound as supportive as possible. "Anne, I need to understand, that's all. I have a feeling there's more to this story. Do you have any more facts?"

Anne felt like crying. "No. I don't have any evidence yet, but I know he did it. He was the only person who would know it was there. I saw him lock the door. Who else could have taken it?"

"Are you asking DNS to take legal action against the Marine Corps? I'll have to have a good case to do that." Joe O'Daniel braced himself for another outburst from Anne; however, this time she paused.

"OK, Joe. You're probably right. I guess I'm just mad at myself for always losing things."

"You get some breakfast, and I'll get some sleep. Call me at the office number in three hours."

"All right, Joe. I'll call you then. Bye."

When Anne walked out the door, the men in line stared and smiled again. This time it didn't bother her. She gave them a big smile and her best walk.

CRED

0730, 10 November 2004
4th Division Headquarters
Camp Baharia, Iraq

After the operations brief, Beck returned to his room to get his battle gear for the convoy into Fallujah. Fortunately, he had everything ready and had packed his Vietnam-era Alice pack with sleeping bag, pad, fleece, GORE-TEX, two pairs of socks, underwear, t-shirt, and his military travel pack. As a result, it took him only ten minutes to double-check his weapon and gear. He headed back to the office, ready to roll.

When Beck walked into the SJA office, Way, Ryan, and Martinez all had looks of doom on their faces. Way motioned towards the door, and the gunny and lance corporal quickly left. Mike continued to walk to the safe, pulled out his SIPER hard-drive, and started toward his desk but was intercepted by Way. This time the look on Steve Way's face made Beck feel ashamed.

"Steve, I'm sorry, but I can't risk getting you involved in this."

"That's bullshit. Mike, you and I go way back, and if you're in some kind of trouble, I have a right to know about it. That reporter was here and claims you stole her camera."

Beck was silent.

"Mike, are you out of your fucking mind? We're lawyers. The Marine Corps is just another client. Even if you know your client is innocent, you don't risk your bar license to win the case."

Beck and Way stared at each other for a long time. Finally, Beck spoke. "Look, old buddy. I know you're probably right, and that's exactly why I can't get you involved. For me, this is different. It's more complicated. It's not money. I think I can save lives. For me, it's worth risking everything."

Steve nodded his head. "All right, Mike. But if you're going down, I'm prepared to go down with you. Promise me that if there's anything in the world that I can do to help, you'll let me know."

"It's a deal."

"By the way, General Scott wants to see you," Way said. "His aide has been here three times and is shitting bricks."

"Did he say what it's about?"

Way looked at Beck like he was nuts and answered. "It's about the missing camera, and you better be prepared to answer the charge of theft. Remember your advice to your clients: Admit nothing; deny everything. And make counter-accusations."

The two managed fake grins.

"Well, I better go face the music," Beck said as he headed out the SJA office and down the hall to the aide's office.

⋐⋙⋘⋙

"Looking for me?" asked Beck.

"Yes, sir," the aide answered. "General Scott needs to see you right away."

Beck looked at the closed door to the general's office.

"You're supposed to go on in, sir."

When Beck opened the door, Gen. Scott, Col. Hall, LtCol. Carter, and Lt. Copeland were seated around the conference table. Hall and Copeland had strange looks on their faces. Carter grinned from ear to ear. Everyone waited for Scott to speak.

"Mike," Scott began, "we have an interesting development. Anne Merrill claims that you stole her camera. Has she talked to you about that?"

"No, sir. I spoke to her this morning and took her over to NCIS before the operations brief, but I haven't seen her since then."

"She says she left her camera in your office and that you must have gone back and taken it after leaving her at NCIS."

Beck continued to try and look puzzled.

"Ms. Merrill is very upset," the PAO chimed in. "She wants something done and says that if she doesn't get her camera back, she's filing the story without the photographs and will claim a Marine Corps cover-up."

At that, Carter started yelling. "Why in the hell would the bitch want to do that? Is she a fucking terrorist? Let me talk to her. By God, I'll kiss her ass, bribe her, threaten her, or do whatever it takes to stop her. We'll threaten her with a fucking injunction or restraining order or whatever the fuck you call it. First Lieutenant Copeland, isn't there something in the goddamn embed agreement to cover this shit?"

As usual, Carter's tirade served as an opportunity for everyone to try and think of a solution. At that point, the aide knocked on the general's door three times and opened it.

"General Scott, Anne Merrill is here to see you."

"Tell her it will be just one minute," the general replied.

The aide closed the door, and Beck started talking. "I think we should offer her the chance to get new photographs and complete the story. I can take her with me into Fallujah. Maybe I can show that the Marine is innocent. If he's guilty, we'll have charges preferred before the story breaks. At the least, she'll be able to report any facts we discover and that we're investigating."

The general, Hall, and Carter all looked at Copeland, who quickly agreed with Beck. Gen. Scott then asked Copeland to escort Anne into the office.

Beck didn't have the courage to look up when Anne came into the room, but she managed to sit across from him, and when he finally looked at her, she gave him a look that made him feel two inches tall. Fortunately, Gen. Scott started talking, and Anne's stare moved to the general.

"The Naval Criminal Investigation Services is conducting an investigation on the loss of your camera," the general said. "If we can find the camera, it will be returned to you immediately."

Anne's expression didn't change but conveyed the message that she didn't believe a word the general said.

"Lieutenant Colonel Beck is heading out to Fallujah to conduct an investigation of the civilian deaths," the general continued. "Of course, it's extremely dangerous in Fallujah, but you've already proven that's not going to stop you. I'm offering you the opportunity to go along with Colonel Beck. You will receive full access to the investigation report, including any photographs or other physical evidence. You can even take additional photographs while you're there. All that I ask in return is that you not release the story until Lieutenant Colonel Beck has an opportunity to investigate."

Anne glared at both the general and Beck. "I don't trust Lieutenant Colonel Beck or you, General. I want my camera back."

The tension in the room was rising, but Beck spoke. "Ms. Merrill, I understand your position, but if you print the story with the wrong facts, you and your newspaper editor will look like idiots. Right now you have nothing by way of motive of why a Marine would suddenly start shooting women and children. You have no source except for a terrorist who has a clear motive to make this thing up. Publishing a story without investigating the facts will do great harm to your country, the Marine Corps, and your newspaper."

No one said anything for a long time. Finally, Anne spoke. "I agree to the terms, but I publish not later than two days from now." Anne then stared directly into Mike Beck's eyes. "And the person responsible for stealing my camera gets prosecuted."

Beck looked at Scott and nodded affirmatively, and the general accepted.

The general continued. "I know that everyone has things to do, so let's adjourn this meeting. Mike, would you stay? I would like to talk to you about some other matters before you leave for Fallujah."

A shiver of fear ran up Beck's back, and he thought about the ass-chewing he was surely going to receive when everyone exited the room.

Scott, however, appeared calm as always. "Mike, I don't want you to say anything, but I know how to read signals from my fellow Marines, and I think I know where you're coming from. I just want to offer some friendly advice as one Marine officer to another."

General Scott rose from behind his desk and came over to sit next to Mike. His voice became fatherly. "Stealing is morally wrong and a violation of the law. I know that there would be absolutely no personal gain for the person that took that camera, and so they did what they thought was the right thing under the circumstances. I'm also sure that they would have known that the incident would have to be investigated. I believe that the person who took that camera did it to save the lives of Marines on the battlefield. But that person needs to ask himself whether the accomplishment of the mission can justify a criminal act. Once you get on that slippery slope, where do you get off? We are the United States Marine Corps, and we're better than that. That person is risking both his military and civilian career. Frankly, I don't know if a court-martial would send him to Leavenworth or give him a medal, but I wouldn't want to find out."

General Scott actually grabbed Beck's shoulder when he concluded. "Mike, I believe there's always a right way to do something. I'd like to see the camera returned to Ms. Merrill immediately."

As he headed back to his office, Beck stopped at the Chief of Staff's office. The door stood open. Carter had two television sets in his office—one tuned to Fox News and the other to CNN. He had three laptops on his desk, one for NIPER, one for SIPER, and one for CINTEX. He received and answered over 100 emails each day.

When Beck walked in, the Chief looked over his glasses for a second and continued to type. "Did the general rip you a new asshole?"

"He wants the camera returned. He made some good points."

The Chief stopped typing and glanced over at Beck. "That doesn't sound good, Judge."

Beck answered unconvincingly. "It's very complicated."

The chief frowned. "Sounds about as complicated as a slow hand job to me. You give the bitch the photographs, and Marines will die that don't have to. Mike, don't let the general or that good-looking reporter fuck with your mind. You did the right thing. There are no free fucking rides in the Marine Corps. There's pain associated with everything." The Chief looked Beck in the eye. "Hell, you just give me that fucking camera. I know what to do with it."

Beck rubbed his head and walked out.

CRBO

0930, 10 November 2004
SJA Office
Camp Baharia, Iraq

As Beck walked in the door to his office, the staff had the same worried looks on their faces. He soon realized why. Anne Merrill sat in his chair.

"Anne, we need to talk in private," Beck said. "Will you come with me?"

Anne said nothing but stood up and started moving to the door. At the same time, Way stood up with his notebook and looked towards Beck. "Sir, do you object if I come along?"

Beck knew it was going to piss off Way, but refused. "I'm sorry, Deputy, but I'm going to need you to stay here until I get back."

Beck walked out the hatch and down the long entryway that led to a small courtyard. In the middle of the courtyard, four plastic chairs surrounded a cheap looking table.

"Welcome to the SJA conference room," Beck said to Anne with a smirk.

Anne glared at him and put her hands on her hips in a motion that Beck noticed pushed her breasts higher.

They sat down across from one another. It felt chilly, but the sun shone bright in a beautiful sky. Beck couldn't speak and just looked in Anne's eyes. Finally, the words came. "I am very sorry this happened."

He continued looking at Anne. "I can tell that you're a good person. But if you release the story and the photographs, it's going to get aired on Al Jezeera. This story can't be released until we have all the facts. Anne, I would do anything to make things right, but I have to protect the young Marines who are still in the fight."

Anne's eyes flashed. "You're so arrogant! I've dedicated my life to telling the truth, straight down the middle. You're just a lawyer, and for you truth is whatever story makes your client win." Anne paused to see Beck's reaction, and continued. "Journalists don't have clients. We report what happens in all its complexities. You know I intend to report what happened yesterday. It's possible that Lance Corporal Case didn't commit those murders. I'll report all the facts when I release my story."

Beck looked beaten, but he continued. "You're right. I've spent my life convincing jurors to believe things that I never believed, and I did it for the money. This is different, Anne. I'm going to get burned for this, but I don't care. I know I can save lives, and I'm going to do whatever I have to do. I know that if your story gets out, there are young Iraqis who will be coming here to kill Americans. Without the story, I believe

there's a chance that we may still persuade them to partici-
pate in the political process."

They sat in the sun for a few moments before Anne ended
the conversation. "I know you haven't destroyed the photographs, and I know you're trying to do the right thing. I'm not
sure how long I can wait."

⚝

1015, 10 November 2004
Phone Trailer
Camp Baharia, Iraq

I hate this business, Anne said to herself as she sat at the one
open spot in the phone trailer. This made the third time she
had returned to the trailer since calling Joe earlier that
morning. She left three urgent messages for him at the
Chicago headquarters, stating that she would try again an
hour later. Each time, she'd received the same speech from
Joe's secretary. "He said he really needs to talk to you, but
he's in a meeting. Please call back in an hour."

Anne picked up the phone and called Joe for the fourth
time. This time, she got through to him. He said he was using
the phone in the conference room with the speaker on. Anne
hated to talk to Joe like that. Although he had worked at DNS
for over 20 years and served as a senior vice-president, he
still sucked up to the bosses and seemed totally phony every
time the bosses listened.

"Hi, Anne. How are you doing in Fallujah? Are you getting everything you need?" Joe's fake sincerity made Anne
want to puke.

Anne started to say, "I could really use the new satellite
phone I asked you for," but she fought back the urge. "Everything is fine here, Joe."

"Anne, we have our legal team working on getting your
camera back. You were right. Frank Tobolski verifies that this
Colonel Beck was involved in the Oliver story. As you may
recall, he's a big time trial lawyer here in Chicago. Frank

thinks he's really a great guy, so he must be getting orders from someone higher up."

Anne now remembered fully how Mike Beck had come to the rescue of Mrs. Oliver. His present demeanor conflicted with his offer to help in Chicago.

"Joe, I want you to hold off for a few days."

"Our lawyers say we don't need to do that, Anne. The Marine Corps is required to turn over the photographs to us right now."

Anne remained silent for a minute. "It's very complicated."

At that point, the President of DNS, Tom Coleman, spoke up. Anne had not known exactly who'd been listening to the conversation. "Now listen, Anne," Coleman said. "There is nothing complicated about this. If you delay the story, we lose credibility, and we're not going to do that."

Anne didn't like Tom Coleman.

"It was wrong for me to take the photographs," she said. "The rules I agreed to follow prohibit filming dead Iraqis, and I have an obligation to delete what I shouldn't have photographed in the first place. Also, I believe that an investigation will clear the young man of any wrong-doing."

Tom Coleman spoke again. "Listen to me. I want your story with the photographs, and I want it today. Do you understand?"

Anne felt anger welling up inside her. "Here is what I understand. I am the only person who knows the story or knows if there are any photographs. I called Joe for help. Any journalist can see there is a great story here, but at present it's a confusing story with some gory photographs."

The phone was silent, but Anne could hear talking in the background. Joe O'Daniel spoke again. "OK, Anne. While we're waiting for this to play out, we want you to do a story on the person who did the shooting. Get his hometown, his training, what led him to join the Marines, and the rest of it."

That was enough to push Anne over the edge. "Have you all lost your minds? You want that boy dead, or are you just plain stupid? I'm not going to release his name to you or anybody. I can't believe I work for such a bunch of cold-blooded people!"

In Chicago, Joe O'Daniel, Tom Coleman, and the other executives stared at each other. Anne could hear only silence on the telephone line. Through the crackle of the satellite connection, Joe finally spoke. "All right, Anne. Let's settle down and think about this for a moment."

From the strain in Joe's voice, Anne could tell he was desperately trying to control himself.

"We would not endanger this boy's life," the CEO finally said. "We'll do this your way."

Chapter 33

When Mike Beck arrived at the Personal Security Detachment barracks, the NCIS agent, Rusty Davis, was waiting outside with an Iraqi interpreter. Davis wore khaki pants, a ball cap, hiking boots, and a black police vest. He carried an AR-15 with a small scope. The interpreter appeared not to be armed and had on a light blue jump suit, a World War II style helmet, and the same type of black police vest.

The PSD Marines were in full gear, checking weapons and installing crew-served weapons into the turret mounts on the up-armored Humvees.

The PSD had the mission of protecting the commanding general any time he traveled. This represented a critical mission in Iraq because the enemy spared no effort to capture or kill American officers. The members of the PSD were carefully selected and highly motivated. They symbolized the best of the Marine Corps.

Beck noticed a female Marine on the PSD. Arguably, this violated the naval regulation prohibiting the assignment of women to combat, but this didn't seem the right time to debate the issue. She wore her blond hair rolled in a tight bun in the back of her head and wore a combat cargo vest over her flak jacket, to which she'd strapped more gear than even Lieutenant Colonel Campbell carried, including a .45 caliber Colt pistol, six magazines, four frag grenades, two smoke grenades, a K-Bar strapped horizontally across the center of her back, a first aid kit, a Vietnam-style butt-pack, flex cuffs, ear plugs, ink pens, climbing swivels, sun glasses, pocket knives, camera, and flashlight. Beck could not even see her body under her battle gear but got excited imagining that it must be rock hard.

A sergeant approached him and spoke. "Sir, you will be riding shotgun in Whiskey Bravo. Can I stow your gear for you?"

"I would appreciate that."

At that point, Gunnery Sergeant Ellis walked up. "Good morning, sir. Do you mind if I tag along for the ride? General Scott and the sergeant major asked me to take charge as your Senior Staff Non-commissioned Officer."

Beck interfaced with Ellis on several issues and already knew that he represented one of the best staff non-commissioned officers in the Division. Ellis held the Deputy Staff Secretary position at the Division and had no responsibility for the PSD. However, he always jumped at any chance to be in the field. He was over 40, baldheaded, and had spent his entire career with the grunts, fighting in every conflict since Vietnam. Ellis was part Navajo Indian and had grown up in the rough neighborhoods of Phoenix, Arizona, drinking, fighting, and breaking all the rules. By the age of 17 he'd been arrested over a half-dozen times and seemed headed for some serious time in prison when he was fortunately rescued by a Marine Corps recruiter who filled his head with stories about Ira Hayes, a Pima Indian and one of the Marines who'd raised the flag at Iwo Jima. Somehow, the Marine Corps had taken all of his anger, hostility, and pointless bravado and focused it in a constructive direction. By this time in his career, Ellis had refocused hundreds of young men that entered the Corps with the same anger and hostility. If Gunny Ellis walked into a room, Marines started working harder and stood straighter. Beck relaxed a little, knowing that he would have Ellis with him in Fallujah.

"Gunny, I'm damn glad to have you."

ڃʀ

1115, 10 November 2004
4th Division PSD Area
Camp Baharia, Iraq

Within minutes, the PSD group squared everything away and huddled around Gunny Ellis for the convoy brief.

"The situation is as follows," Ellis began. "The enemy forces are actively engaged in combat operations against coalition forces in Fallujah in two to ten man elements, with massed forces as large as thirty. Enemy forces include foreign terrorists, Islamic jihadists, former regime elements, and criminal groups. The most probable attack will be pre-planned ambushes with improvised explosive devices, indirect fire, and small arms fire.

"The enemy capabilities and limitations are teams lead by extremists who seek martyrdom and death. The enemy will likely see this convoy as a target of opportunity. The enemy avoids tanks and heavy weapons, and the enemy may withdraw if decisively engaged with superior firepower.

"The enemy course of action is to deny the Iraqi People a free and democratic society, and the enemy will attempt to destroy one or more of our vehicles and kill our personnel by deliberate ambush. The enemy's most likely course of action is to detonate IEDs and conduct small arms and indirect fire attacks.

"The friendly situation is as follows: Higher Units are RCT-9 and RCT-4, which will continue to clear in zone. Higher Commander's Intent is to kill or capture all enemy forces in Fallujah. Adjacent Units include the BCT-23 conducting combat operations outside Fallujah to the south. RCT-15 and RCT-11 are operating at our eastern boundary. Security consists of internal and vehicle-mobile quick reaction forces. There are no attachments or detachments.

"The mission is to move to the Al Hareery School building at grid 0385703853, gather intelligence, conduct a crime scene investigation, recover the bodies of Iraqi civilians, evacuate any wounded insurgents, kill or capture any enemy occupying the school, and evacuate to Camp Baharia.

"The commander's intent is to make a tactical forced march to the school building, complete the mission, and exit as quickly as possible. When the convoy reaches the school building, the first fire team will post at the front door while the second fire team creates a perimeter at the north side of the school. The third fire team covers the south side. Once we dismount, the first fire team will enter and clear the building as rapidly as possible. As soon as we have surveyed the school, examined the bodies, collected all physical evidence, and interrogated any wounded, we will egress to Heyal Sinala Street in proper order of march and head north for approximately 3400 meters, crossing route Duster, and turn east at the northwest corner of the mosque. Once we have turned east, the convoy will head to the canal crossing, and then maneuver north to RCT-9 Headquarters at the train station. The commander's guidance for fire support is that air and artillery assets are available on call. I will call in all fires, with Sergeant Smith as my alternate.

"The coordinating instructions are as follows. H-hour is in three minutes. I have already gone over the route. The planned formations during movement are tactical column and wedge as dictated by terrain and buildings. In case of near ambush, assault through. In case of far ambush, break contact on order of squad leader. For incoming rounds, all members will seek cover and remain until fire stops. We will remain in place to ensure security and to repel any enemy assault that may ensue. If we make contact with enemy forces, we will attempt to detain or kill if necessary. Lieutenant Colonel Beck will determine all other actions.

"The administration and logistics are as follows. Casualties will require self-aid, buddy aid, and corpsman aid. If a casualty is taken, we will win the fight and call for an immediate extract. All prisoners will be treated humanely and moved by the most expeditious means to the nearest coalition holding facility for further processing.

"Ammunition is combat load. Chow and water are full camelback. Sergeant Smith will pass out command and signal cards for all personnel. The challenge and passwords are 'here comes' and 'the judge.'

"The succession of command is as follows. First, Lieutenant Colonel Beck. Second, myself. Third, Sergeant Smith."

⋙⋘

As soon as the brief concluded, the PSD Marines started climbing into their vehicles. When Beck headed for his vehicle, he saw Campbell running toward him in full battle dress and carrying a pack. "Sir, you have to take me with you. I've cleared it with the Chief."

Campbell seemed to hear every piece of scuttlebutt, but he astounded Beck by finding out about this investigation so fast. Beck started to say no, but he hesitated. "I guess you've earned it."

Beck shouted at Gunny Ellis. "Do we have room for your boss? "

The gunny yelled back. "There's a space in your vehicle, sir."

Ellis came over to give Campbell an abbreviated brief. As the three stood next to the Humvee, Ellis noticed Beck staring at the female Marine's rear as she bent over to set ammo cans in the Humvee. The gunny whispered in a low voice. "Sir, that's a hard target for a lieutenant colonel. You better be careful."

At that point, Beck and Ellis saw another Humvee approaching the PSD area, which Beck quickly recognized as the worn-out Humvee assigned to the SJA office. Lance Corporal Martinez drove, Major Way sat in the front passenger seat, and Gunnery Sergeant Ryan manned the turret. Beck used the SJA Humvee just to get around Camp Baharia, but somehow Ryan managed to borrow a 5.56mm SAW from the Seabees as the turret gun. The Humvee pulled up beside Beck, and Maj. Way jumped out with a grin and smartly saluted.

"Sir," Way said, "Deputy SJA and staff reporting as ordered by the Chief of Staff."

This really irked Beck. First, he started to walk over to the headquarters building and have it out with the Chief of Staff, but after a couple steps decided he didn't have the time. He stopped and walked back toward Way. By this time, he looked fighting mad, with a red face and purple cords for a neck.

"You work for me, and I don't give a flying fuck what the Chief says," Beck said sternly. "I've already decided that someone has to stay here and run the SJA office. So you just get your dumb ass back inside that Humvee and take the lance corporal with you. And that's a fucking order, Major."

Way's face turned as red as Beck's. He slowly scanned the area like he was looking for a place they could talk in private, but seeing that was impossible, he walked up to Beck and spoke right in his face. He even doubled up his fists. "Look, you crazy bastard, I don't give a rat's ass if you like it or not. Colonel Moore is sending over Lieutenant Colonel Hanson from I MEF to run the SJA office, and Carter speaks for the general. I'm going on this mission. So fuck you, asshole."

The PSD Marines stared in shock at the two officers as they argued.

"We don't have time for this shit," Beck said. "I'll take this up with the Chief when we get back. Major Way, you're going, and you're going to do exactly what I tell you to do. If you fuck up one time, I'll have your ass. Let's get the fuck out of here, Gunny."

Gunny Ellis ushered Way back to the SJA Humvee, and Beck climbed into the passenger side of his Humvee. The seat was narrow and he could barely get his legs in, and there was little room for his M-16A1. He started to shove the heavy ballistic glass window up, but looked around and decided to wait and see if the other Marines slid theirs up or left them down.

Campbell jumped into the seat behind him, and Anne Merrill got into the rear driver's side. The turret gunner already stood at his post in the center of the vehicle, with only his feet and legs visible.

The female Marine sat on the driver's side and immediately introduced herself. "Good morning, sir. I'm Lance Corporal Bell. I will be your driver for this convoy."

She then started tuning in the radios, changing frequency settings, testing microphones, and listening for radio checks. She removed a microphone and carefully brushed the connection with a toothbrush before screwing it back on—something Beck knew that Marines had been doing since the Vietnam War.

He heard the turret gunner working the bolt on the M-240G 7.62mm machine gun and realized the PSD was going to condition one—magazines inserted, round in chamber, and weapon on safe.

გ8ა

The convoy proceeded through a series of Jersey barriers and checkpoints until pulling out onto a dirt road leading to an Iraqi freeway. The interior checkpoints were manned by Marines, followed by Iraqi Security Forces and Iraqi police. At each checkpoint there stood a guard tower manned by one or two Marines. The convoy kicked up dust as it sped towards the freeway.

Within minutes, the convoy arrived at ECP-1, or Exit Control Point One, on Route Wisconsin at the east end of Fallujah. Before the start of Operation *Al Fajar*, the Iraqi name for the Second Battle of Fallujah, this site represented the most dangerous place on the face of the Earth, and Americans were under constant surveillance and subject to sniper fire.

The planned route traveled through ECP-1 and straight down Wisconsin to the 3rd Battalion Headquarters. However, the sergeant in charge of ECP-1 reported to Beck that his orders were not to let anyone pass under any circumstances. The insurgents had infiltrated the area, and 4th Battalion Headquarters remained cut off. The sergeant recommended going to 4th Regiment Headquarters to wait for the area to be retaken. It sounded like a good idea to Beck.

It took half an hour for Ellis to radio in the change in route and get authorization to proceed to regimental head-quarters. The route lay north on the freeway, then west along the old railroad tracks to the train station, which was now the 4th Regiment Headquarters. The PSD convoy found a good place to park, out of the way in a deep wash, and Beck and Ellis walked a half mile to the train station. Inside, they spoke to the S-3 officer and waited another two hours before they were cleared to proceed to the 3rd Battalion Headquarters. Finally, the PSD convoy joined a re-supply convoy for the trip into Fallujah.

As the convoy approached Headquarters, it passed through a checkpoint manned by Iraqi Security Forces. This was a hub of activity in the area, with Seabees using bulldoz-ers to push up security berms. Iraqi troops filled sandbags and constructed guard positions on the tops of the buildings. Jersey barriers were being unloaded off lowboy trailers, and engineers were stringing up concertina wire.

The convoy drove straight to Headquarters and stopped.

ભ્&

1730, 10 November 2004
3rd Battalion Headquarters
Fallujah, Iraq

The Fallujah Government Center, the site of 3rd Battalion Headquarters, sat in a large building that curiously had an American-style boxing ring in the middle of an atrium. The building appeared to be in good shape with little battle damage. The back door opened into an entryway, and in the next room Beck heard a tactical briefing in progress. He noticed an officer that he instantly identified as the battalion commander by his demeanor and interaction with the other Marines.

Lieutenant Colonel McCall seemed like a man who would normally smile a lot. He was medium height, thick necked, and although he was 25 pounds underweight, he had a fleshy face. It looked like he hadn't had much sleep for several days, but he sprang to his feet and extended his hand to greet Beck. "Welcome aboard. I'm glad to see you here. Let's go chat in my office."

The two walked into a room that McCall used as both his office and living space. Beck sat on the end of the sleeping cot and took out his hardback green notebook. McCall sat on the edge of a field desk.

Beck spoke first: "Tell me what you know."

"Not enough. On Monday an armored battalion took fire from a school, a prepared battle position with six insurgents. The school was taken with main tank gun. Not that much structural damage, but three of the enemy were killed and three were wounded. The wounded were assessed as routine and treated, but the battalion's flank was seriously exposed, so the CO had no choice but to leave the wounded to be picked up later by Third Battalion. Before we could evacuate the wounded, insurgents re-infiltrated the area.

"Yesterday, we sent Kilo back to re-sweep the area. We had intelligence that schools were being used by the insurgents as command and control centers and had a pre-planned assault, including use of a STA team. Kilo immediately received small arms fire from the school, and it was engaged again, this time by infantry with .50 cal and small arms. Kilo had an embedded news reporter. When they went in the second time, there was a massacre site. An old man, two women, two girls, and a boy shot in the back of the head, execution style. The embedded reporter took photographs of the bodies."

"Did anyone out here see the photographs?" Beck asked.

"No. I don't think they pushed the issue. The platoon commander saw the whole thing and thinks it's going to get real ugly. I know the smart guys in Camp Fallujah think that having embedded reporters is the way to go, but I honestly don't understand how PAO could have cleared a woman reporter in combat."

McCall waited for an answer.

"I understand," Beck said. "It's a sad story with a lot of hairy fists pounding tables—and no good answers. In fact, it gets worse. Believe it or not, I have her with me right now."

"Well, as they say, that's beautiful, Just fucking beautiful."

"Yes, it sucks, but there's not a damn thing the Division can do about it," Beck said, grimacing and shaking his head. "You know anything about Lance Corporal Case?"

"Nothing, except that the STA team was just cleared on a detainee abuse investigation, and they feel like the Marine Corps has it in for them."

"If I were the Marine's commanding officer, this would piss me off, but believe me, I have no choice in the matter," Beck said. "I'm going to need the lance corporal's pistol for a ballistics test."

McCall disgustedly nodded his head. "Check."

Beck followed him around the atrium into an auditorium where four Marines slept near the wall. McCall kicked the boot of the Marine nearest the door.

"Corporal Nelson, this is Lieutenant Colonel Beck, the Fourth Division Staff Judge Advocate. He's here to find out what happened at the school. I want you to cooperate with him."

Nelson opened his eyes, then leaped to his feet and stood at attention. "Aye aye, sir!"

The three other Marines also sprang to their feet and stood at attention as McCall marched out of the auditorium.

"You have everything you need here, Corporal?" Beck asked.

Corporal Nelson looked straight ahead. "What we need is a ride back out to Kilo Company. Our unit needs us in the fight."

"That may take some time, but we'll get you back there as soon as possible."

"With all respect, sir, this is bullshit," Nelson asserted in a voice ten decibels louder. "Lance Corporal Case didn't shoot those Iraqis."

Beck moved closer and stared Nelson in the eye. "Well, I'm glad we can talk straight. Don't think for a second, Corporal Nelson, that General Scott would take your team out of the fight if it weren't absolutely necessary. So I suggest you stop whining so that we can work together to get this investigation over with as soon as possible. Check?"

"Check, sir," Nelson replied in a respectful but determined voice.

ᏣᏍᏬ

An enormous explosion suddenly shook the Government Center so violently that it seemed it would fall down. Beck instinctively flinched and glanced up at the ceiling. Dust filled the room so that it was difficult to breath. He noticed that the four grunts stood calmly waiting for him to finish the conversation, so he did his best to continue. "I'll need written statements from all of you."

Another explosion rocked the building, but this time Beck forced himself to ignore it. "For now," Beck said, "stand by in the auditorium. Lieutenant Colonel McCall and I have to take care of some things. I'll be back shortly."

When he returned to the Battalion Combat Operations Center, Beck paused to watch the S-3 Officer coordinate the counter-battery fire operation. The Fire Support Coordination Center immediately cleared a battery of Paladins to engage the point of origin. Standing in the COC, Beck soon heard the counter-battery fire landing about two kilometers away. The S-3 officer stayed on the radio, talking to the Fire Support Coordination Center for about five minutes. When he got off, he grinned and spoke. "Sir, a UAV got a picture of the insurgent mortar crew getting blown to bits."

Beck headed to McCall's room and explained that he needed to proceed to the school as soon as possible. The other man looked upset.

"Mike," McCall said, "with the conditions we have now, there's no way I can let you go driving around my area of operation at night with just the PSD Marines. That would be tactically crazy and too dangerous for you and my men. I'm sorry, but I don't have the assets to provide you any backup. If you're thinking about doing it, I strongly suggest that we wait until tomorrow morning and see what develops. I would hate to see the mujahideen cutting your head off on the six o'clock news!"

Beck now felt weary. "I agree that we should stay here tonight. If you can spare any assets tomorrow, I would really appreciate it. If you can't, I'll make do with the PSD. My team will finish the interviews here tonight and launch first thing in the morning."

"How many people are you going to talk to?" McCall asked, regretting that he'd gotten excited.

"This is big enough that I will have to talk to everyone that knows anything. It will probably be the entire platoon. Maybe we can do a squad at a time. I have the PSD outside in dispersed battle positions. You got somewhere I can let them throw their packs down?"

"Sure. Mi casa es su casa." McCall motioned for the S-3 to take care of the task.

Beck started to feel confident, like being back at the office in Chicago. His mind raced. What was the winning strategy here? He looked around and found a seat in the COC and took out his green notebook. He wanted to think about things.

After about 20 minutes, LtCol. Campbell and Maj. Way came in to talk.

"Sir, we have inventoried the weapons that Kilo Company took out of the school yesterday and have sworn statements from the supply sergeant," Campbell said. "We recovered twelve AK-47s, two SKSs, one Kalashnikov assault rifle, one Al-Kadesian sniper rifle, one Drogunov sniper rifle, one Mark One Lee-Enfield .303, and two Tokarev 7.62 automatic pistols."

Beck checked off the items in his green notebook.

Ɑ჻ᲙᲝ

1800, 10 November 2004
3rd Battalion Headquarters
Fallujah, Iraq

At 1800, the S-3 officer came into the room where Beck sat outlining questions for LCpl. Case. "Sir, First Squad, Third Platoon is here."

Beck picked up his flak jacket and helmet, grabbed his Alice pack, and walked down to the auditorium. He chose an inside wall to stow his gear and planned to sleep in the same spot that night. After stowing his gear, Beck took a deep breath and walked across the auditorium to talk to Anne Merrill, who sat typing on her laptop.

"I don't want to make you angry, but I need to talk to you," Beck said.

Anne seemed calm but not overly friendly. She stopped typing and stared intently at Beck.

"We're bringing the Marines here for interviews," Beck explained. "Some of them are here now, and the others should arrive within an hour. Unless any of them objects, I'll let you listen to all the interviews."

Beck, followed by the squad leader and Anne Merrill, headed toward a group of offices located next to the auditorium. In the first room, he saw LtCol. Campbell interviewing a witness, and as they passed a second room, he observed Way interviewing a lance corporal.

The room chosen by Beck had a large window with the glass blown out, and gusts of wind blew in, so that it felt very cold. There were built-in bookshelves next to the window, an old desk with the drawers missing, and two chairs. He sat in the desk chair and told the squad leader to have a seat in the chair across from him. He then took out a half-dozen blue chem-lights and spread them around the room—on the bookshelves, the desk, and the floor. The effect appeared the same as the black lights popular at colleges in the sixties.

Beck tried to break the ice. "All we need are posters and a bong to have a party."

No one smiled.

The interview of the squad leader took about an hour. The squad leader didn't know Case since the STA team had never been assigned to the squad until that morning. He was present in the school and heard shooting, but he didn't see Case or the Iraqis.

After the interview, Beck went outside to bring in another witness to interview and discovered that Campbell and Way had, in the same time period, completed three interviews each.

The second witness had difficulty finding the chair and kept dozing off. It seemed obvious that he was not able to answer questions. After five minutes, Beck decided that the witnesses would have to get some sleep before they could be interviewed, so he headed back to the auditorium. On the way, he ordered Campbell and Way to secure for the night.

Chapter 34

1900, 10 November 2004
Al Hareery School
Fallujah, Iraq

Haitham Rasheed slept all day, but when the temperature started dropping at dusk, he awoke. He was hurting. After a few minutes, Haitham raised his hand to his face and felt the hole next to his right eye. It took all of his energy and will power to turn his head a few inches to the right. His eyes were open, but he saw only darkness. He tried the left and could not see anything.

He tried to sit up, but he didn't have the strength. He felt cold but could do nothing. He lay on the floor, freezing.

ભ્૰

2200, 10 November 2004
3rd Battalion Headquarters
Fallujah, Iraq

By the time Mike Beck and Anne Merrill returned to the auditorium, all lights were out and the room felt like an icebox. Everyone seemed to be asleep. Beck used his key chain light to guide Merrill back to her gear, returned to his spot, and pulled out the two luxury items he'd brought to Iraq: a Prolite sleeping pad and Mammut goose-down bag rated to minus 35 degrees Fahrenheit. Both looked like Marine Corps-issued items but were 100-times better.

As he pulled off his boots, blouse, and pants, Beck felt a sudden chill and hurried to get inside the bag. He zipped up the bag and fell asleep in two minutes.

An hour later, he felt someone gently shaking his shoulder and heard a whisper. "Let me in, Beck."

He opened his eyes, but in the darkness he could only discern that someone knelt next to his bag.

"Come on, Beck. I'm freezing to death! It's not worth it."

Beck thought he recognized Anne Merrill's voice. He unzipped the bag and, without thinking, whispered, "Take off your boots and jacket. You'll start sweating in this bag."

He waited as Anne Merrill sat on the floor, unlaced her boots, and pulled them off. Next, she unzipped her jeans, slipped them down, and placed them on top of her boots. She slid her legs into the bag, took off her jacket, and rolled it up as a pillow.

Beck tried to zip up the bag, which seemed too small to accommodate two people. He lay on his side, with Anne's back snuggled up next to his chest. She shivered violently from the chill, and her back felt like ice.

The narrow bag naturally pressed their bodies together, and Beck's arm wrapped around Anne. He rubbed her body with his right hand with the innocent intention of creating more heat to stop her shaking, but in the process figured out that she wore only a bra, long sleeve T-shirt, and panties.

Anne felt the warmth of the goose down bag and kept wiggling closer to Mike to maximize body heat. It wasn't long before Anne stopped trembling. Within five minutes, they were both warm.

Beck suddenly felt terrified that one of the Marines would see Anne in his sleeping bag. He considered getting out but lacked the willpower.

As she lay in the warm bag, Anne unconsciously arched her back and pushed her rear against Mike. They were separated only by the thin fabric of their undergarments. She sensed herself reaching for Mike, then started to get out of the bag but stopped. She lay there, paralyzed between the thought of having sex with Mike and the possibility that he might think she planned it from the beginning.

Similar thoughts went through Beck's mind. He also thought of all the times he'd leered at his secretary, Brenda

Higgins, a woman who exuded sensuality. He recalled looking at her black bra when she'd dropped him at O'Hare. All of his life he had taken great risks for sex—the risks of divorce, sexual harassment lawsuits, losing law partners because of affairs with their wives, and even disbarment for sleeping with female judges, attorneys, clients, and witnesses. Indeed, it was a miracle he hadn't bedded Brenda yet, not that he hadn't been tempted a dozen times. But tonight he told himself that he could not risk the lives of the Marines in Fallujah. He tried to calculate the result of having sex with Anne Merrill. Would they get caught? Would she get angry again? Would she fall for him and give him the photographs?

He didn't know and would not risk letting the Marine Corps down. Mike stayed awake all night, just touching and smelling Anne.

 C380

0400, 11 November 2004
3rd Battalion Headquarters
Fallujah, Iraq

Beck carefully maneuvered his arms outside the sleeping bag to look at his watch. This required him to slip his arms above Anne's head so that he could push the light button with his left hand. The attempt not to wake Anne failed, and she moaned a sleepy moan and started wriggling in the bag. It was 0400.

Anticipating that the battalion would call reveille at 0430, Beck whispered in Anne's ear, "I need to get up. Take my bag. I can get it back later."

Anne rolled over to face him, and for a moment she felt somewhere else. She and Mike had been lovers. She looked Beck in the eyes with the most intimate of smiles. Then she remembered that they had not had sex. That was only a dream. Beck had been a perfect gentleman.

She turned, unzipped the bag, climbed out, quickly put on her jeans and coat, and started lacing up her boots. She spoke coldly to Beck. "Thanks, I appreciate the favor."

After dressing, Beck walked to the COC. He noticed a large green insulated carrier full of hot coffee. As he stood looking at the coffee container, a COC Marine read his mind. "Sir, you need a cup of coffee?"

"Sergeant, I'd cut off my left nut for a cup of that coffee right now."

The sergeant brought over a stainless steel insulated mug with the words I LOVE NEW YORK on the side. Beck made a mental note to add a coffee cup to his combat pack list.

"Sir, there's a box of MREs in the corner," said the sergeant. "Better grab one before they get possum-fucked by grunts."

The breakfast of hot coffee, peanut butter, jelly, and crackers would be described by the wives of the firm's partners as "to die for."

While Beck continued eating, Gunny Ellis came in the COC with a wide grin on his face. "Did the Lieutenant Colonel get some good rack time last night?"

Beck realized that rack time meant sex, and that the gunny knew Anne had shared his sleeping bag. He started praying that none of the others had seen them. He figured he couldn't explain what happened to the gunny and decided to play it cool.

"I've had better," Beck said.

Still with a grin on his face, Gunny Ellis pushed on. "I'm sorry the accommodations were not to your liking, sir. Your bag looks to be a little small for your use."

"Yes, just another sacrifice for the Corps, so you can stop worrying about it. Check?"

"Check, sir. Subject closed."

Campbell charged into the room. "I have all the situation reports, detailed maps of the area, and written statements from the platoon commander and all of the squad members. No one seems to know anything. With your permission, I'd also like to get a statement from Anne Merrill."

Beck sat astonished at Campbell's efficiency. "I knew there was a reason I brought you along. Good work."

Beck thought for a moment and decided that even though he'd promised Anne she could be present, he would interview Case alone.

"Lieutenant Colonel Campbell," Beck said, "I want you to interview Anne when she wakes up. Don't tell her, but I'm going to interview Case by myself."

"Gunny Ellis," Campbell said, "get Lance Corporal Case and escort him to the interview room."

"Roger, sir."

೧೮೮

Beck liked the way that Case entered the room—but witnesses had fooled him on more than one occasion. "Have a seat Lance Corporal Case. I'm Lieutenant Colonel Beck, the Division Staff Judge Advocate."

"Yes, sir."

"Do you know that Anne Merrill has a photograph that looks like you are shooting an Iraqi family?"

"Yes, sir. That's what I've been told."

"General Scott sent me here to try and resolve this before we have another Abu Ghraib scandal. You understand?"

"Yes, sir."

Beck thought that Case was acting a bit too calm. He'd learned in his law practice in Chicago that some people could be as cool as they needed to be, regardless of whether they were telling the truth or not. "I don't want to scare you, Lance Corporal Case, but I have to ask you if you know your Article 31 rights."

"Yes, sir," Case replied as Beck handed him an Article 31 rights waiver.

"You read every word of this and then you tell me if you fully understand it."

"Yes, sir." Case blinked twice in a row.

Beck was a master of reading body language. Was Case playing him?

He looked up from his green notebook while Case read over the Article 31 rights waiver form. "Sir, I understand everything on here."

"OK. Now then, if you're innocent, I would like to talk to you. I will do everything in my power to *prove* you're innocent. I will do that because I believe in doing the right thing and because I don't want to lose this fight because of some public relations catastrophe. Check?"

Case cleared his throat. "Yes, sir."

"On the other hand, if you are guilty, then the smart thing for you to do is keep your mouth shut and wait and talk to a lawyer. If you try to bullshit me, I'll find out, and I'll use everything you say against you. Check?"

"Yes, sir."

"I want you to know that I will do everything I can to win this fight. And if you fucked up and shot innocent Iraqis, then the way I see it, I have to make sure you go down. In that case, I'm going to do everything I can to hang your ass. I believe in the system, and no one is going to hold it against you if you just want to talk to a lawyer before you make a statement. As a matter of fact, that would be a pretty smart thing to do. You think you have a good idea where I'm coming from?"

"Yes, sir."

"Do you think it's a good idea to talk to me?"

"Yes, sir."

"Do you want to sign that piece of paper?"

Case glanced at the waiver and paused. "Yes, sir."

Beck considered Case's hesitation. Was he being cautious or evasive? "Then sign it and tell me what happened."

"Yes, sir."

Case signed the Article 31 rights waiver and handed it to Beck, who looked it over carefully to make sure it was completed correctly. Then he looked Case in the eye. "Start talking."

Case looked dumbfounded. "Talk, sir?"

Beck then said, "Just tell me what happened in the school."

Case spoke of entering the Al Hareery School. The two went over every minute, movement, and detail. Beck wrote everything down in his green notebook. "Have you told me everything, Lance Corporal?"

"Everything that I can remember, sir."

Beck was frustrated. "Does that mean that there are things you *can't* remember?"

"No, sir. I mean...I mean that I've told you everything that happened."

"Have you talked about this to anyone else?"

"No, sir."

"None of your STA team members?"

"No, sir."

"What else should I know about this?"

"That's it, sir."

Beck stood, walked away, and then wheeled around. "Are you being straight with me, Lance Corporal?"

"Yes, sir."

"Why did you join the Marines, Case?"

"To make a difference, sir. I was laid off, and then I walked by a recruiting station one day."

"And have you made a difference, Lance Corporal?" Beck asked.

"Yes, sir. I've made a difference."

Beck wasn't sure what to think. What *kind* of difference had Case made? Was the lance corporal being honest or elusive in his plain-spoken manner?

 príprava

0800, 11 November 2004
3rd Battalion Headquarters
Fallujah, Iraq

When Beck walked into the Combat Operations Center, he heard McCall talking on the radio to the Echo Company commander. Beck walked over to a tactical map on the wall and waited for the man to finish his conversation. McCall put the radio mike down and came over to Beck.

"I need to talk to you, Mike," McCall said. "If you have a minute, let's go in my office."

McCall led the way wearing a concerned look. "You better close the door," McCall said.

This made Beck more anxious. "What's up?"

"Third Battalion is in a world of shit this morning. The mujahideen are crawling out of their holes like rats. Our area of operations has been swept, but it looks like we have more enemy now than we had yesterday. My intelligence officer says he is ninety-nine percent positive that the enemy has reoccupied the school. I have radioed all of my company commanders, and there's no way I can clear that area today. Mike, you're going to have to wait here until tomorrow."

Beck stood silent for a long time and then looked McCall in the eye.

"The reporter has an agreement with General Scott that she won't release her story until tomorrow. If we sit here and she releases that story without having more facts, it's going to look like a Marine murdered innocent Iraqi civilians. What do you think will happen if a story that an American massacred civilians gets published around the world, a story with photographs?"

McCall looked sick. "Is it that bad?"

"If it gets released, the story will be repeated around the world, and the photographs will be shown twenty times every hour on the BBC and Al Jazzera. We'll have extremists coming to Fallujah to join the fight from all over Iraq and the Middle East. The Prime Minister could call this off again. Hell, we could have another Vietnam, with peace marches and the whole nine yards."

Beck realized that he sounded just like Carter. He could tell that McCall was convinced. He asked another question. "Do you know if any of our people have been back to the school since yesterday?"

"No one has been back," McCall answered. "The area is too hot. As I said, we know that the mujahideen have re-infiltrated, and that's why I am going to need today to get this organized. Every unit in the battalion is heavily engaged. When we pause tonight, I can shift a platoon to provide security for you. There just isn't anyone to do it until we get through today's operations."

The two men stared at each other before Beck spoke again. "I understand. I just can't risk waiting that long, and I'm going in with the PSD. I'll be taking full responsibility. When we go back, you get the Regimental CO on the horn, and I'm going to tell him that I made the decision against your recommendation."

"Mike, with all due respect, you're a lawyer and I'm an infantry officer. It's fucking suicide for you to go to that school today. If you just give me until tomorrow, we can do this thing the right way. I just can't organize anything any faster. Maybe the reporter will wait another day."

"Honestly, I think she would if she could, but she can't. We can't wait until tomorrow. Let's call Colonel Allen, and if he needs to, he can call General Scott."

The two walked back to the Combat Operations Center and got Colonel Allen on the radio. Beck did the talking. "Sir, I have to examine the crime scene, and I need to do it today. It will be dangerous, and I need all the help I can get. Lieutenant Colonel McCall is doing the same thing I would do, but the general's PSD is packing up now, so if you want to try and talk to General Scott, I don't have a problem with that."

Allen answered without hesitating. "That won't be necessary. Can you put Lieutenant Colonel McCall on the net?"

Beck handed the radio mike to McCall, who said "Yes, sir" three times and hung up.

McCall looked at Beck and shook his head. "Mike, if you run into insurgents, there's not a damn thing I can do to help. Our air support is already committed, and I can't put together a QFR. The best I can do is pray for you."

"Well, hopefully that will be enough."

અઢ

0900, 11 November 2004
3rd Battalion Headquarters
Fallujah, Iraq

The 3rd Battalion's S-3 Officer accomplished all necessary
coordination in record time, and at 0900 Beck walked out the
back door of the Government Center towards the vehicles. It
surprised him that Gunny Ellis called "Attention on Deck"
when he walked up.

"Sir, are you ready for the confirmation brief?" Ellis
asked.

"Go ahead, Gunny."

The confirmation brief made Beck feel 20 years younger,
and he had no second thoughts about his decision. He
considered Gunny Ellis a great NCO, but he never realized
that any man could appear as brave, determined, and
competent. The brief covered the mission, fire team tasks,
call signs, radio frequencies, vehicle assignments, immediate
action drills, casualty procedures, adjacent units, fire support, close air support, and every other detail that anyone
might possibly need to know. Every member of the PSD
listened intensely with determined looks on their faces.

The gunny concluded, "Sir, do you have any comments?"

"This is a dangerous mission," Beck added. "However, I
think the risks are justified. Our mission here is to defeat an
insurgency. To accomplish our mission, we must have the
support of the Iraqi people and the American public. If we
can prove what really happened at the school, I believe we
can keep their support. If they hear lies and see misleading
photographs, we could have a big problem. I won't ask you to
do anything that does not have to be done or stay any longer
than necessary. Are there any questions?"

Beck looked up to see Anne Merrill walking out of the
Government Center, wearing a protective vest and carrying a
helmet and pack. She looked stunning. When she approached the group she smiled. "Colonel Beck, I guess I
overslept. You weren't going to leave without me, were you?"

"Gunny, this won't take but a minute," Beck said, glancing sideways.

Beck motioned for Anne to follow him back inside the Government Center and walked into one of the vacant offices. "The insurgents have infiltrated the area," he said. "It's going to be extremely dangerous out there. I'm sorry, but you'll have to wait here for us to return."

It surprised Beck that Anne remained calm.

"Mike, I helped create this mess, and I have the right to help fix it. You're smart enough to know that if you go back without me, it won't mean a thing. Do you think Al Jazeera is going to just take your word if you find something?"

After looking away, deep in thought for more than a minute, Beck decided Anne was right.

ᘓᘔ

0920, 11 November 2004
3rd Battalion Headquarters
Fallujah, Iraq

At 0920, the convoy pulled out with three up-armored Humvees, a hardback Humvee, and the SJA Humvee. The up-armored Humvees all had turret-mounted crew-served weapons: two .50 caliber heavy machine guns and one M-240G 7.62mm machine gun. The hardback had a pedestal-mounted M-240G machine gun and a side mounted SAW light machine gun. The SJA Humvee had the turret-mounted SAW.

McCall allowed the STA team and two members of the 3rd Battalion Combat Operation Center to volunteer for the mission. Gunny Ellis left the STA team as a functioning unit in the back of the hardback Humvee. He assigned one of the COC Marines to an up-armored Humvee, and one climbed into the SJA Humvee, which meant that Lance Corporal Martinez was driving, Major Way had shotgun, Rusty Davis was claiming the rear passenger seat, and the COC Marine,

Private First Class Collins, was sitting in the rear driver's side. Gunnery Sergeant Ryan climbed into the turret.

Ellis knew that it would be easy to get lost in Fallujah. The streets weren't laid out like an American city. Roads that seemed to go in one place suddenly slanted off in a different direction. Gunny Ellis did everything he could to determine exactly where the convoy needed to go and pre-planned numerous alternative routes to get there. The primary route ran down Andalusa Street, turning on to Al Busha Street and then down Industry Avenue. The alternative routes were all marked out and identified as Bravo, Charlie, and Delta so it would be easy to direct a change of course. Ellis planned to have the lead vehicle stay three blocks ahead of the convoy. This was not part of standard convoy operations and put the Marines in the scout Humvee in extreme danger. Ellis felt the risks were justified.

A scout Humvee would be the best way to warn of insurgents, and the PSD would try and stay away from the mujahideen if possible. If the scout were attacked, it would radio back for an alternative route. Both the scout and the convoy would quickly divert to the new route and hopefully avoid the enemy. If the scout got into trouble, the convoy's quick reaction force would race to the scout's rescue.

The scout and the convoy would drive as fast as possible to the school, set up a defense, complete the investigation, and get back as quickly as possible. The tactical plan emphasized avoiding contact with the enemy and get in and out as fast as possible.

As the convoy pulled out, the team members contemplated their individual fates. Ellis had trained for missions like this his entire adult life. For him, combat existed as a grim necessity, part of his job. Years ago in other actions, he had weighed the risks of being a Marine and had accepted them.

Mike felt apprehensive but determined. He realized that he was out of his league, but remained confident that he could rely on Gunny Ellis to accomplish the mission. Besides, he had never heard of a Marine Lieutenant Colonel getting hurt in combat and that made him feel invincible.

Way sat in the SJA Humvee, trying to understand what had made him lose his mind the day before and why he had insisted on the SJA office going on the mission. He figured he had a right to get himself killed but now felt terrible about Gunny Ryan and LCpl. Martinez. He prayed that they would all make it and promised himself that he would never leave the SJA office again except to go home.

Lieutenant Colonel Campbell double- and triple-checked his weapons and assortment of high-speed gear. He tried to shake the feeling that he was out of place. Here he sat, having spent most of his career just trying not to get kicked out of the Marine Corps, headed into combat to do something really important. Through an incredible chain of crappy assignments and lucky breaks, he finally considered himself a real Marine.

Chapter 35

T he lead vehicle headed down Andalusa Street as fast as the PSD driver could maneuver, with everyone else trying to keep up. Andalusa Street was lined with one- and two-story houses made of cement blocks and stucco, each with fenced courtyards. Most of the walls were uneven and had metal gates. The construction, while in some cases ambitious, appeared unplanned and uncontrolled.

The drivers had to work hard to keep their positions and avoid hitting the burnt vehicles, cinder blocks, and general debris in the roadway. After three blocks, they passed the body of a dead Iraqi on the side of the road. Everyone knew that the convoy was traveling way too fast, but no one wanted to slow down. Regardless of the risk of an accident, the drivers wanted to get to the school as fast as possible.

In the SJA Humvee, LCpl. Martinez felt so pumped up that he stayed within ten feet of the PSD Humvee in front of him, tracking its every move like a NASCAR driver in the slingshot. Gunny Ryan had a grin on his face and was in full Ninja mode, moving the turret side to side to scan both sides of the street. Maj. Way had Martinez's M-16 pointed out the passenger window and still prayed to himself that no one would get hurt.

At Jabail Avenue, the scout vehicle turned left and radi-oed back on the net. "Turning onto Jabail. All clear."

Jabail Avenue turned out to be a four-lane road with a wide median, but it was in worse condition than Andalusa Street, with garbage, litter, and old tires scattered every-where. Some of the drivers were unable to react fast enough and ran over the rubbish, curbs, and barriers. Beck thought about ordering everyone to slow down but decided to leave that up to Gunny Ellis, who had said nothing so far.

The scout vehicle turned onto Heyal Sinala Street after 20 minutes, and Beck figured they would be at the school in another ten minutes. It seemed almost too easy.

A minute later the smoke trail of an RPG caught the corner of Beck's eye. He followed it as it zipped past his vehicle and exploded on the opposite side of the street. At the same time, he saw several grenades plop onto the street from behind a fence next to an alley. He recognized the grenades as the kind used by Germans in World War II movies, soup cans on a wooden stick. Some didn't even explode, but two did. Luckily, the blasts were far enough away so that none of the vehicles were hit.

At first, Beck couldn't see any enemy, but the turret gunners opened up with the Browning M-2 .50 caliber heavy machine guns, M-240Gs, and SAWs. The gunners were spraying the fence, alley, and nearby houses as the convoy raced past. Then he saw an insurgent about two hundred yards down the street stick his head out from behind a wall and snap off a burst from his AK-47. Dirt popped up on the side of the road next to Beck's vehicle, and he could hear the snap and crack of the rounds passing close.

A second insurgent stepped out from behind a fence at the same location as the first and let off another burst of rounds. This time, Gunny Ryan had a bead on him with the borrowed 5.56mm SAW, and the insurgent danced a death dance as the rounds tore though his body. Being his first time, Beck had expected that witnessing a man being shot would require a moment of soul searching, but today he didn't give it a second thought.

He could see rounds fired from other locations impacting the sides of the scout vehicle, and he got a glimpse of insurgents running in or out of alleys.

At the next intersection, things continued to get hot for the convoy. About four or five insurgents darted from houses, shooting bursts from their AK-47s and running back to cover.

The enemy fire remained wildly inaccurate, generally not even hitting the vehicles. Still, with all the bullets flying, it was hard to believe that no one had been hit. Beck realized that this was going to be one hell of a gunfight. He struggled to stay calm, kept track of what was going on, and tried to look like he knew what he was doing.

At that moment, he saw an improvised explosive device detonate on the lead vehicle. It looked like four bombs linked together as a chain and buried 100 meters west of the intersection of Jabail Street and Heyal Sinala Street. He figured it was made of mortar rounds and had been intended to damage personnel, not vehicles. The explosion didn't damage the scout vehicle, but it proved enough to cause the driver to swerve and lose control. The Humvee bounced over the curb, flipped over, and continued sliding upside down until coming to rest against an electrical pole on the opposite side of the street.

Gunny Ellis radioed the net. His voice was calm and matter-of-fact. "IED attack. Vehicle disabled. Commence immediate action drill."

The quick reaction force assumed blocking positions in the front, rear, and sides of the convoy, and the vehicles grouped at 50-meter intervals. Beck and Ellis jumped out and ran to the disabled Humvee while the STA team and COC squad fanned out around the vehicle. Before they could get across Heyal Sinala Street, the convoy started taking small arms fire from a house on the west side of the street. The bullets hit the disabled Humvee.

In a fraction of a second, Gunny Ryan returned fire from the SJA Humvee using the 5.56mm SAW. A half second later, the Browning machine guns in the PSD Humvees joined in. In a minute, the house was shot to pieces, and the firing stopped. Beck realized that this aspect of combat had not changed since Vietnam. No insurgent force could match U.S. firepower, and the firefight stopped as quickly as it had started.

The front passenger of the scout vehicle, a lean tough-looking PFC, only 20 years old, crawled out and sat on the side of the road. Blood ran from his nose and mouth, signs of the blast concussion caused by the IED. The corpsman was there first and knelt beside the wounded man, saying, "You'll be all right in a few minutes."

Beck headed straight for the disabled Humvee. As he ran, his respiration accelerated, his jaws clenched, and anger energized his mind and body.

Amazingly, the driver and second passenger were not hurt and were crawling out without assistance. The good news was quickly followed by bad. The turret gunner lay inside in a twisted ball.

Gunny Ellis yelled at several Marines who'd taken cover and were adding to the barrage of fire from the Humvee turret guns being aimed at the last sighting of the enemy. "Save your fucking ammo and get your asses over here," Ellis screamed.

The men came running.

"When I give you the word," Ellis said, "you're going to raise the side of this vehicle."

Six men instantly took hold of the Humvee and waited for the command. A corpsman crawled inside. Everyone waited as time stood still.

Beck joined the corpsman inside the Humvee.

"Sir, there's no pulse," the Corpsman told Beck.

"Well, let's get him out," Beck said, squatting so he could see the corpsman better. "Let me know when you're ready."

At that moment, Beck saw Anne Merrill standing with the six men, ready to lift up the Humvee.

The corpsman nodded, and Beck relayed the signal to Gunny Ellis, who barked, "Lift!"

The two-ton vehicle heaved three feet off the ground.

Beck pulled the turret gunner's body out, and the corpsman reexamined him for a pulse, but it was obvious from the deformation of the man's head that he could not have survived. Beck saw that the turret gunner wore private first-class rank insignia, and his nametag said "Mayberry." Gunny Ellis identified him as a member of the PSD.

"Gunny, have this Marine placed in the back of my Humvee." Beck spoke conversationally and calmly, although his stomach was in painful knots.

"Yes, sir."

Without any further command, the men carried PFC Mayberry's body to Beck's vehicle and rolled the scout Humvee back on its wheels. The only damage seemed to be to the turret, so Ellis assigned a new crew, and the Humvee was moved to center position in the convoy. Another PSD Humvee assumed the lead position.

Ellis reluctantly radioed in the information. He knew that radio operators all over the battlefield could hear the report and that the operators at the Division Combat Operations Center monitored all bands. In no time, everyone at Division headquarters would know what had happened.

At the same time Ellis made the report, Beck ordered the convoy to resume course. As the convoy proceeded, Beck sat in his Humvee, asking himself if PFC Mayberry would be alive if he had ordered the convoy to slow down. Gunny Ellis was asking himself the same question.

They would think about that question for the rest of their lives.

Cℨ℘

0935, 11 November 2004
Jabail Avenue
Fallujah, Iraq

As the convoy started moving again, the SJA Humvee slipped into a position directly behind Beck's Humvee. Way and Martinez had a clear view of Bell, Beck, Campbell, and Merrill.

Martinez had been wildly scared ever since the shooting started. He'd never felt that way in his life, and now he thought he might die from fright. It felt hard to breathe, and his heart banged in his chest. He kept thinking to himself, *We're never going to make it to that fucking school and are just going to drive around until we're fucking dead.* He struggled to keep the SJA Humvee on the road and was about ready to pull over, get in the back, and let the gunny drive when the shooting started again.

There were so many rounds coming towards the convoy, kicking up dust and ricocheting off walls, that if felt like the SJA Humvee had crashed into a barrier. Worse, this time the insurgents' aim was much better. Bullets ripped across the hood of the SJA Humvee, shredding the right front fender and blowing off the driver's side rearview mirror next to Martinez, causing glass and metal to plaster his face. He screamed in pain and terror. He felt paralyzed with fear, but in that brief moment, his fear went away. He had a sudden realization that he wasn't the only one in danger in the SJA Humvee and that if he didn't drive like hell he might kill everyone. He determined to do his job and knew that all that mattered was his fellow Marines. They would not get hurt because he failed to do his part—he'd make sure of that.

In the back seat, Collins was suddenly hit by a bullet in his shoulder, which slammed him against the seat. "I've been shot!" he screamed.

As usual, Ryan spotted the insurgents first and opened up on them. They stood inside windows, shooting from the second stories of two houses. In seconds, the insurgents faced a crushing wave of lead from the Humvee windows.

This time, the rear vehicles in the convoy took the brunt of the insurgents' fire. Another RPG skimmed across the hardback Humvee's front fender with the sound of grinding metal. It exploded on the opposite side of the street. The explosion lifted the hardback in the air, after which it bounced off the block wall onto the street, throwing the STA team into a pile on the floor and then crashing into the back of another Humvee. Hale was thrown three feet in the air, fell out the back of the hardback, and landed on the side of the street before tumbling another ten yards. The driver of the rear Humvee saw this and slammed on his brakes. The passengers scrambled out, picked up Hale, and put him in the back seat. Amazingly, he was still conscious. "I'm OK. I'm OK," he yelled. "Where's my fucking rifle?"

Rusty Davis struggled in the confined space of the rear seat of the SJA Humvee to apply a pressure dressing to Collin's bleeding shoulder. Way looked back and spoke on the radio. "Judge to Six. COC Marine took a round in the shoulder. He needs a corpsman."

Beck responded on the radio net. "Halt at the next intersection. Disabled vehicle drill on vehicle number three. Corpsman up."

The quick reaction force assumed blocking positions in the front, rear, and sides of the convoy as the vehicles grouped at 50-meter intervals around the SJA Humvee. Again, Beck and Ellis jumped out and ran to the SJA Humvee while Nelson, Goldman, and Case bailed out of the hardback Humvee and fanned out around the vehicle. Before anyone got there, Collins stepped out and lay down on the pavement next to the SJA Humvee. In five minutes, the corpsman had the bleeding stopped and Collins crawled back inside the SJA Humvee.

The convoy resumed its movement to the school and kept moving fast, turning east and south. Beck felt bad about Mayberry and Collins but thanked his good luck. With all the bullets and RPG's fired at the convoy, it was a miracle there had been so few casualties.

Chapter 36

I n accordance with the operation plan, the scout vehicle radioed back to the convoy leader four blocks from the school and slowed down to allow the convoy to catch up so that all Humvees would arrive at the school at the same time. As the Humvees pulled up, Ellis and Beck sprang out of their vehicles. Beck assumed tactical command, and Gunny Ellis became the assault force commander.

When Beck exited the Humvee, he noticed that Lance Corporal Bell followed close behind. She kept her rifle at her shoulder and scanned in all directions for enemy snipers or other threats. Beck moved cautiously but without fear. By this time, he felt bulletproof and strode confidently into the schoolyard.

The task force quickly surrounded the school with the Humvees, two parked to the south side, one to the west, and the rest on the east. Ellis planned the geometry of fire so that insurgents would be forced out the rear of the school and could be engaged by two of the .50 caliber machine guns.

The PSD formed into stacks at each of the two front gates, with Way standing at the front of one of the stacks. Before anyone could stop her, Anne lined up at the end of a stack, but Beck noticed that for the first time that she appeared scared. Ellis gave the command, and both stacks charged inside the gates and ran to the front door and side windows of the classroom building. Ellis gave the second command, and the stacks burst into the classroom simultaneously. Once inside, the STA team ran to the roof to set up an over-watch position, and the rest of the unit started clearing the class-room.

As Beck entered the school, he heard Ellis shout. "OK, assholes. You know your job. Give me some security here. Get two of the fifty cal Humvees inside the wall and get your perimeter defense up. Now!"

Gunny Ellis dashed back outside, followed by a half-dozen Marines.

Campbell, Way, and Davis commenced the investigation. Agent Davis dictated notes into a small recorder as he carefully examined the bodies of an old man, two women, two girls, and a boy. He carefully removed a bullet lodged in a dead woman's arm and placed it into a pre-marked plastic bag.

At the same time, Campbell snapped photographs, and Way examined the insurgent bodies. Everyone expected an insurgent attack at any moment, and they all worked as quickly as possible.

It appeared that the victims had been lined up facing the wall and shot in the back of their heads. During his 30 years as an NCIS agent, Rusty Davis had observed hundreds of gunshot wounds from 9mm pistols. He concluded that the victims' wounds were not from a 9mm and suspected that the victims were shot with Russian 7.62mm Tokarev pistols. He yelled at Beck. "Mike, I need a detail to police this area for brass."

Beck relayed the request to Ellis, and the men methodically policed the classroom for bullet casings. They didn't find a single U.S. 9mm Beretta casing, but found six 7.62mm Tokarev casings on the floor next to the Iraqi bodies, and one more a few feet away.

Rusty Davis found Iraqi ration cards on the old man and two women that identified them as members of the Saddaq family. He placed the cards inside the evidence bags. The bodies of the victims were quickly loaded into the hardback Humvee.

 C3&O

During the night, Haitham Rasheed lapsed in and out of consciousness, and he lay comatose on the floor of the school at the time the task force first entered. As the task force conducted the investigation, however, he started to regain consciousness. Soon, he heard shouting and opened his eyes. Haitham immediately started praying. "Please, God, save me. I will not sin again. It is your will that I survive."

Finally, he got the strength to raise his arm about six inches.

One of the PSD marines saw Haitham move, and yelled. "We got a live one!"

Four rifles were instantly pointed at Haitham. When Haitham dropped his arm, he hit the extra AK-47 magazine he carried in his pants pocket. It hit the marble floor with a metallic sound and slid towards Beck. One of the men overreacted and yelled, "Grenade!"

Bell jumped three feet, knocking Beck to the floor and covering him with her body. Everyone else dove on the floor and waited for the explosion. After several seconds of silence, a Marine stood up. "It's only a rifle magazine," he said.

Beck remained on the floor, sprawled out on his back with Bell lying on top, trying to shield him with her body. She held onto him as tightly as possible, so that her face remained buried against his neck, her legs wrapped around his sides. He gently tapped her arm, but it took her a moment to relax and look at him.

Beck smiled. "That was above the call of duty, but thanks."

Beck recalled that Bell had been called a "hard target." That's how he'd thought of her ever since—as Hard Target.

By the time Bell managed to move off, Ellis stood next to Beck, grinning. Anne glanced at Beck with a raised eyebrow and shook her head.

Beck got to his feet and yelled for a corpsman. "He better not die!"

The corpsmen worked furiously. In minutes, he completed an assessment of Haitham's medical condition, had

Haitham on an IV, and started cleaning and dressing his wounds.

Haitham tried to raise his hand again. He lay surrounded by Beck, Campbell, Way, Anne, Rusty Davis, and the interpreter.

"Please, I want to surrender," Haitham said. "I can give you information. Please."

Beck and the translator moved over to Haitham and took out his green notebook. "Do you know who murdered the women and children?"

It hurt to talk, but Haitham answered. "It was Kamis Hadeed."

"Did you see an American shoot the women?"

"No. It was Kamis Hadeed."

"Why did Hadeed kill them?"

"To make it look like the Americans did it. The Hadeeds hate the Saddaqs."

"Who are you?"

"I was kidnapped and forced to come here," Haitham said. "I am not a terrorist. I am a Rasheed, and I hate the Hadeeds. I killed Laith Hadeed."

"All right," Beck said. "That's enough for now. We're going to take care of you."

Haitham continued to talk. "I am not one of them. My cousin was here. Can I look for him?"

Beck looked at the corpsman, who nodded and lifted Haitham into a sitting position.

Pointing at Sdeek's body, Beck asked, "Is that your cousin?"

"No. He is an outsider. A jihadist. He came here from Saudia Arabia, and his name is Sdeek. He was a good man. He wanted to die. He was crazy. He came to be a martyr to make his father happy."

Haitham tried to point towards Ahmed's body. "That is my cousin."

A Marine gently rolled over Ahmed's body.

Haitham spoke again. "Yes, that's my cousin. Will you bury him?"

The Marine glanced at Beck, who nodded as two men put Ahmed's body into a body bag and carried it to the hardback.

"Gunny," said Beck, "let's get the rest of these bodies in the hardback and get the hell out of here. Rusty, are you ready to roll?"

Rusty nodded.

"Lieutenant Colonel Campbell, do we have everything we need?" Beck asked.

Campbell looked around the classroom and at Rusty Davis. "Yes, sir."

Beck then addressed Way. "Major, are we ready to roll?"

"Yes, sir."

"Then let's get going!"

ᏽᏬ

1300, 11 November 2004
Al Hareery School
Fallujah, Iraq

The first mortar round hit before the corpsman had finished putting a new bandage on Haitham's wound. Beck thought he was getting used to the sounds of battle and, after noticing that the gunfire that hurt his ears earlier now sounded muffled, determined that his ears must have adjusted. However, this sound was different and knocked him down. Bell looked horrified again and ran to help him up.

The STA team ran down from the roof and, along with the men inside the classroom, took cover next to the walls in the same spots that Haitham, Ahmed, and Sdeek had two days before. Beck looked around the classroom for Anne. She wasn't there. He ran outside, followed by Bell, and found Anne standing next to the front wall.

"Damn it, Anne!" Beck yelled. "Get your ass inside the school!"

Beck grabbed her hand, pulled her back inside the school, and shoved her down on the floor next to the south wall.

The second mortar round came quickly, followed by the third. Beck heard a crack, and a Marine next to the north window went down. The corpsman rushed over, followed by Beck and Anne. When the corpsman unfastened the Marine's flak vest, he found no blood and no evidence of a wound. The shrapnel had been deflected by the SAPI plates inside his protective vest.

The third mortar round hit Ellis's Humvee, scattering it over the schoolyard and causing secondary explosions from the 240 Golf ammunition in the back. The shrapnel from this explosion hit Nelson in the left arm, and he went down.

Beck yelled for Campbell. "You're a grunt. Can you call in counter-battery fire?"

Campbell had a scared look on his face, but he could see his duty. "Yes, sir! I can do it."

The area east of Andalusa Avenue fell within the boundary of the adjacent regiment, so Campbell had to contact the Fire Support Coordination Center to effect cross-boundary coordination. He gave the position of the school to the FSCC and notified it that the unit was receiving enemy mortar rounds. As usual, the counter-battery radar quickly located the enemy mortar crew, and the Marine artillery battery at Camp Fallujah commenced firing the counter-battery mission in seconds. The mortar attack ended.

Beck heard the automatic fire of several AK-47 rifles from some distance to the south, and rounds started hitting the school. Way, Ryan, and Martinez returned fire from the classroom windows.

Martinez regained control of himself and started doing things right. He looked like a drill instructor giving instruction to new recruits at the rifle range. He knelt on one knee with his left hand against the window sill and returned single rounds of well-disciplined fire, just the way Marines had been taught since World War I. Every time an insurgent exposed himself to crank off a burst, Martinez took careful aim, squeezed the trigger of his M-16, and watched the insurgents go down.

Ellis moved over to confer with Beck and yelled into his ear. "Sir, this is a coordinated attack, and I estimate thirty to forty enemy moving in from the south!"

The blast of the .50 caliber machine guns outside interrupted their conversation. One of the PSD Marines, seeing that the mortar attack had ended, climbed back into an up-armored Humvee and used the turret mounted .50 caliber to engage the insurgents from house to house. The big gun punched right through the concrete block structures. Unfortunately, he failed to notice that shots were coming at him from a different angle across the schoolyard.

Ellis stood up, grabbed Martinez's arm, pulled himself next to his ear, and pointed with his free arm at the Marine on the .50 caliber. "Cover his left flank!"

Martinez ran out the door and took up a position at the rear of the Humvee in order to engage the insurgents shooting from the east. Several members of the PSD joined him.

Four insurgents stumbled out from an alley and walked down the center of the street, wildly firing their AK-47s toward the school. They appeared stoned, with crazy looks on their faces, and their rounds were way off target. Martinez and the other Marines seemed stunned and just stared at the spectacle. Finally, Ellis took control. "What are you waiting for, you dumb shits. Shoot the motherfuckers!"

The Marines fired at once, and the four insurgents went down.

Beck yelled and motioned for Campbell. "Campbell, call in artillery on those bastards to the south."

While Campbell reviewed his call-for-fire card, Bell located the correct radio frequency. Beck continued to obtain glimpses of the enemy maneuvering south of Andalusa Avenue.

By studying his map of Fallujah, Campbell identified the location of the enemy. He simply used the streets as grid boundaries. He quickly wrote out all the information he needed to do the call-for-fire and then radioed the fire mission in to the FSCC using the grid method as an adjust-fire engagement. He estimated that the enemy fell within the "danger close" range and so informed the FSCC. After he transmitted the call for fire, a single artillery round impacted 200 meters south of the school and north of the enemy location.

He then changed the adjustment of fire from grid to polar. He radioed an adjustment of 3,200 mils and a distance of 200 meters and called for another round. This hit on target, and Campbell called fire for effect. This resulted in a barrage of artillery shells encompassing an area large enough to cover the entire enemy position.

Next, Beck heard someone yelling for a corpsman. He looked and saw that Way had been hit, apparently by small arms fire. Way had been crouching at a back window, firing his M-16 rifle. He now lay flat on the floor, trying to regain his senses.

Beck rushed over to Way, who lay propped up, resting against one of the pillars and holding his left hand. A large pool of blood formed underneath his hand. Beck lost his temper.

"Goddamn it, Steve!" Beck shouted. "You dumb-ass son of a bitch! I told you to stay at Camp Baharia. I better not have to explain this to Wendy."

Steve Way just smirked. "Don't get your panties in a wad, Beck. It's just a scratch, and Wendy will never know about it."

The corpsman stuffed the hole in Way's hand with Curlex bandages, applied antiseptic, layered the top with gauze, and wrapped the hand and left arm in duct tape.

From that side of the classroom, Beck could see the enemy relocating to buildings east of Andalusa and north of Hulsa Street. Campbell called in another adjustment in order to track the movement of the enemy. The artillery fire did the trick. Within minutes, the enemy was leaving the area, and Campbell called in an end of mission.

Ellis returned to Beck's side. "Sir, this might be a good time to get the hell out of here."

It was an easy decision for Beck. "Let's get moving, Gunny!"

Ellis started yelling instructions and everyone ran for the vehicles.

ⱭⱭ

1330, 11 November 2004
Al Hareery School
Fallujah, Iraq

As soon as he got inside the Humvee, Ellis started issuing orders on the radio. His new plan was to head straight for the Forward Aid Station at the Government Center. From there, the wounded could be air-evacuated to the Bravo Surgical Center at Camp Fallujah.

The convoy would not use a scout vehicle for the exfiltration. Instead, all of the vehicles would maintain an equal distance of 30 meters to provide mutual fire support in case of attack. This time, Ellis's vehicle took the lead, with Beck's vehicle in second position. The SJA Humvee assumed third place, followed by the hardback Humvee with the corpsman and Haitham Rasheed.

After issuing the convoy orders, Ellis got on the radio and sent in a report to 3rd Battalion: three wounded in action, including Maj. Way, PFC Collins, and Cpl. Nelson; one wounded detainee, Haitham Rasheed; and one KIA, PFC Mayberry. The corpsman assessed Way, Collins, and Nelson as "critical," which meant they required evacuation, but none of the injuries was life-threatening. Haitham's condition, however, *was* life-threatening and assessed as "priority." Ellis also reported that one Humvee was totally destroyed and another damaged.

After PFC Mayberry's death, the convoy had slowed to 25 miles per hour. However, for the exit run, Ellis's driver went as fast as he could, and again, Bell, Martinez, and the rest of the drivers had to work hard to keep up.

The return route followed Nazal Street to Bazarr Avenue and then straight to the Government Center. Basal Avenue appeared to be in terrible shape, worse than Jabail Street or

Andalusa Street and resembled something out of a *Mad Max* movie, with wrecked automobiles scattered along the street. The drivers were forced to weave in and out of the roadway, driving into yards and increasing the risk of another IED attack.

Gunny Ellis used the radio to call in the convoy's position every five minutes, and the 3rd Battalion COC reported that, because of the number of WIAs and Haitham's condition, they had the medical-evacuation helicopter standing by so that it would arrive at the Government Center at the same time as the convoy. For a long time there was no sign of insurgents on the trip out. Then Ellis made a mistake. He turned right on Bazarr Avenue instead of left and headed back into the city.

After three blocks, a large group of insurgents stood in the road in front of the convoy. It appeared to be the same group of insurgents that had attacked the school from the south, and they seemed startled to see the Humvees barreling toward them. They all scrambled for cover and started firing their AK-47s at the convoy.

As the turret gunners opened up on the insurgents, Ellis realized he had headed the wrong way but decided they would have to run the gauntlet before they could do anything about it. The convoy and the insurgents traded broadsides of small arms fire. When Beck's vehicle passed, Anne lay down on the floor, and Campbell fired his M-16 out her window. Rusty Davis fired his AR-15 out the SJA Humvee. They figured that if they kept shooting, at least they might keep the insurgents pinned down as they drove past.

Ellis silently cursed, frantically staring at the map in his lap and trying to decide what route to take back to the Government Center. He knew that Bazarr Avenue would be clear but had no idea what the convoy might run into if he changed routes. He also worried about friendly fire. He saw that the convoy had entered the traffic circle at Nazal Street, so there wasn't any time left to think about it. He grabbed his driver's shoulder, pointed, and yelled, "Hang wide around the circle and head back the way we came in!"

As Ellis's vehicle cleared the circle, it passed the vehicles in the rear of the convoy. He tried not to look but could not help but see the stunned look on the Marines' faces. Most of them had felt a rush of excitement at first contact with the enemy, and the excitement and confidence had continued. Now, some were starting to doubt themselves and were thinking that, in a matter of time, someone else would be hit. The realization that the convoy had made a wrong turn further eroded their confidence.

૭૩૪૦

After running into the convoy, the group of insurgents took shelter in a room in one of the houses on Bazarr Avenue. They sat against the walls, exhausted, breathing hard and sweating. Two were seriously wounded, bleeding on the floor and on the verge of passing out. All of them had cuts, bruises, and other injuries from the firefight. They felt ready to give up and head for the river. Then, as they reloaded their magazines and checked their weapons, they heard the convoy head back up the street. For a long time they just starred at each other, trying to decide whether to run, hide, or fight. Finally, one of the insurgents grabbed his rifle, stood up, and bellowed. "These Americans are playing with us."

They all ran outside just in time to see the convoy pass. They ran into the street and fired a burst of rounds at the rear of the convoy. The convoy continued to speed up Bazarr Avenue without even bothering to return the fire.

૭૩૪૦

Fifteen minutes later, the convoy drove through the check-point at the Government Center and proceeded into the parking lot at the rear. Mike Beck jumped out and scanned the sky for the Medevac bird. It didn't take him long to spot the CH-46 helicopter that had been circling for five minutes. The shadow of the big chopper glided over the sides of the bombed-out buildings and into the Government Center compound.

"Gunny," Beck said, "go ahead and pop green smoke over there on the side of the building. This area looks safe for landing, and there's no need to delay for radio contact."

"Sir, should we put our Fallen Angel on the chopper?" Ellis asked.

"Roger," Beck replied. "It's against the rules, but I think they have the room. If they object, we'll take Mayberry back with us."

As soon as the Gunny popped the smoke, the chopper started descending, and the Marines carried Nelson, Collins, and Haitham Rasheed out on stretchers. Way insisted on walking. Four Marines carried the body of Mayberry and lay him near the landing area. When the CH-46 landed, Beck ran up and asked if they could take the Fallen Angel.

"No problem, sir," said the pilot. "We have plenty of room. We can take you and anyone else you want."

Beck started to run back, and the Crew Chief yelled at him. "Sir, you'll have to send a security guard with the wounded Iraqi."

Beck asked Ellis to pick a guard. "Sir, how about the STA team? I'm positive they'll make sure nothing happens to the Iraqi."

Without thinking much about it, Beck agreed. Ellis yelled at the top of his voice. "STA team up!"

Case, Hale, and Goldman ran up to Ellis.

"Lance Corporal Case, you're the team leader," Ellis said. "I want the STA team to escort the wounded. Don't talk to the Iraqi and don't let him out of your sight until relieved by Lieutenant Colonel Beck. Check?"

"Check."

The Fallen Angle, Haitham Rasheed, Nelson, Collins, Way, one of the corpsman, and the STA team were aboard the CH-46 in less than a minute and headed for Bravo Surgical Center at Camp Fallujah.

Beck followed the CH-46 with his eyes until it was out of sight and then turned to look at the Marines gathered around the Humvees, staring at him.

"Marines, this was a no-fail mission," Beck said. "I'm proud of you for accomplishing it."

ೞೲ

1400, 11 November 2004
Aboard Medevac Three
Above Fallujah, Iraq

The chopper ride back to the hospital at Camp Fallujah took less than five minutes. Case stood facing one of the side windows, feeling the wind through the open door. As they took off, he thought he could see the school and tried to retrace the route of the convoy.

The STA Marines all rode silently. They were exhausted and no one wanted to try to scream over the noise of the engines.

Steve Way sat in a pool of hydraulic oil and could hardly breathe because of the smell of aviation fuel and exhaust, but he didn't care. It felt good to be getting out of Fallujah alive.

ೞೲ

1330, 11 November 2004
MSR Copper
Fallujah AOA, Iraq

After traveling in almost total silence, the convoy returned to Camp Baharia, the men balancing the choice of inhaling the stench of their own bodies or the taste of dust from the roads. Their canteens were empty and their mouths felt dry.

Beck considered himself wildly, incredibly lucky. With all the shooting, it seemed a miracle that casualties were not higher. Strangely, being in command of Marines—and being so close to death—made him feel completely alive. During

the hours on the streets in Fallujah, he was not the trial
lawyer from Chicago who got himself sent to Iraq by mistake.
He'd been something entirely different. He had experienced
a state of complete mental and physical awareness, with no
connection with the rest of the world—no clients, no dead-
lines, nothing.

Mike had never thought about death. He'd simply felt he
would live for a very long time. Having narrowly escaped
death, he sensed his mortality. He would never be the same.

Chapter 37

B eck's vehicle peeled off the convoy at Camp Baharia and drove straight to Bravo Surgical Center at Camp Fallujah. The hospital building had been an old Iraqi barracks with the usual brown stucco walls and concrete roof. All of the windows were blocked with sandbags. An uneven, cracked sidewalk ran towards the front door, and gravel had been spread in what used to be the grass yard. Four field ambulances were parked out front, and there was a small light over a sign on what looked like the front door: THIS IS NOT AN ENTRANCE.

Lance Corporal Bell drove around to the rear and Beck, Anne, and Ryan got out and walked inside. Surprisingly, Nelson, Collins, Way, and Haitham Rasheed all lay in one room and had IV packs hanging next to their beds. All of the patients except Way appeared to be asleep. Case stood guard.

"How is the Major?" Beck asked the young doctor in a low voice, as if the major weren't lying on the bed awake.

"The major is fine," the doctor said. "In fact, they're all doing well and should be ready to be med-evaced to Germany soon."

After looking at the patients for a few more minutes, Beck, Anne, and Ryan returned to the Humvee. Beck got on the radio and called Lieutenant Colonel McCall to let him know of Collin's condition. McCall appreciated the call-in.

"You're one lucky rogue lawyer, Beck," McCall stated. "I'm glad you're on our side on this thing."

Bell drove back to the PSD barracks at Camp Baharia.

The PSD Marines had the gear and weapons removed from the Humvees and spread out next to the building and were busy surveying, cleaning, and packing away everything. They methodically stripped down, cleaned, and re-lubricated every weapon, followed by a function check. Gunny Ryan got out, walked over to the PSD Marines, and yelled, "Corporal Nelson is doing fine. He'll be back to duty in a few days."

Anne looked at Beck, realizing for the first time that, when she'd gone into the field, her room at Camp Baharia had been reassigned. "I don't have a place to stay," she said.

"Follow me," said Beck, "and I'll see if I can get you a shower and a warm bed."

Beck led Anne around the PSD compound to the head-quarters building and walked inside to the command deck to the G-4's office. It was past midnight, but he knew that the most senior woman Marine in the Division, Lieutenant Colonel Becky Wick, would be at her desk, responding to emails. Her job as the logistics officer had nothing to do with billeting at Camp Baharia, but Beck knew that Wick con-trolled everything related to women at the camp, and if anyone could get Anne a decent room, it would be her.

"Lieutenant Colonel Wick," Beck said, "can you find a room for this news reporter?"

Wick smiled at Anne and Beck. "Have a seat. This may take a few minutes."

"Why don't you wait here while I drop off my gear in my office?" Beck said. "I'll be right back."

He walked to Gen. Scott's office, looking to see if he was working late. No one seemed to be around, and Beck didn't see any point in waking up Lt. Lewis. Instead, he decided he would report the first thing in the morning.

When Beck returned to the G-4's office, Wick and Anne were chatting.

"I'm having someone bring over a key," Wick an-nounced.

Beck poured himself a cup of coffee and waited another 20 minutes for a sergeant to show up with the key.

It took ten minutes to walk from the G-4 office to Anne's new room, located in the center of Camp Baharia and about 300 yards from the mess hall. There were 50 white rectangular trailers—living containers—interspersed with shower and head trailers. At one end, four large generators roared, and the usual two inches of gravel covered everything.

Beck had trouble finding Anne's trailer. After walking around for a few minutes, he figured out that the letter B on the key meant that Anne would have the west end. He located the trailer, opened the door, and handed Anne the key. He started to speak, but Anne interrupted him. "You want to come in?"

A bolt of excitement hit Mike Beck. He had not thought about his feelings for Anne all day, but suddenly he felt like he had to touch her. When Anne stepped up to go through the door, Beck couldn't help but focus all of his energy on looking at her shapely rear and imagined how it looked under her jeans. After following Anne inside, he closed the door, locked it, and turned to face her.

"I see you're always alert, Colonel. Locking my door in case there's a terrorist aboard the base?"

Mike took a step, wrapped his arms around her, and slowly moved his lips to hers. She felt incredible. At the same instant, Beck got a whiff of his rank body odor and felt embarrassed about how filthy he was after the trip into Fallujah. He couldn't stand the thought of grossing out Anne and broke off the kiss while mumbling, "I have to go."

Mike walked out the door and headed for his room. This was one of the few times in his life that he'd ever walked away from a woman. He wondered what had gotten into him.

CBEO

0130, 12 November 2004
4th Division Headquarters
Camp Baharia, Iraq

When he got to his room, Mike took off his helmet and pulled his dog tag chain over his head. In the field, he kept his room key, a crucifix, and a Saint Christopher metal on the chain around his neck.

He hung his helmet and vest on the 782 gear rack made by the Seabees out of four-by-fours—it looked like a grave cross—and slowly sat on the side of the bed. It hurt to bend over and untie his boots, but it was marvelous to get them off. He considered just crawling into bed and avoiding the five-minute walk to the shower trailer, but he realized he couldn't sleep with the stench. It took five minutes to pull off his digitals and to put on running shorts and flip-flops. He put his vest and helmet back on, grabbed his 9mm pistol, and headed for the shower.

It was 0200 by the time Beck returned from the shower and slid into his bed. It felt great to stretch out, and Mike expected that he would be sound asleep in 30 seconds. This time he couldn't go to sleep. Mike kept thinking about Anne. He replayed kissing her over and over in his mind. He mentally debated walking back over to her room. Mike desperately wanted to talk to Anne, touch her again, and kiss her.

He lay awake all night.

ᘓᘔ

0400, 12 November 2004
LtCol Beck's Quarters
Camp Baharia, Iraq

At 0400, Beck gave up trying to sleep. He planned on putting on a clean uniform and heading straight to Gen. Scott's office to wait there until someone showed up. He had his running shorts on, and his blouse lay on his rack. He started pinning on his silver oak leaves when he heard a soft knock on the door, followed by a whisper.

"Sir, it's Lance Corporal Bell. May I come in? I need to talk to you."

Beck answered in a quiet voice. "Sure, Lance Corporal. What's up?"

Bell wore running shoes, green shorts, and a green t-shirt. She had her hair up in a baseball cap. The shorts and t-shirt were two sizes too small and gave Mike his first look at Hard Target's body. It seemed almost as perfect as he had imagined. She had long muscular legs, a tiny waist, and firm pointed breasts. Her skin looked incredibly smooth, with a blond complexion. She wore no makeup, and her face seemed soft and feminine. Hard Target looked very young and stunningly beautiful. She was, in some ways, a younger version of Brenda Higgins.

Beck hung up his blouse and sat at the end of his rack, expecting Bell to sit at the other end. Instead, she sat beside him so that their bare legs were touching, removed her baseball cap, let her hair fall down, and shook her head so that her long blond hair draped over her shoulders. Mike Beck could smell perfume, and the fact that their bodies were touching, even if only leg-to-leg, drove him crazy. He tried to sneak looks at her gorgeous legs and could see her nipples protruding through the T-shirt.

She turned toward Mike, and he could feel her breast lightly touch against his arm.

"Sir, you left your logbook in the Humvee," she said. "I thought you might need it to brief the General."

Bell handed Beck the small green notebook that he carried everywhere and stared him in the eyes.

In the last 20 years, Mike had been in this situation 100 times with 100 women in 100 different circumstances: clients, witnesses, court reporters, wives, and barflies. He had always made a move, usually an embrace and a kiss. He felt some supernatural force pulling him toward Bell and telling him to kiss her, but even though he felt completely aroused, he didn't. For the first time, he resisted the force. Instead, he focused and tried to talk in a normal voice. It wasn't easy.

"Thanks. Good thinking, Bell. Having the logbook will make things a lot easier."

Bell looked Beck in the eyes for a long time, but she said nothing.

"I'm sorry, Lance Corporal Bell, but I have to get going for that meeting with the General." Beck stood up and headed for the door.

In a moment, Bell followed. At the door she smiled. "Maybe we could run together. I see you running all the time."

Beck smiled. "I'd like that, but not here at Camp Baharia. Maybe when we get back."

Bell walked out the door, and Beck continued to stare at her body as she sauntered down the hallway. He sat down on his rack and spoke out loud to himself. "Beck, you must be the biggest asshole in the Marine Corps or else the biggest homo. First, you walk out on Anne and now you're thinking about hitting on a lance corporal who is only trying to do her job."

As he put on his uniform, he thought of Anne. Hard Target was beautiful, but he'd restrained himself. He wasn't sure what it meant.

❦

0430, 12 November 2004
4th Division Headquarters
Camp Baharia, Iraq

When Beck arrived at the command deck, the aide sat at his desk, working on his laptop. "Lieutenant Lewis, I need to talk to General Scott as soon as possible," Beck said.

"Sir," said Lewis, "he's out running with the sergeant major. They should be back in a few minutes."

"OK. What's on his schedule?"

"Just the morning brief."

"Great. I'm going to talk to the Chief. The second the general gets here, let him know that I need to see him, and then you come find me. This is a critical matter that General Scott will want to hear about ahead of everything. Check?"

Lewis looked curious but responded. "Check."

When Beck looked in LtCol. Carter's office, he saw him doing what he did every morning—reading and answering emails. Carter stopped, walked to the coffee pot, and poured Beck a cup. He then sat back in his chair and grinned.

"Beck, you're now a fucking Marine Corps legend—a real live combat lawyer."

They both chuckled as Carter continued. "Lieutenant Colonel Campbell has made a full report and is demanding a Combat Action Ribbon and a Bronze Star with combat V. And you know he's going to drive me fucking crazy until he gets both."

They knew it was true.

"More importantly," Carter said, "you have the respect of Gunny Ellis, and that means a hell of a lot to me, Mike. Damn it—I don't give a two-toned horse shit in hell what they say about fucking lawyers. It's an honor and privilege to serve with you, by God!"

Beck laughed again. "Damn, Vic. You're starting to scare me. You're not going to ask me to volunteer for a *real* job, are you?"

Both men were still laughing when they saw the sergeant major walk by in his running gear, headed to Gen. Scott's office. The Chief motioned for Col. Hall to follow as they walked past his office.

"Do we need the PAO?" Hall asked the Chief.

"That would be a good idea."

Scott, Hall, Carter, Beck, and Copeland gathered around the general's conference table.

"Mike," Scott said, "the scuttlebutt is that you and the PSD had a hell of a fight in Fallujah. I already know that you accomplished your mission. The sergeant major says you have three wounded and that your Deputy took a round in the hand. I'm glad that they're expected to fully recover. I'm going to write to PFC Mayberry's parents. He was one of our best. I would like to hear from you now, Mike."

"General," Beck said, "there's overwhelming evidence to dispute any allegation of a war crime. We found a wounded

Iraqi at the school who witnessed the entire incident. This was a deliberate attempt by terrorists to stage an atrocity, and to do that the terrorists murdered innocent women, children, and an old man. The insurgent we brought in the first day is a member of the Hadeed Terrorist Cell. The victims are members of a rival tribe, the Saddaq.

"There is also substantial physical evidence. There was not a single U.S. 9mm casing found in the school. On the other hand, we found Russian-made 7.62mm pistol casings, one for each victim and the one used by the Hadeed to shoot himself in the shoulder. We recovered two Russian-made Tokarev 7.62mm pistols and are completing autopsies and ballistics tests. The NCIS agent is certain that the wounds on the civilians are from the Russian pistols. General, I could keep going, but the bottom line is that the evidence clears the Marine, and a report will be on your desk by tomorrow."

General Scott addressed Lt. Copeland. "Is this thing wrapped up for PAO?"

"Yes, General," Copland answered. "I've seen Anne Merrill's story, and it's consistent with Lieutenant Colonel Beck's investigation. In fact, it's a masterpiece on explaining what is really happening here. It addresses the violence within Iraqi society, and I believe it portrays the Marine Corps in a favorable light. The newspaper story is being run in all major newspapers in the United States and in many others around the world. Ms. Merrill also completed a video report, which is airing on all major television networks. She wants to re-interview the wounded Iraqi that Lieutenant Colonel Beck brought in, and her story is so popular that her boss wants her back in the States as soon as possible. I'm arranging transportation for her. I'm hoping she feels we honored our agreement."

"First Lieutenant, hope is not a course of action," Scott asserted. "Talk to her and make sure we've lived up to everything we promised. Specifically, I want to know her position on the camera theft."

General Scott paused and looked at Beck, then towards Copeland. "Check?"

"Yes, General," said Copleland. "I'll get right on it."

"Also, if she has the time," Scott continued, "I would like her to stop by before she leaves so that I can personally thank her for her heroism and cooperation. Gunny Ellis tells me she's one hell of an American."

General Scott then stood up and extended his hand to Beck. "Mike. You did one hell of a good job out there. Thank you."

C3&D

0530, 12 November 2004
4th Division SJA's Office
Camp Baharia, Iraq

When Mike Beck walked into the Staff Judge Advocate's office, he could see six large stacks of documents on the table. LtCol. Campbell sat at Beck's desk, typing furiously on one of Beck's laptops. Ryan and Martinez scanned piles of documents into computers. Lieutenant Colonel Hanson, the I MEF Deputy Staff Judge Advocate, sat on a folding chair next to Beck's desk, talking on the telephone.

"Anything to report, Lieutenant Colonel Campbell?" Hanson asked.

"No problems, sir."

Campbell spent an hour briefing Beck. Four NCIS agents from Camp Baharia and Camp Fallujah were working the case. One was on a chopper with the bodies and headed for Baghdad for completion of the autopsies. Case's weapons and the Russian Tokarev pistols were in Baghdad for ballistics tests and coordination with the autopsies. NCIS expected the results the next day.

The brass casings recovered by Agent Davis were already identified as Russian 7.62mm pistol rounds and matched the two pistols recovered from the insurgents.

The I MEF G-2 confirmed that the Saddaq and Hadeed tribes were rivals and that both were engaged in terrorist activities, including smuggling, kidnapping, assassinations, and extortion. The families had a long history of tribal war.

In the medical officer's opinion, Kamis Hadeed's wound appeared self-inflicted.

Haitham Rasheed seemed to be recovering nicely at Camp Fallujah. He'd been re-interviewed by the I MEF Staff Judge Advocate and had provided a complete story of what happened in the school. He was to be transferred to the hospital in Baghdad at 1500.

Finally, Hanson had drafted a press release to go out as soon as the results of the ballistics tests and final autopsies came back from Baghdad.

Beck extended his hand towards Campbell. "As always, Ed, your speed is amazing."

CℨℬƆ

0630, 12 November 2004
LtCol Beck's Quarters
Camp Baharia, Iraq

Beck felt guilty as he walked out of his room to go for a run. He and Way always ran together, and Beck worried about Way's injuries. The hand wound might be permanent. Plus, Way had turned out to be a great Deputy, always willing to help. He had worked his ass off.

The six-mile runs were one of the few things that Beck liked about Camp Baharia. As he started running down the asphalt road leading to the dirt perimeter road that circled Camp Baharia—his favorite running route—he carefully jumped over the worn-out tank tracks that were used for speed bumps and darted in and out of Humvees. Running alone constituted a violation of camp rules, and hopefully he wouldn't be spotted by an enlisted Marine.

Beck immediately started thinking about Anne. She seemed a most incredible person. Aside from being drop-dead gorgeous, she was intelligent, honest, brave, and determined. He felt a desperate longing that he'd never felt before.

When Beck turned the corner onto the perimeter road, he instinctively looked at his watch. He did this every day at the same four spots—at the start, at the helipad, at the corner, and at the finish. It was 0630. Was it too early to go to Anne's trailer? He knew that he had to see Anne, but he didn't want to scare or annoy her. From what Copeland had said, Anne probably was busy preparing and filing her reports.

At that point, Beck stopped running. He stood in the dust of the perimeter road, trying to make the right decision. He turned and started running back to camp, back to Anne's trailer. Then Mike stopped again and started talking out loud to himself. "Why don't you wait until after lunch, you stupid bastard? You're going to fuck this up."

Beck knew that he should wait, but he couldn't help himself. He had to see Anne. He started running toward Anne's trailer as fast as he could.

ᚳᚱᚾ

0700, 12 November 2004
Transient Quarters
Camp Baharia, Iraq

Beck stood at the door, out of breath from running, and knocked. He listened for any noise inside. Anne opened the door, wearing shorts and a t-shirt, her hair wrapped in a towel. It seemed obvious that she'd just returned from the shower. She looked down at Beck from inside the trailer and flashed a big smile.

"Good morning, Colonel Beck. Is someone chasing you or did you forget something?"

Beck felt awkward looking up and couldn't think of a witty reply. "Anne, may I come inside?"

A serious and painful look formed on Anne's face. She stood in the doorway, thinking. Beck's heart stopped, and he felt he would die if she said no. Finally, Anne looked around and answered. "I don't think that would be a good idea for either of us."

Mike had to beg. "Anne, I'm sorry. I know this sounds over-dramatic but I'm afraid that I might not see you again and there are some things I need to say to you."

Anne carefully looked up and down the spaces between the trailers as Mike continued to plead with her. "Anne, please trust me. I just want to talk."

The two stood in silence for a long time. Finally, Anne spoke. "We're just going to talk?"

"I swear, Anne. I just need a chance to square some things between us. I promise that's all I will do is talk."

Anne stepped back, and Mike climbed into the trailer. Anne's laptop and a stack of papers were spread out on her bed. Her backpack lay open and there were little piles of papers and clothes on the floor. Anne closed the door, and they faced each other.

Without saying a word, Mike moved closer, embraced Anne in his arms, and kissed her.

Anne cocked her head. "I thought we were just going to talk for a..."

Beck ignored her, but she offered no resistance. He pulled Anne's t-shirt over her head, removed her bra, and started kissing her breasts. Anne responded by ripping Beck's shirt off. He pulled down her shorts. She then helped him out of his shoes and shorts. In seconds they stood naked in front of the bed. As they made love, the laptop and papers flew to the floor.

After the lovemaking, they both fell asleep. Mike slept for an hour without moving. At 0845 Mike woke, remembered he had a staff meeting at 0900, and quietly dressed. He left the trailer without waking Anne.

CR&O

0845, 12 November 2004
4th Division Headquarters
Camp Baharia, Iraq

After stepping out of Anne's trailer, Beck ran as fast as he could to his quarters. He was sweating profusely when he threw on his uniform and laced his boots. He ran to the Headquarters Building and even ran down the hall to the conference room. When he got there, he looked at his watch. It was 0903 and he could hear that the meeting had started. No one had ever been late for a staff conference.

He had to make a decision. He thought about just leaving and missing the conference. He could always make up some story that there had been an emergency in his office. He rejected that idea because he knew he needed to attend. He took a deep breath, walked into the conference room, and headed straight for his chair.

General Scott glanced at him with a curious look on his face. Carter appeared visibly annoyed. The other staff officers had knowing grins on their faces.

Beck sat in his chair thinking to himself *That's just like you Beck. You went from hero to shit bird in less than two hours.*

෨෧෩

0845, 12 November 2004
Transient Quarters
Camp Baharia, Iraq

Anne sat naked on the bed in the barren trailer and tried to comprehend everything that had happened to her in the last week. She tried to decide if she was in love with Mike Beck and what that might mean for her future. It seemed preposterous, of course, to think that they could have a permanent relationship.

For a moment she considered that she was not on birth control and this was the worst time of the month. Then she laughed at herself, speaking out loud. "Yesterday I had a hundred terrorists trying to kill me, and today I'm worried about getting pregnant. I was married for three years and it never happened, so it's not going to happen now."

Anne knew that she couldn't stay at Camp Baharia. Sooner or later, she and Mike would get caught. That wouldn't help her credibility as a reporter and would be bad news for Mike. He could even get court-martialed or disbarred as an attorney.

Anne thought about embedding with another unit not located at Camp Baharia. She didn't think the Marine Corps would let her do that, and besides, the big story was over—the Second Battle of Fallujah—and DNS wanted her back in Chicago.

In the end, Anne decided it was time to go home.

Chapter 38

T he rest of the staff had gone to lunch, and Beck sat in the swivel chair, reading situation reports, when Anne walked into the SJA office. She looked amazing.

"I came to say goodbye," Anne said. "Lieutenant Copeland has me on a flight to Baghdad from Camp Fallujah at three o'clock."

Beck was instantly overwhelmed with emotion. This had never happened to him, and it scared him. He felt like he might get tears in his eyes. "Do you have to leave?"

"Yes. I have to get back to Chicago. I guess General Scott is happy to get rid of me since Lieutenant Copeland wasted no time in getting me out of here. "

Mike still felt stunned, but tried to talk. "Did you know that Chicago is my home town?"

"Mike, I'm a news reporter. Frank Tobolski and I have a file on you."

Mike Beck sat for a moment putting two and two together. Without asking a question, he realized that Anne had worked with Frank Tobolski on the Oliver case. Beck stood up.

"I'll be back in two seconds."

He walked out of the office and returned with Anne's camera. "Here. Someone turned it into an amnesty box."

They both knew that most camps had wooden boxes for people to turn in extra ammunition, booze, or other contraband items.

Anne smiled. "That's convenient. I guess we'll never know who took it." She then pulled out the memory chip and handed it to Mike. "This may be useful in the investigation."

"Won't you need it for your story?"

"No. It was a violation of my embed agreement to take photographs of the dead. Besides, photographs of Iraqis killed by Iraqis are a dime a dozen and not considered news by my editor."

"Anne, can I drive you over to Camp Fallujah?"

"I'd like that a lot."

○380

1400, 12 November 2004
SJA Office
Camp Baharia, Iraq

Mike and Anne walked out of the SJA office and climbed into the SJA Humvee. Amazingly, it still ran. They joined the PAO convoy headed for Camp Fallujah and drove straight to the landing zone, a section of abandoned road with a tent located inside a large number of Texas blast barriers. A large group of Marines and Iraqi soldiers stood next to the tent. It was a beautiful day, so Beck and Anne got outside the Humvee.

Beck saw an ambulance headed toward the landing zone. The driver missed the turn and had to drive all the way around the landing strip before turning into the road next to the tent. When the ambulance stopped, Case jumped out, followed by Goldman and Hale. The corpsmen carried Nelson, Collins, and Haitham Rasheed on stretchers. Steve Way had a bandage on his left hand, but stepped out of the ambulance and walked toward the tent.

Beck realized that he'd forgotten that he had assigned the STA team as Haitham's guards. Obviously, Case and the STA team intended to continue guarding Haitham until properly relieved.

Case walked over and saluted Beck. "Sir, the medical officer instructed that we are to turn the detainee over to the flight crew. Do you confirm?"

"Roger that, Lance Corporal," Beck said. "Have you been able to get chow and billeting for your team?"

"Yes, sir. We've been rotating the watch. Sir, would it be possible for the STA team to return to Kilo Company?"

"We'll take care of that as soon as we leave here."

"Aye aye, sir"

Beck walked over to Way. "Someday you'll learn to listen to me."

"Yeah. And someday I'm going to stop pulling your ass out of the fire. You know I lost my little finger, right? My golf game is ruined."

Beck grinned. "Steve, you never had a golf game. At least now you have an excuse for letting me beat you all the time."

"Keep laughing, Beck. I'm going to be drinking German beer before you go to sleep tonight. Hell, what am I saying? With me gone, you aren't going to get the chance to sleep tonight."

"Seriously, Steve—you did one hell of a job here. I am damn proud of you."

Beck shook Way's good hand and then walked over to Nelson.

"Corporal Nelson," Beck said, "I can't explain all the shit that happened to your team. The STA team never did anything wrong and yet endured two investigations. Believe me, I wish we could leave your team alone so that all of you could just do your jobs. Thanks for your service here, and I wish you the best."

"I understand, sir. Shit happens. Thanks for bailing our asses out each time."

Next, he walked over to the group of Iraqi soldiers and asked if anyone spoke English. Several nodded, and Beck asked one to help translate. They walked over to Haitham Rasheed, who sat with large bandages over his left eye, on his left shoulder, and on his right leg.

"Mr. Rasheed," Beck said, "I want to say a few things to you before we take you to the hospital in Baghdad. Your cousin received an Islamic burial. His grave is marked and the family can obtain the marker identification here at Camp Fallujah. You're going to Baghdad to see an eye doctor, and we'll do everything we can to treat your wounds. We will take care of you until you're well. You're a brave and honest man. I believe that with men like you, the Iraqi people will soon have a great nation. Before you leave, please tell me if there is any thing I can do for you."

Haitham took some time to answer. "Thank you for burying my cousin, Ahmed Rasheed. He died to protect Iraqi women and children. God has willed that I should live to do the same. There must be an end to the killing, and there must be law and order. Families should not kill each other, and the police must protect all Iraqis. I want you to help me join the National Police. I want to come back to Saqlawiyah and protect all the innocent."

Beck shook Haitham's hand. "I will do everything I can to help you join the police."

Suddenly, Beck heard the two CH-46 helicopters flying in from the north. Soon, he could see them, flying fast and low. The corporal in charge of flight operations started yelling over the noise for everyone to line up. Beck walked Anne over to where the line formed. He planned to ask if he could see her on his return to Chicago.

It was too late. The CH-46s roared into the landing zone, performing a rapid series of maneuvers, turning sharply, slowing down, and descending while creating a huge cloud of dust. The helicopter engines appeared to be at full throttle as the helicopters set down on the old pavement. The rotary blades kept spinning and the line started moving, dragging Anne Merrill along with the group. Beck cussed himself for not saying goodbye earlier and stood there helpless to stop what was happening.

Then he saw Anne run to the Crew Chief on the CH-46 and yell something in his ear. The Chief nodded his head, and Anne started running back to Beck. A second later, Beck ran toward Anne. They met in the worst possible spot. The noise was deafening, and the rotor wash blasted their faces with dust and gravel.

While the CH-46s sat on the runway, Anne jumped into Beck's arms. He held her as close as he could for a long time and then kissed her. He shouted as loudly as possible in her ear. "I'm in love with you, Anne."

Anne looked up and smiled.

The pilots, crewmen, Way, and the rest of the Marines and Iraqis sat aboard the choppers, watching, but Beck didn't care. He shouted again.

"I mean it," Beck reiterated. "I love you. I'm absolutely crazy about you."

Anne pulled herself up to Beck's ear. "I love you, too. I'll see you in Chicago."

She then wiggled loose, turned, and ran to the CH-46. Beck watched as the Crew Chief helped her aboard and the choppers lifted off. In less than a minute, the CH-46s were out of sight.

Beck stood looking at the horizon for a long time, then turned and headed back to the Humvee.

Case came over and saluted again. "Colonel Beck, I wanted to thank you for saving my ass."

"No problem, Lance Corporal Case. Let's get the STA team back to the fight."

About the Author

J. W. Stone is an exceptional author with 30 years of military service. He was with the Marines in Iraq during the Battle of Fallujah and developed a unique perspective on modern warfare. His writing brims with action, real characters, and a deep understanding of courage and commitment, both from the perspective of the grunts on the ground and the highest ranking officers.

CPSIA information can be obtained
at www.ICGtesting.com
Printed in the USA
BVHW031829170622
640082BV00011B/165